THE BETRAYAL INCIDENT

THE INCIDENT SERIES, BOOK THREE

MARLA HOLT

TINY DINO PUBLISHING

eBook ISBN: 978-1-7338518-7-9

Paperback ISBN: 978-1-7338518-8-6

Cover Design by: Suite Six Studios

Tiny Dino Publishing

Berryton, KS

To Find out more and for exclusive sneak peeks at Marla's newest work, sign up for her newsletter

🌸 Created with Vellum

for the ones afraid they don't deserve to be chosen
(you do)

CONTENTS

PROLOGUE

PROLOGUE

August 2019

Van Birch Goes Viral

Pop star Vanessa Birch is doing everything she can to stay in the headlines lately.

First, in her typical tabloid style, she fired her longtime manager, Henry Bishop, the same day she filed sexual assault charges against him. Then she almost single-handedly spearheaded the rebuilding efforts when her hometown of Wellville, Kansas was devastated by an F-5 tornado, and hired her boyfriend, Bryant Wilder, and his construction company to do it. Then yesterday, in possibly the juiciest gossip day of all time, not only did photos surface of Van and her stepbrother, Clay Noble, getting cozy on a

stoop, but a sex tape featuring Van and Bishop (yes, the same man
she filed sexual assault charges against) also went viral.
We have so many questions, but we'll start with these three:
How does a busy megastar have time to juggle three men?
Did Bryant know before yesterday that Van was cheating on him
with his best friend and business partner?
And what repercussions will Van's actions have on her dad, Robin
Birch, who is rumored to be planning a run for Congress?
Of course, Van could not be reached for comment.

"This doesn't look good, Robin," John said.

Robin Birch leaned back in the plush leather armchair in his home office. An ache formed behind his eyes, and he'd been fighting tension in his shoulders for days. He would have asked Phoenix to rub them for him. She gave phenomenal massages, but well... Phoenix was in L.A., and when she got back, she likely still wouldn't be speaking to him.

"Do you think I give a fuck what it looks like?" Robin asked.

"I'm just saying that if you want to represent the people of Kansas, it doesn't look good for your daughter to have a sex tape."

Twenty years of friendship or not, if John had been standing in front of Robin right then, Robin would have knocked him the fuck out. He leaned in toward the phone on his desk so his friend wouldn't mishear him. "First of all, Van didn't put this tape out there. It was filmed without her consent, released without her consent, and the only reason it went public is because it's one of the only ways we're going to nail Bishop for what he's done to my daughter. And if I hear one more comment from anyone about Van or about Van's body or about what happens in that video, I will slap them with a lawsuit so fast, they'll be drowning in legal fees before they can even take a breath. I don't care if it holds water or not. Do you understand me?"

There was a long pause. Robin imagined his friend loosening his tie the way he always did he was uncomfortable. "And second?" He sounded breathless. Good. Robin wasn't willing to take shit on this subject from anyone.

"Second," Robin had to stop and take a deep breath. "If I'm going to be held accountable for whatever's going on with my daughter, then perhaps a political bid isn't the best idea."

It pained Robin to say it. He'd always intended to get into politics. The plan since college had been law school, practice, local politics, state politics, senate. He was a little bit further behind than he wanted to be. He'd announced his candidacy for city council the year Caroline, his first wife, was diagnosed with ovarian cancer. He'd dropped out to take care of his wife and daughter. Caroline had passed only a few months later, and all of sudden he'd found himself a single father. It took him a few years to find his footing, and by then he was on the board of the local historical society and worked with the state historical society as well. Another city council seat opened up by the time Van was sixteen, and he'd served his two, four-year terms. For the last year, Robin has been biding his time until the 2020 election. There was a Kansas seat open in Congress, and Robin wanted it. He hadn't announced anything yet, but there had been local gossip, not that he'd be running for the Representative seat in particular, but that he would be running for something had been deemed inevitable, especially with how visible he'd been during Van's ongoing rebuilding effort.

Robin was proud of his daughter, and he'd been glad when she'd come home for a few weeks. He'd needed her to come home. Even internationally known pop stars needed their father when times got hard. And the Birchs' world had imploded all at once. Van's assault and the tornado had happened the same night. Clay, Robin's stepson, had lost his house and was living in his high school bedroom at Robin's house while he decided what to do next.

Back when Phoenix was still speaking to Robin, before he'd screwed that relationship all to hell, she'd mentioned that Van was working on getting Clay a deal with some home improvement network to fund his rebuilding his house if they could film it. Robin thought it might be a tough sell for Clay, but if it guaranteed him more time with Van, Robin could see Clay accepting. He was prideful and hated being on television, but Robin had never doubted how much Clay loved his daughter. Whether Van returned those affections, well, Robin would deal with that if it came up. It's not like he could throw stones. Robin's relationship had been just as taboo. He'd been sleeping with a woman twenty-five years his junior for the last six months, which might not have been so bad if she wasn't also his daughter's business partner.

"I'm not saying you should give up," John said. "I'm just wondering if there's a way we can somehow distance you from the Hollywood side of things."

"Van will always have my full support, no matter what she does," Robin said. It wasn't even a question. It had just been him and Van for years. She was his entire world, and if it came to choosing between Van and politics, Van would win out each time. No question.

Robin ignored the part of his mind that nagged at him that if he'd given Phoenix the same consideration, his heart might feel slightly less obliterated as he dealt with this sex tape madness.

He'd taken the next few days out of the office, but he'd barely manage to leave his desk at home with the way his phone hadn't stopped ringing and his email hadn't stopped pinging since the sex tape had dropped that morning. He'd known it was going to be like this, but he'd hoped by the time this happened, he and Phoenix would be handling it together. Instead, he'd consulted with the lawyers in L.A., spoken to his P.I., and there had been a seemingly endless supply of information from Phoenix's assistant, Amanda.

Amanda.

Robin hadn't even ever fucking met Amanda. She lived in L.A. and had never once traveled with Phoenix and Van to Kansas. Robin had never asked why; he'd known that Phoenix had a staff, but that they were invisible was something he'd never thought about. He hadn't needed to. Robin tried to keep himself in an entirely supportive role when it came to his daughter's career. And Phoenix had never hesitated to contact Robin directly before—even before they'd ever met, before Van had landed her recording contract, Phoenix had called him and told him when he and Mary Beth, his second wife, were going to come visit Van in L.A. at Christmastime. She already had the plane tickets booked and the hotel room reserved, he just needed to reimburse her.

He and Mary Beth had laughed at the time about how bossy she was, but they'd gone along with the plans. Robin had been pleased his daughter had found someone so fiery and commanding to represent her. But when that was turned against you? It was nothing but ice.

"And I'm not saying I think you shouldn't support your daughter," John said. "It's just, she complicates things."

"Are you saying I should find a more capable campaign manager?" Robin asked.

John chuckled into the phone. "Honestly, your girlfriend would do a better job at getting you elected than I can, but I doubt you can afford her."

Robin stiffened. The reason Phoenix was no longer speaking to him was because she'd overhead his conversation with John on the phone last week. That had been a disaster on all fronts. "I thought I made it clear that Phoenix was off-limits."

There was enough bite to Robin's words that John said, "Fine. Fine. I'm just saying that someone will bring this up, and you'll have to be prepared to talk about it, in public, without losing your temper."

"I can do that," Robin said, but he even sounded pissed off to himself.

John sighed on the other end of the line. "Look, professionally? I have no doubts. In a courtroom you are unflappable, but when it comes to your family, you turn into a bit of a territorial asshole, and you can't do that on television is all I'm saying."

"You forget I have practice being on television."

"But live interviews are different from semi-scripted reality television."

Robin ground his jaw. He understood what his friend was saying. He didn't like it, but he pretty much hated everyone and everything at the moment. And he needed a break.

"Look, I'll practice not being a territorial asshole in case someone asks me about Van after I announce my candidacy in six months. But right now, I need to go take care of my family."

"Right. Of course." John sounded embarrassed. Good. "I'll see you Saturday?"

"Make sure there's plenty of Scotch. The good stuff too. Not that crap you usually buy."

"Not everybody lives with a rock star," John said with a laugh, and Robin knew he'd be drinking the same old swamp swill on Saturday.

"See you then," Robin said and cut the connection.

He leaned his head back against his chair and closed his eyes, the headache was only going to get worse, he could tell. Robin needed to call Van, but he'd wait until after lunch.

He wanted to talk to Phoenix, both for personal and professional reasons, but the one time he tried calling each of her multiple phone numbers, he was sent straight to voicemail on every one. Each time, it felt like somebody had stacked another brick on his chest. He didn't want to be here. After Mary Beth had passed, he'd sworn off women for good. It was better for him, better for any woman he was involved with. Clearly, he was cursed. What kind of man was a widower twice over in the twenty-first century?

It was almost as ridiculous as a man in his mid-fifties dating a twenty-something redhead.

That wouldn't do his political career any favors either.

But fuck, had Robin let Phoenix down.

And he'd give just about anything to make it up to her.

CHAPTER 1

DECEMBER 2018

*R*obin raised his glass, lifting one eyebrow. Phoenix wasn't sure if it was that arched steel-gray eyebrow or if it was the carafe of mulled wine they'd shared, but the tingles lit a storm down her spine. She knew she was behaving badly. In all the months that Robin had been giving her the tingles, Phoenix had never once been this close to giving in to them. That was because feeling the tingles from Robin was neither safe nor smart. For a million reasons.

He was Van's father. He was in his fifties. Twice as old as she was, practically. He lived half a continent away from her. He was widower twice over. And he was twenty-five years her senior. That point needed to be counted twice, because oh my God, stop being an idiot, Fe.

But Phoenix handed over her empty wine glass anyway.

Robin turned the carafe upside down to fill their glasses. "Well," he said. "That's the last of it. We'll have to drink something else tomorrow."

They hadn't finished the wine on their own. Everybody

else had drunk a glass while they'd waited for Clay, Robin's stepson, to show up. But it was a big carafe and everyone else had given up waiting for Clay hours ago. The asshole hadn't come over for Christmas Eve like he'd promised he would. Not that Phoenix had wanted to see him; she hadn't. But Van had, and goddammit if her best friend wanted to see her stupid, predator stepbrother on Christmas, then she was going to get to see him on Christmas.

Bryant had been the first to leave, driving his mom home after the carol singing had wrapped up. Bishop and Van had escaped up to her room for some ill-concealed sexy times next. Phoenix had stayed so she could chew Clay out for being an insensitive bastard, but she'd known he wasn't coming.

She'd really stayed because Robin hadn't shown any indication of budging from his stool, and Phoenix wasn't strong enough to leave. Not when it could just be the two of them for the first time, possibly ever.

She was at cross-purposes with her companion. Robin had said he wasn't ready to give up on his son, and while Phoenix thought it was sweet Robin had regard for the idiot, she was ready to lay into Clay for being a coward for not being able to even confront Van. Phoenix knew why Clay avoided his stepsister. It was obvious to anyone but Van that he was totally into her. That didn't make him any less of a bastard—probably more of one actually. Was he really going to let Bishop scare him away?

Though, if Phoenix were being honest, she'd been avoiding Robin for months, because she was afraid of how appealing she'd found him recently. The difference was that Phoenix wasn't mad about it and taking it out on everyone she cared about. Robin had been giving her the tingles since

July, and she was dealing with it by pretending it hadn't happened.

Now, if only she could forget it.

He hadn't done anything in particular, just spent an afternoon by Phoenix's pool with Van and a few industry friends. Everyone had been showing off their designer swimwear, and the results of their long hours at the gym. It had been the first time Phoenix had seen Robin without a shirt on. He'd always been tall and lean and well dressed, but she'd never noticed his body composition before. She hadn't expected to be so fascinated by the subtle motion of long, lean muscles under tanned skin. He even had a spray of silver chest hair she found herself wanting to run her pointed nails through.

The discovery that Van's dad was a man had left her feeling stunned for the rest of the afternoon. She'd had to take a dip in the pool to clear her head. When she'd hopped out and headed toward the bar, Robin had dropped a fresh towel over her shoulders.

It could have been a fatherly gesture, but it hadn't been.

For the first time all afternoon, Phoenix was aware of how much of her body her navy blue bikini left bare. She was not a self-conscious woman, and she worked hard to remain toned and lithe, but she hadn't been trying to impress anyone. All Phoenix had wanted was to take a break before they hit the road again. She'd been trying to fly under the radar if anything, but the second the fluffy white towel had settled on her shoulders, Phoenix had known that Robin had seen her. Not just her body, but her.

Phoenix wasn't sure anyone had ever properly seen her like that. That's what had been dangerous about it, because the man who saw her was supposed to be the man she spent the rest of her life with, not her best friend's dad. She wasn't supposed to get the tingles over someone who could never be more to her than a fling. So Phoenix's mind disregarded what her body had to say and kept as far away from Robin Birch as she could.

Avoiding him wasn't that difficult when they lived 1500 miles apart most of the time. But the few times they had met in the last six months, Robin had given her the tingles. Every. Single. Time.

Not just he-could-be-a-good-time tingles, but put-a-ring-on-it tingles, because that connection is once in a life-time. Which of course meant she'd completely stopped feeling the tingles for anyone else. Which also meant that Phoenix hadn't had sex in the last six months, because her love life lived and died by the unconscious reactions in her body.

It was why it was so easy to reject potential lovers. If they didn't make her skin prickle and set butterflies free in her stomach from across the room, they weren't worth her time. But as Robin rejoined her at the breakfast bar and set his glass down beside hers, Phoenix's whole left side radiated heat. She'd already had to do away with the chunky cardigan she'd worn all day and was only in her flimsy white V-neck T-shirt. The collar had started slipping over her left shoulder. She was thankful for the cool air on her neck, even though it was as cold as the devil's heart outside. Phoenix could also feel Robin's gaze on her bare skin. She flicked her eyes sideways as she sipped the warm wine. His eyes were rapt, as if he were playing dot-to-dot with her freckles.

Phoenix had always hated her freckles, even though they were in fashion now and she'd learned how to play up the ones that were still visible over the bridge of her nose. The rest of them never faded, no matter what combination of sunless tanner and sunscreen she used. Her pale complexion was still covered in red spots that nearly matched the vibrancy of her hair. And even though she'd learned how to sculpt her body and dress so she was no longer the gangly, skinny, awkward girl she'd been growing up, she still hated the freckles.

She shifted on her stool, facing Robin, and watched as his eyes traced the constellations over her collarbone and down the neckline of her shirt, where he seemed to get lost in ogling her breasts. She hid her smile behind her wine glass as she took another sip. She had to give him that one. When her breasts had finally showed up, they'd come in spectacularly.

She recrossed her legs so the toe of her boot skimmed his shin, and Robin shook himself from his stupor. "Have you spoken to your parents?" he asked.

They'd been talking about safe topics up until now—the spring schedule for filming Van's reality show, *Pop Star*, what Van's summer tour was going to look like. Keeping Van between them was smart. It was the way it had always been, everyone being there for Van, but now? With them all alone, and Robin asking about her family? It was almost too much. Did he know anything about her family? Was he actually curious or just being polite?

"I received the yearly deposits they call Christmas gifts," she said with a shrug of her shoulder. He frowned. "And my stepmom offered to send me a pound of marijuana."

Robin choked on his wine, and Phoenix patted his back as he wheezed. "They're growers," she said as he spluttered back to breathing, and she had to bite her lip to keep from laughing. "Licensed and everything."

"I still forget," he said, then coughed.

She rubbed his back and wondered how much of his job had been defending local people on petty drug charges. A pound of marijuana in Kansas was probably enough to get you put away for dealing. But her stepmom, strangely the only one of her four parents who bothered to communicate with her on a regular basis, had texted her photos of her father proudly standing in front of stacks of pallets as tall as he was for distribution all up and down the West Coast.

Robin cleared his throat, and said, "Thanks."

Phoenix knew she should stop touching him, but her body was slow to follow through. The wine had her feeling heavy and relaxed, and the gorgeous warm wave of tingles that were streaming from his back, through his delicious checked navy shirt and into her palm made her reckless. She couldn't stop rubbing his back. If she didn't pull back before his breathing returned to normal, the potential for awkwardness grew. There was also the possibility that Robin would like her to continue touch him. The idea softened the press of her hand against his back. Phoenix knew she should pull her hand away now.

Except.

Would it really be that big of a deal?

They were both adults. Both single. What was a little age gap in the grand scheme of things? What would it hurt to explore what was unfolding between them?

Robin, his breathing even again, glanced at her over his shoulder, a question in his eyes at first. Then she could tell the tingles had caught him too, because he raised that mischievous eyebrow again. All Phoenix's inhibitions dissolved into a rush of pins and needles.

This was happening.

Where the flat of her palm had been against his back, she now traced lines up and down his spine with her fingernails. She'd chosen the sparkling red manicure because she'd seen Robin's gaze catch on her nails a time or two, and though she'd never planned on acting on the attraction, Phoenix wasn't above trying to tempt him.

Because yes, she wanted this. Phoenix had wanted it for a while, and maybe it had taken a bottle of mulled wine to admit that to herself, but Phoenix wanted Robin Birch with a ferocity she'd not been sure she was capable of. She wanted to know what it felt like to have those sturdy, wise hands in her hair, on her breasts, nestled between her thighs. She wanted to hear him sigh at the rightness of their joining and then groan into the pleasure of it.

Her fingers traced back up his spine into the short steel-colored hair at the back of his neck. She raked her fingernails over his scalp, marveling at the way his hair transitioned from a dark steel gray at his neck to silver on top. From the photos around the house, Phoenix knew his hair had been nearly black when he'd been younger and the silver had started in his beard then slowly spread.

Part of her wanted to climb into his lap and see if she could count the hairs that were still black, one by one, her nose pressed against his, their breath shared as she shifted her hips down and into his.

Robin sighed and dropped his head back into Phoenix's touch, then rotated his head and brushed his lips against the inside of her wrist. The tingles erupted into their own drunken revelry, and Phoenix felt a tremor run through her entire body. Robin's lips curled into a sly smile as he turned on his stool to face her and place a trail of kisses up her arm to where her sleeve ended at her elbow. He skipped up to her bare shoulder, his lips soft, his breath warm as she shivered. She was ticklish there, but the tingles overpowered the urge to squirm away. Instead she tilted her head back, inviting him to kiss his way up her neck.

His hand landed on her waist pulling her closer as he trailed kisses to her ear. He nipped the lobe, just below her row of piercings, and she couldn't help the whimper that escaped from her lips.

That seemed to be what he was waiting for, because the hand at her waist pressed her between his spread legs and into his arms as his lips met hers in a hungry kiss.

Phoenix couldn't remember the last time she'd been kissed like this. Hell, she couldn't remember the last time she'd been kissed. She wasn't much into emotional involvement. She was more likely to go down on a guy than she was to kiss him. But this?

This was magical. Her whole body was paying attention to the points where they connected. His lips on hers, his hands on her back, his thighs pressing against her hips. He felt so good. Solid. Strong. Sturdy, but not overpowering. Robin smelled like the spices in the wine and something earthy and fresh. She found out as his tongue slipped between her lips, he tasted that way too. She moaned as his tongue met hers, then pressed her chest into his.

One of Robin's hands found its way inside Phoenix's shirt, his fingers warm and comforting against her fevered skin. She thought she might be sweating; she definitely knew she had too many clothes on for this. Her body felt tight and frantic, like all of her nerves were firing at the same time.

She lapped at Robin's lips once, twice more, then pulled back at the same time he did. Their gazes met. His gray eyes were enchanted, yet somber, and Phoenix felt the same way. Awed at the fire between them, but frightened.

"We shouldn't be doing this," he said, his voice barely a whisper.

Phoenix traced the corner of his mouth with the tip of one nail, outlining the part where his lips ended and his beard began. "I have wanted you for months," she said.

Then she placed one slow, chaste kiss to the corner of his mouth and dragged her nails lightly down his throat to where the top two buttons on his shirt were undone. His hands fell into his lap as she stepped back from out between his legs, letting her nails graze down his chest, then over the top of his thigh as she stepped toward the stairwell that led to the basement apartment where she always stayed.

Robin stared after her as if nothing but his eyes could move. "Are you coming?" she asked over her shoulder as she descended the first step. "I won't wait long."

That was all it took for him to follow her all the way to her bedroom.

He should not be doing this. That was the only coherent thought in his head as he followed Phoenix down the stairs and into the apartment beyond. The rest of his mind was a dark swirl of desire and temptation that propelled him forward when she bypassed the living room entirely and made straight for the bedroom at the far end of the hall. The one she'd claimed as her room the first time she'd visited with Van all those years ago.

She'd been barely more than a child then. In her early twenties and already formidable. She hadn't let anyone in Hollywood tell her what she could and couldn't do, and he'd been grateful at the time that Van had found a friend to guide her.

Phoenix had been nothing to him but Van's friend then. Mary Beth and he had still been married. They'd still been happy. Before the arguments had started, before she'd told him she wanted a divorce. Robin had never had a chance to move past the sinking feeling in his gut when she'd told him she was leaving him. That she found their relationship more suffocating than freeing. That she needed to be out on her own.

She'd never had a chance either. She'd died less than twenty-four hours later in a car accident, and Robin hadn't known where to start unpacking his grief. He'd lost his wife twice in two days, and become a widower for the second time over. He'd sworn off love forever.

That had been almost two years ago. And Robin had stuck to his word. He'd remained celibate. He hadn't dated. He hadn't wanted to.

But his body had started to become physically aware of Phoenix sometime over the last six months. Whenever she was near, he was able to pin-point exactly where she was in the room. He knew exactly what she was doing. He could remember every dress she'd worn, the way her tall body had the ability to fold in on itself when she relaxed with Van, like she carried zero tension in her muscles despite the fact that she never put down her tablet.

She had already kicked her boots off and switched on a

lamp by the time Robin closed the bedroom door behind him. She was three inches shorter without the boots, putting her forehead at perfect kissing level. He should only be kissing her on her forehead. She was his daughter's best friend for chrissake, but when Phoenix whipped her shirt over her head to reveal the blue and black satin bra, Robin stopped thinking with his brain.

He hadn't been tempted like this in years. He'd loved Mary Beth, but she had been right, the last couple years of their marriage, they'd become more friends than lovers, and trying to force the romanticism had been crushing him too. He'd never strayed. Never looked for fulfillment outside his marriage. Robin wasn't built that way, but he had wanted to want his wife like this.

Now his erection strained the fly of his jeans as he watched Phoenix shimmy her leggings over her hips and down her long, toned and freckled legs. God, she didn't have panties on. She grinned up at him as if she knew what that knowledge was doing to him.

She flicked her hair over her shoulder, then turned her back on him and undid her bra dropping the garment on the ground with an outstretched arm while Robin ogled her ass. He'd known that Phoenix took care of her body, but seeing the softness of her skin, her full, round ass on top of her muscular thighs, the flex and pull of the lithe muscles in her back. He'd had no idea just how well-formed she was. Better than all of his fantasies.

Robin's mouth actually watered as he took a step toward her. She gave him a grin over her shoulder, watching him approach as if knowing that he wouldn't be able to resist touching her once he saw her naked.

She'd been right.

He wrapped his arms around her waist and pulled that perfect ass up against his hips and pressed his erection into her. She sighed and guided his hands to her breasts. They were the perfect handful, and he let out a quiet groan as he her hard nipples pressed into his palms.

He massaged both breasts as she writhed against the ridge in his jeans. His left hand drifted down her tight stomach and the thin strip of red hair at the apex of her thighs. She bucked into his hand as his fingers grazed over her folds.

God, she was so wet. He shouldn't be touching her like this. Part of his brain still told him that he shouldn't want her, that the twenty-five years between them should forbid this sort of connection, but then Phoenix whimpered his name, and he was back in the power of the temptation.

The danger, the alcohol, the fact that this woman was only a few years older than his daughter only made her gasp of pleasure that much sweeter as he sunk a finger into her depths. God, it had been so long, and he wanted to feel more of her, hear more of her, see more of her.

He nibbled her neck and rolled her nipple with his right hand as his left thumb found her swollen nub. Her head fell back against his shoulder, and his cock pulsed in his jeans as her breath sped. She was melting against him now, taking away the glorious friction of her ass against his bulge. He'd thought it had been torture, but now that it was gone, Robin ached to have the pressure of her body back against his. The only acceptable alternative was to be inside her, and he would be soon. Only Robin wanted to feel her come on his fingers first.

He bit his lip as Phoenix gripped his wrist, pressing him more firmly inside her, her clit gliding over the base his thumb. Robin hooked his fingers up, and Phoenix's gasp of pleasure sent a surge of pure desire straight to his dick. She was close, and Robin only stopped moving his hands when Phoenix trembled, then stilled. She mewled then sighed, then drew his hand from between her legs and turned in his arms. A languor he'd never seen in her movements before only made him want her more. Robin had never seen Phoenix truly relaxed, but now seeing her tipsy and love drunk, he never wanted to see her any other way.

Her eyes were sparkling as she wrapped her arms around his shoulders. "You're wearing too many clothes," she said, playing with the collar of his shirt.

Robin didn't care. The feel of her breasts pressed against his chest was too delicious. The silken feel of her skin beneath his fingers was driving him wild. And all that was between him and her, truly, was his zipper.

But Phoenix had already started undoing his buttons.

"Do you remember the pool party over the summer?" she asked as she worked her way down his shirt.

Did he remember the pool party? She'd worn a navy-blue bikini. Her red hair had been braided over one shoulder like an amber rope. That had been what had drawn his attention, noticing the contrast of her vibrant hair against the night-sky color of her swimming suit and the subtle glow of her skin. The combination was mesmerizing, even as he thought she was trying to be invisible at her own get-together. She wore a high-waisted suit that only let glimpses of her belly button show, and the top was modest, with a vintage cut.

Robin had always known that Phoenix worked hard, but he'd never noticed before how little credit she took for all she did. Sure, she'd hired someone to grill for them and had sushi catered and even a bartender on site, but she spent most of her time making sure her guests were taken care of. She'd billed the afternoon as a break from production for cast and crew, a chance to lay around her pool and relax, but the only time Robin saw Phoenix relax was when Van pulled her down onto a lounge and shoved a White Claw into her hand.

And after she'd taken her one and only dip in the pool, cleanly gliding three laps through the mostly abandoned water as everyone else was drying off and grabbing food, Robin couldn't help but do something to take care of her. He had dropped a towel over her shoulders as she'd gotten out of the pool and approached the food spread.

She'd smiled at him over her shoulder, so naturally and unguarded, as if she'd genuinely been delighted by the gesture. Robin had felt his whole world turn sideways. Since then, he hadn't been able to stop thinking about Phoenix, trying to see her, trying to divine if she wouldn't just body slam him and crush her heel into his crotch for even entertaining the idea.

This was more than he'd ever hoped for. That Phoenix might see him as more than Van's dad. As more than an aging, but ambitious, small-town lawyer, but as a man.

"I remember."

Her fingers had finished with his shirt and moved onto his belt. Then his fly. They both watched her hand dip behind his open zipper and pull him free. Her eyes met his again as her fingers closed around him and squeezed. A pleased smile crossed over her lips, and Robin's breath left him in a *woosh* when she stroked up and then down.

"If we had been alone," she said, "I might have done this to you in the pool."

He jumped in her hand, and she giggled.

"I would have liked that." His throat felt like sandpaper, and his eyes could see nothing but Phoenix's hand pumping over his length, but his arms were already slipping his shirt to the floor.

"To think we could have been doing this for six months already," she said.

"Then we have a lot of time to make up for," Robin said and brought his lips back down to Phoenix's. She surged up on her toes and wrapped her arms around his neck. His cock pressed against her soft warm belly, her breasts flattened against his chest, and he couldn't wait any longer.

He kissed his way down her neck, whispering, "I don't have any condoms."

Phoenix nipped his shoulder. "I have you covered." She wiggled her eyebrows at her pun, then backed to her bedside table and opened the drawer.

Robin took the opportunity to take off his shoes and kick off his jeans. The hungry look in Phoenix's eye as she watched him made him want to hurry, but he slowed himself. Despite being almost twice her age, Robin felt like a teenager again. Desperate to impress the woman in his bed. Desperate not to make a fool of himself. He tossed his jeans into in the corner and stood tall, proud.

Phoenix didn't hide her admiration as her eyes swept over him from head to toe. She centered in on his erection as she caressed him again, then rolled the condom on him herself.

Robin was torn between taking his time and savoring his first sexual encounter in almost two years or pushing Phoenix backwards onto the bed and jumping on her in his eagerness.

Phoenix's impatience didn't leave him time to decide. She pulled him down on top of her and wrapped her long legs around his hips so he couldn't get away. He chuckled in her ear at her antics. He'd forgotten that sex could be fun. That it could just be about pleasure. Not expectation. Not obligation, just the joy of mutual pleasure.

Phoenix arched her back, pressing her mound against him, and she loosened her legs around him just enough for him to slide into the right position. Robin navigated himself inside her by feel. He wanted to watch her face as they joined, and he wasn't disappointed as her eyes darkened, as desire swirled in the deep blue and eased into awe.

The grin that spread over his lips was involuntary until he moved in her and Phoenix threw her head back, arching into his thrust, her eyes closing, her mouth open. Robin was destroyed.

The excuses he'd been using to combat his attraction since July, the ones that had fired again when Phoenix's palm had landed on his back, that she was interested in a male body, not necessarily his, that she wouldn't be interested in his old ass anyway, fell away. Phoenix was here with him because she wanted this with him. And he was not a decent enough man to not take advantage of her want.

He covered her lips with his. Their tongues mingled as their hips kept pace with each other. Her nails bit into his shoulders. Robin dug his finger into the sheets on either side of her shoulders, to leverage the pace she demanded.

Phoenix's breath hitched in the same way it had before and knowing she was close brought Robin to the edge. Her moans grew quieter as she seemed to concentrate all of her energy inward. Her mouth opened in a silent scream as her body clenched around him. Robin said her name but had to bite his lip to keep from roaring his release and waking the whole house up.

Spent, Robin collapsed onto Phoenix. She curled her arms and legs around him as her entire body shook with laughter. Robin was almost too exhausted to move, but again, he couldn't help the smile that overtook him. He even kissed her shoulder with smiling lips.

"What's so funny?" he asked.

"Oh, God," she squeezed his hips with her thighs, still laughing. "That was just so good. Jesus."

Robin kissed her shoulder again, still grinning. "It was." And he was determined that it would happen again. Perhaps the next night. After everyone had gone to sleep, and he'd had a good long nap. He could barely keep his eyes open long enough to get cleaned up and collapse back into bed next to Phoenix who draped herself over him. He fell asleep to her running her nails lightly up and down his thigh.

When Phoenix woke the next morning, she was alone. Disappointment threatened to overtake the continuous full-body tingles still flowing through her. But she told herself to be realistic, even as she sat up in bed and the sharp pain in her head reminded her that alcohol had played a large part in their liaison. And they hadn't made each other any promises. And even if they hadn't, things were still complicated.

How did one tell their best friend and business partner that she'd just slept with their dad?

Phoenix didn't want to say anything just yet. Whatever was going on between her and Robin, she wasn't ready to share it, not even with Van. Especially not with Van in this case. Possibly later, when everything was less fresh. Less new.

She was pulling on her yoga clothes before she saw the package on her nightstand. That had definitely not been there the night before. It was the kind of Christmas card she'd received from Robin every year. Only this time, it was taped to a small rectangular package, and when she opened the card, a hand-written note fell out.

Phoenix,

I've been debating with myself over whether to give you this gift all month. Whether it was too extravagant or inappropriate in some way. Perhaps before last night, it might have been. I hope you get some use out of these before they disappear. Merry Christmas.

Yours,
   Robin

"He didn't," she said aloud as she tore the paper from the package.

But he had.

He'd purchased her two—TWO—of the newest, top-of-the-line styluses she preferred. Because she'd complained off-handedly over Thanksgiving that, despite her best efforts, she inevitably lost her favorite stylus and had to use crappy cheap ones as substitutes.

So he'd bought her two.

None of them had worried about money since Van's first album, but still, the styluses weren't cheap, hence her complaining. And Robin and Phoenix had never exchanged more than cards or a bottle of wine at the holidays.

This was big. Good, but big.

She held the boxes and the note to her heart, then, in her elation, texted a photo of herself blowing a kiss to Robin's phone.

She was going to drink a glass of water, ignore her headache and knock out her morning yoga. Then she was going to pretend like her life hadn't transformed overnight. Somehow.

CHAPTER 2

*R*obin hadn't been hungover in a long time. The long day of delivering presents to local shelters and watching his daughter perform for Christmas services at the big church in town left him feeling queasy and exhausted. Even then, Robin couldn't keep his eyes from straying to Phoenix over and over. She wore an ugly Christmas sweater and a green Santa hat that made her hair shine in contrast.

They all wore ugly Christmas sweaters and Santa hats, even Van. It had been her idea, and then she'd forced them all together to take a photo that she posted on her social media like a Christmas card. This year there had even been a dusting of snow on the porch steps when they'd all posed in front of his house.

The photograph had looked wholesome and sweet. Like a traditional Midwestern Christmas. Someone had made a joke that if Van's dad would only gain a hundred pounds, he could play Santa. Robin had not been amused. His beard might be going silver, but he didn't feel old enough to be anyone's Santa. Well—most of the time. After he'd removed his red Santa hat, only to have Van place it back on his head, telling him that they were all Santas for the day, he'd felt every day of his twenty-four years of fatherhood and more. There were days when he felt ancient, and being thought of a benevolent, jolly, granter-of-material-wishes didn't seem so bad.

But even as Van smiled and kissed his cheek, something in Robin rebelled against the idea of being relegated to the sexless, grandfatherly role. Even if, until the night before, Robin had been celibate and satisfied with it. This morning, he was different. Last night had changed everything.

Robin felt himself wanting again. Not only wanting Phoenix, though he did, desperately. Something else he couldn't name yet had roused within him. A restlessness he hadn't felt in a long time. Like a part of him that had lain dormant since Mary Beth was coming to life again. There had been a point after Caroline had died where he'd felt like a bear shaking off the winter's hibernation. Was that what this was?

Had Phoenix reawakened him?

Phoenix had caught his eye as he swiped the hat off his head again, their naughty secret dancing in the corners of her smirk, as if she understood exactly what he was thinking.

They hadn't spoken yet today outside the usual niceties. He'd offered her cinnamon rolls and fruit salad. She'd only taken the fruit salad and helped herself to some of the yogurt she'd moved into his refrigerator. Then she'd poured them both a cup of coffee without a word. She'd taken her usual place next to Van at the dining room table, and Robin had sat back to observe Van with Bishop. Van had only admitted to him over Thanksgiving that they were an item, and that she hadn't expected to develop feelings for her manager but that she was happy.

Robin could see that Bishop was protective of his daughter, but he also didn't miss the way he antagonized Bryant and sometimes Clay. As if he were taunting the both of them that he'd won Van's affections despite her long history with them. It was a part of the man's personality that Robin didn't understand. He'd prefer a man in his mid-thirties be above that sort of petty behavior, but then again, most of the people he'd met from L.A. were unapologetically competitive. That might be it, but Robin hadn't made his mind up yet. Bishop had always treated Van well professionally, fighting for and booking her the best venues and guest spots.

Phoenix might know how to navigate the Hollywood machine, but Bishop knew how to work the music side to Van's advantage, and Robin knew Van owed a good portion of her success to the man. He only hoped that Bishop continued to treat his daughter well now that they were together. Perhaps he'd ask Phoenix what she saw. She probably knew both of them better than anyone else. And Van would confide things to Phoenix that she wouldn't want her father to know.

He'd watched the steam swirl out of the rim of his coffee cup as he wondered how what was happening between him and Phoenix would affect Van's relationship with Phoenix. Not that he was necessarily after a relationship with Phoenix. He wasn't sure what he wanted. What was appropriate. He'd bought that stupid gift for her on Black Friday, mere hours after hearing Phoenix complain about losing her favorite stylus—again. Robin knew he wanted Phoenix's attention, and he didn't want whatever was happening to end with last night, but what would the consequences of such an affair be on his ambitions? Would he lose the respect of his community? And more importantly, what would happen to his relationship with his daughter? Would Van start censoring herself around her friend so that Phoenix wouldn't confide the wrong things in him? He and his daughter had always been close. They'd had to be. But the friendship Van and Phoenix shared was the kind that kept no secrets.

Robin hadn't had that since Caroline had passed away. He didn't expect to find that sort of connection again, but as the days passed, and he wondered how his relationship with his daughter might change if she found out he was sleeping with her best friend—which she inevitably would—he found that, for the time-being, he was more interested in exploring the reawakening, so long as it was private, than worrying about what Van might say once it was over. Phoenix could be discreet. Robin knew that. There was no reason anyone needed to know what was beginning between them, at least not yet.

Phoenix probably didn't think of his old ass as anything more than a holiday fling—though even as he thought it, Robin recognized that it didn't feel true. There had been a connection between them. Something he knew from experience could be nurtured into more. But the two of them lived in different states, different worlds really; they probably didn't have anything in common outside the bedroom, and Robin had stopped believing in happiness. At least the kind that was derived from a partner. Even after they promised to stay forever, they never did.

He couldn't let his heart get involved in this thing with

Phoenix, but that didn't mean he couldn't explore it, couldn't allow himself to revel in the bacchanalian celebration that was his own personal spring. After he finished sleeping off his hangover.

When they finally got home, Robin blinked and nodded his way through the Christmas dinner they'd had catered, then excused himself to bed almost immediately. Maybe he wasn't too old to be relegated to sexless benevolence, but he was definitely too old to function on only three hours sleep and a belly full of mulled wine. He fell asleep the moment his head hit the pillow.

He was awakened by the soft click of his door snicking shut, and the subtle creaking of wood as light feet crossed his bedroom floor. It was a sound he associated with Van. Not Van as she was now, but as she had been as a scared and lonely child who had lost her mother. She'd climbed into Robin's bed every night for a year. There were nights when she would cuddle up to him and weep. Robin's tears had never been far behind.

Caroline's illness had been swift and brutal. Her ovarian cancer had taken her within months of her diagnosis. Robin had barely been able to function. He could only imagine how alone his daughter felt without her mother. Until Caroline got sick, Robin had been a largely absent father. He hadn't meant to be. He'd been around for the important things, piano recitals, school presentations, but on the day-to-day, Robin had spent most of his time downtown. He'd been building his law practice, supporting his wife and daughter. It had been Caroline who had cooked, cleaned, and spent quality time with their daughter. The year after Caroline died had been long and anxious as he'd gotten to know his daughter while balancing out his grief with the new anxiety he carried about what it meant to be a single father and widower.

They'd eventually connected over their love of music and started playing the piano together every night, but Van had been twelve before she'd stopped sleeping in his bed at night. She'd come to him the night of Mary Beth's funeral, but that had been for his benefit.

Now it was Phoenix who had woken him and spread herself over mattress. She smelled like fresh, sweet flowers, and the skin on her midriff was bare and so soft. He caressed his fingers over her waist then around so he could stroke her spine.

"How are you feeling?" she whispered.

"Sleepy" was the only word he could muster. His mind was at once sluggish with sleep and abuzz with flipping through the reasons Phoenix would have for sneaking into his bedroom in the middle of the night that he couldn't keep up with them.

Phoenix snuggled in closer and ran her fingers through his hair. "I didn't think everyone else would ever go to bed."

"Were you waiting for me?" Robin asked.

"I wanted to say thank you for my gift. I feel bad that all I gave you was a card and a hangover."

That made a smile spread over his lips. "I gave myself the hangover, and—" He'd been going to say something teasing about how what they done last night had been worth it, but Phoenix's lips landed on his, and Robin stopped thinking.

Phoenix had been itching to touch Robin all day. Not just touch him but launch herself at him the way teenage girls did to movie stars. She wanted to suction herself to him and rub all over him. She was fairly certain he wouldn't mind, but the doubt she'd never been able to banish, that tiny part of her that still harbored fear, thought that despite last night, despite his gift, that maybe he didn't want her again. That she had been a novelty. A conquest, and that one taste was all he'd needed.

But he was shirtless and pulling her on top of him in his bed. The comforter maddeningly separated their lower halves. She'd put on a fresh set of yoga clothes, which could pass for pajamas if she was caught sneaking around the house in the middle of the night, but she wanted to know what Robin wore to sleep. The thought that he might be naked under the covers sent a thrill down her spine.

Robin mistook her shiver for her being cold and pulled back the comforter, inviting her inside. He was not naked, but his dark boxer briefs were an acceptable alternative. It was too dark to see, but Phoenix could feel. The sheets were warm with his body heat and crisply clean. His body radiated warmth, and when Phoenix's hand roamed over his hard length, they both groaned in anticipation.

She chided herself for wasting so much time in avoiding him these last few months. His body was amazing. Not amazing for a man twice her age, just fucking amazing. She'd been reliving the feel of him on her all day, reveling in how his lean muscles felt flexing under her fingers. He felt real. Not like the boys she'd been hooking up with in L.A. over the last couple of years. They'd pumped themselves up and only wanted to talk about the gym and the kind of water cut they were doing for their photo shoots. But Robin felt strong and stable, like a deep-rooted tree, and Phoenix couldn't get enough of him.

She pushed her hand beneath his waistband as they kissed, and his cock was hot against her palm. She almost couldn't wait for the time it would take to disrobe and take him inside herself. She used her other hand to reach between her boobs and pull out the string of condoms she'd hidden there. She tossed them onto Robin's chest as she shimmied her way down his body.

A chuckle cut through the delicious rustle of sheets as Phoenix peeled his underwear down his legs. She heard the crinkle of foil as he picked up the strand. "This is optimistic," he said.

Phoenix shrugged, but she wasn't sure if he could see her. She'd brought five condoms with her, which, she'd admit, was a lot for one night. "Now you have your own stash."

If he was going to say anything else, Phoenix didn't give him the chance as she closed her lips around his tip. He groaned, and Phoenix smiled around him before sliding down his length, taking him as far into her mouth as she could. Robin cursed, and his hand came down to land on the back of her neck. She thought he might be trying to signal for her to stop, but instead he held her in place as he flexed his hips beneath her.

Giving head was her specialty, and as much as she wanted Robin inside her, Phoenix wanted to show off. She wanted Robin to know that whatever this was that was happening between them came with all the benefits. Her throat relaxed, and Phoenix was able to take him in almost to his base, and by the way his body tensed beneath her, she could tell he was enjoying himself.

"Phoenix," he said, his voice was a harsh whisper, bordering on a gasp. She didn't stop as his fingers curled into her hair. God, it felt so good to give him pleasure. Phoenix wasn't sure when she'd last been this turned on stone cold sober.

"Phoenix," Robin said, and the urgency in his voice told her she had him exactly where she wanted him. She grinned as she pushed up to her knees and flung her sports bra across the room, then shimmied out of her yoga pants and slid back up his body, making sure her breasts grazed his skin every step of the way.

She brought her lips to his and swept her tongue into his mouth. Robin banded his arms around her back and kissed her like she was his salvation, and Phoenix grew heady with power. Clearly, he'd needed to be reminded about this side of himself. Phoenix had the feeling he'd forgotten how good sex could be, not that she blamed him, but she was absolutely on board for taking her time to remind him.

She could feel his erection against her leg and wiggled so that she could smooth her wet center over the length of him, teasing them both.

Robin cursed again, and one of the condoms that was still in his hand crinkled as he ripped it open. Phoenix swiped it and sat back on her heels to roll it on to him. Then she positioned herself over him and pushed his cock inside her.

This was where she'd wanted to be all day long, and the satisfaction of him filling her was even better paired with the lingering soreness from the night before. Phoenix was loathe to admit how long it had been since she'd hooked up with anyone. Since she'd developed her crush on Robin, no other man had been able to distract her from wanting this man and this man only.

She moaned as Robin squeezed the tops of her thighs,

but a quick finger at her lips reminded her to be quiet. They weren't in her apartment but in the main part of the house. Van and Bishop only slept two rooms away, and the last thing Phoenix wanted right now was for Van to catch her fucking her dad's brains out. Even though that's what Phoenix planned to do every chance she got for the foreseeable future. She silenced herself and sucked Robin's finger into her mouth, mimicking the way she'd sucked on his dick only a few minutes before. She had to silence him with a nip this time.

He hissed and pulled her down to his lips so he could return the favor by pulling her bottom lip between his teeth, and Phoenix's heart soared. God, why had she wasted so much time thinking this was a bad idea? She'd never had a lover who just seemed to get her like this.

She felt Robin kick one of his legs, then the comforter settled down over her shoulders and Robin pulled it over their heads, and they were cocooned in their own little world. It was stuffy and sweat began to form between their bellies, but it was so dark and so isolated that everything had become pure sensation as Robin grabbed two handfuls of her ass and pushed and pulled her up and down over him. Phoenix latched onto his shoulder with her teeth, and he hissed again, but she didn't relent. She wasn't biting him hard, just enough to scrape his skin when he pulled down.

"Fuck, Phoenix," he said, and she was learning that he liked to talk as he got close. And that was all her body needed to explode around him. To keep from letting loose the screams of pleasure that wanted to erupt form her throat, she plastered her lips to Robin's and kissed him hard as her world darkened to contain only the eruptions happening inside of her.

Robin's fingers grabbed her ass harder, and she knew he'd lost the battle for duration and was chasing her over the edge.

"Jesus fucking Christ," Robin said after their bodies finally stilled.

Phoenix grinned and pinched his side in agreement. She couldn't even talk yet. Her vocal cords might never work again, that's how good it had been.

Eventually, Robin slid out from underneath her and disappeared into the en suite bathroom. Phoenix had stretched out in the bed, luxuriating in the afterglow before spying Robin's robe hanging on the back of the bathroom door. She'd seen him wearing it before. It was a dark hunter green robe made of soft cotton, and the bed, while comfortable, lacked warmth without him in it.

She was just tightening the sash around her waist when he emerged from the bathroom. He was so tall, the robe was comically oversized on her, but that made it all the cozier. Robin smiled when he saw her and pulled her into his arms with a tender kiss to the top of her head.

Phoenix kissed his bare chest in return, even as she could hear the questions well up inside him. What are we doing here? What is this? What happens when you fly back to L.A. tomorrow? Is it over?

Phoenix didn't even need him to ask the questions to know what he was thinking. She was thinking the same questions. Questions that she didn't have any answers to outside the fact that together, they were capable of some of the best sex Phoenix had ever had, and she didn't want to give that up after just two nights.

Phoenix didn't have a solution to the fact that she lived in a different state, and as much as she liked to plan, this was so new, so vulnerable, she didn't want to press it too hard. It was like a balloon, Phoenix was afraid if she squeezed it too hard, it would pop and disintegrate before it had even had a chance to become something less fragile.

Instead, she slipped into the bathroom. And when she emerged a minute later to find Robin sitting at the end of his bed, still nude, hands folded in his lap like he didn't know where to go from where they were, Phoenix slipped into his bed, still wearing his robe, and waited for him to snuggle up next to her before she fell asleep.

CHAPTER 3

*W*hen Robin woke at dawn, it was to a frantic Phoenix searching for her yoga pants. He was too disoriented at first to be of much help, and her whispers were too difficult to make out over the sound of the radiator in the corner knocking to life.

Eventually he realized that she was trying to sneak down to her room before Van woke up for their morning training session and Phoenix couldn't find her clothes. Robin's boxer briefs were at the foot of the bed, but her pants were nowhere to be found. He pulled his underwear on and helped her search. They found her sports bra in the corner, but there weren't many places for things to hide in Robin's tidy room.

They both froze as they thought they heard a noise down the hall. "Go," Robin said, not wanting to be found out any more than it seemed Phoenix did. "Keep the robe."

Phoenix nodded and was almost at the door when she doubled back threw her arms around him to pull him into a kiss. "Last night was amazing," she said as a dreamy smile parted her lips.

"It was," Robin agreed. He wasn't sure he'd ever had sex like that. He'd had plenty of good sex, but experiences that powerfully raw and explosive had been few and far between.

"We should do it again sometime, yeah?" she asked.

"I'm all yours, Fe."

Phoenix smiled at the nickname, something Robin had heard Van call her. He hadn't been sure it would be welcome from him, but he'd always liked it.

"Likewise," she said, before kissing him one last time and dashing out of his bedroom on near-silent feet.

Robin hadn't found Phoenix's yoga pants until the day after she'd left when he'd stripped his bed to change his sheets. They'd been sandwiched between the sheet and the comforter at the foot of the bed.

He'd texted her a photo of the blue and green Lycra.

Her response had been, *I guess there's no choice but for you to bring them back to me. Saturday maybe?*

Five minutes later, Robin had purchased his plane ticket. He did not pack the yoga pants. Those he was keeping for himself.

She'd sent a limo to pick him up from the airport, but when he climbed in and found her curled up in the far corner, a glass of champagne in each hand, his heart jumped into his throat.

"Happy New Year," she said with a grin as bright as the full moon.

Technically, the New Year wasn't for another two days, but Robin didn't give a goddamn. He would take advantage of any reason to celebrate with this woman while he could.

Only Robin didn't have patience for the champagne. He'd been thinking about nothing but her since she'd last left his bed. Robin set the glasses in the cup holders, pulled Phoenix into his arms and kissed her. She giggled into his lips and could barely kiss him for her wide smile. By the time limo reached her Malibu beach house, Robin was already spent and dozing, and a satisfied Phoenix in rumpled clothing sagged into his side as she napped. They escaped inside her home with the champagne untouched.

They'd spent the rest of the weekend in bed together.

Robin felt like he was twenty-five again. Insatiable and all-consumed with his lover. Just when he'd felt that time of his life was behind him, he'd found someone who'd renewed his interest not just in sex, but in life. Phoenix was vibrant and bossy but giving. The way she approached him, it was like she didn't believe there was any reason he couldn't keep up with her appetites simply because he was older. Robin was surprised by his own ability to rise to the occasion, but he didn't dare complain. With each shared orgasm, Robin was reborn and reenergized, like there was nothing he couldn't tackle.

He knew he should talk to Phoenix about the limits of what this relationship could and could not be. Warn her that there were limits to what he could give and how long he could give it, but he wasn't ready to let go of her yet.

"Where have you been lately?" Van asked as their coffee and post-yoga snack was delivered. They were cozied up in their favorite booth at the coffee shop next door to the yoga studio, the one in the back with the tall seats so they couldn't be photographed from the window.

Phoenix looked pointedly toward the window, then down into the rosette at the top of her coconut milk latte.

"Don't pull that shit with me, you have been MIA the last three weeks," Van said, blowing across the top of her own latte.

"When in the world would you have had time to notice? Every time I've tried to get ahold of you, you've been riding Bishop."

Phoenix didn't speak loud enough for anyone to overhear, but Van shushed her as she glanced over her shoulder in an exaggerated manner anyway. It was the usual post-hot-yoga high. They were always a little extra silly afterwards, but Phoenix was not prepared to answer these exact questions.

Especially since she'd spent the last two weekends screwing Van's dad's brains out. She'd gone to him in Kansas this past weekend and had gone down on him just before her car service had come to pick her up for the airport yesterday morning. She could still taste him in the back of her throat. While Phoenix didn't share a lot about her love life, she would have normally told Van that there was a guy who was regularly blowing her mind, even if she wouldn't have told her who. Not that a guy had regularly blown her mind in years. Dudes were usually after Phoenix for the novelty of her body or her proximity to the Van Birch fame machine. It had been ages since she'd fucked someone who was just into her for herself. But Robin? Jesus. Phoenix hadn't stopped tingling since Christmas Eve.

That shit was unprecedented, but she didn't know how

to talk to Van about it. If she started, Phoenix was going to gush. And Phoenix did not gush.

"I've been busy negotiating you more time to write your album," Phoenix said with raised eyebrows that told her friend to drop it.

In typical Van fashion, she wasn't fazed. "See, I would believe that if those douchebags ever worked on the weekends, but they are waaay too important for that. What have you really been doing?"

Phoenix mimed zipping her lips, then put her full attention on her latte. She was contemplating giving Van a hint about who she'd been doing, but Bishop slid into their booth, having apparently appeared out of nowhere.

"Hey, baby," he said to Van, then kissed her hard on the mouth. Van lit up at his attention, and Phoenix had to fight the urge to pretend to puke. She was glad that Van was happy, but sometimes the two of them could be disgusting together. Plus, Bishop was always pushing what he could get away with in public.

Phoenix shot them both a glare. Van unplastered herself from Bishop's side and flashed Phoenix a wicked grin as she innocently picked up her mug. Bishop pretended not to notice Phoenix's policing. Sometimes she thought he wanted a scandal. She could see him causing a big uproar that would push Bryant and Van's farce of a relationship to the sidelines once and for all so Bishop and Van could be together in public.

Phoenix got it. She really did. Even though her affair with Robin was new and she wanted to keep it just between them for now, she knew that after months and months together she would want everyone to know. But it had always been Van's call about when to put a stop to her fake relationship with Bryant, and so far, she hadn't made it.

Phoenix only hoped Bishop didn't get impatient and do something stupid.

"What are you two up to?" he asked as he slouched against the seat and threw his arm over the back of the booth. Not quite around Van's shoulders, but close enough he could still pull the fake-a-sneeze-and-grab-her-boob move. He also spread his legs so wide underneath the table that Phoenix had to tuck her feet up against the side of the booth to avoid bumping his knees.

"I was just getting ready to ask Phoenix who her new boy toy was," Van said and added waggling eyebrows to her wicked grin.

"Nice," Bishop said. Settling further into the booth as he swung his eyes to Phoenix. "Spill, Fe."

"What are you even doing here?" Phoenix asked. "I thought you were supposed to have a meeting with Gavin Mercany about getting on board to produce the next album."

Bishop sat up, grabbed a cucumber from their hummus platter, and said, "He's on board, but there's only so much to talk about when we don't have a projected schedule." His eyes never left Phoenix's, but she knew his words were for Van. Bishop was the one feeling the most pressure from the label to make Van's third album happen as soon as possible. They'd wanted her to record it in January for a spring release followed by a summer tour, but as far as Phoenix could tell, Van hadn't even started writing.

Right now, Phoenix's focus was getting enough off of Van's plate to make sure she had time and energy to write, but with the Grammys just weeks away and all the endorsement work they had lined up, she didn't foresee room in their schedule until the spring. Instead of band practice, Van was going to be attending launch parties, red-carpet soirees, and photo shoot after photo shoot. Phoenix would be too exhausted for creativity too.

"There's nothing wrong with buying a song or two to get us started," Bishop said.

"No fucking way," Van said. "I have always written my own music. I'm not going to start phoning it in just because I have a little block."

"Then let's at least get you in the studio with the band. Maybe it will spark something."

"We'll talk about it after the awards season is over," Phoenix said. "We're booked solid through then."

"The label isn't going to be happy with that," Bishop said.

"Well the label can kiss my ass," Van said. "They pushed these other commitments."

"With the understanding that there would be another album," Bishop said.

"There will be another album."

"This year."

"There will be another album this year," Van said. "I'm not flaking, I just need a little bit more time." Van skimmed her fingers up Bishop's arm, over his shoulder, and tugged on his man bun. "You've seen how hard writing is for me lately."

Bishop flashed Van an indulgent grin, and Phoenix had to look away. The moment wasn't exactly intimate, but it was difficult to deny that these two people knew each other. And sometimes Phoenix's old crush snuck up on her when she least expected it.

Before she'd met Bishop, back when she'd followed him

in the local tabloids because of his face and his body and his tattoos, Phoenix had thought he was gorgeous. He was even more good-looking in person. But once she'd met him? The tingles weren't there. Not even a little bit. Most of the time he drove her crazy. She was so not attracted to his personality that sometimes, like now, his pleasant physical attributes took her by surprise.

"I know, Little Bit, but I'm only going to be able to keep up with business as usual for so long."

If Bishop was pulling out his pet names, Phoenix needed to bail or she really might puke. She took a long sip of her latte, then slung her yoga bag over her shoulder. "I have to get back to work. No PDA, you two. There are paparazzi outside."

Then Phoenix walked into the crowd of photographers and pretended they weren't taking photos of her ass as she walked away. Joke was on them, Phoenix's ass was spectacular, and she knew it.

Three days later, Robin sat on Phoenix's patio, drinking coffee in nothing but a pair of gray sweatpants. The morning air was still chilly. Phoenix wore a fluffy bathrobe, but when Robin had emerged with his cup of coffee, he'd chuckled and said, "It's practically summer out here."

"You're such a tourist," she said.

Robin had stretched and claimed the only other chair at the patio table that sat in a patch of sunlight. Phoenix sat across from him and sipped her coffee, watching him watch the waves crash against the sand below. Since it was still early, and cold, no one was out yet. Sometimes Phoenix would run up and down this beach in the mornings, but mostly she did exactly this. She luxuriated on her patio and enjoyed the ocean air, the ambient sound of the waves and delighted in the satisfaction that this little slice of the world was hers. She breathed in the salt air and reminded herself that these calm quiet moments were the reason she worked so hard.

Phoenix had never shared those moments with anyone before. Even when Van stayed over, she usually slept in as late as she could. This space was precious to her. Phoenix had never wanted to share it before, but it felt right to have Robin next to her now. His eyes crinkled as he smiled into his mug.

"I've always enjoyed living on the prairie," he said, "But I can see the appeal of the ocean."

Phoenix didn't see the appeal of Kansas at all. It was either hot and sticky or so cold she couldn't feel her toes. But Van liked it there, and there were parts of Wellville that were cute. Robin rested his mug on the table and stretched his arms overhead, like a cat arching into the sunlight. Phoenix watched the show of his abs under his skin and decided it should be illegal for a man to be so cavalierly attractive.

"What?" Robin asked when noticed her staring at him.

She shook her head and took a sip of her quickly cooling coffee. "Nothing."

"No, you were thinking something, you had that look in your eye you get when you're plotting and you think no one's watching."

"I was wondering if you were too old to try surfing."

Robin let a loud, barking laugh. "Do you surf?"

Phoenix grinned out at the ocean. "No. I'm more of a yoga-on-the-beach sort of girl."

Robin cocked an eyebrow, and Phoenix could read the *I'd like to see that* in his curious expression.

He stood, collecting his empty mug and rounded to her side of the table. "I'm not too old," he said. "Just a landlocked guy who's not sure he trusts all that water." He ducked his head to touch a quick kiss to Phoenix's lips. "Now, how do you like your eggs?"

That was new. Robin had never cooked for her before. They'd usually spent so much time in bed that they just ordered a bunch of takeout and ate on that all weekend. "Over easy, with avocado toast."

Robin blinked. "Do you have any avocados?"

Phoenix grinned. "I do. And in couple months you'll be able to pick them out of the tree in the front yard."

"Huh. Well, you'll have to instruct me on the toast, but the eggs I can handle."

Phoenix tapped him on the nose, then scraped her nails lightly up his arm as she stood and eased past him on her way back into the house. "Come on then," she said over her shoulder.

When Robin was stationed at the stovetop, cracking eggs into a pan, and Phoenix was slicing an avocado at the kitchen island, she got up the guts to say, "So this seems to be sticking, yeah?"

She watched the muscles across his back go taut, then his shoulders dropped, just a fraction. "Yeah, it does."

"And I'm thinking I'd like to see where it goes," Phoenix said, pissed that her heart was hammering so hard. She didn't want to be as invested in this as she was. This should just be a fling, something stupid that she did once upon a time for fun, but she couldn't make herself feel that way about Robin. Maybe the first time had been daring and forbidden, but ever since then, she'd only had big feelings about him that she wasn't comfortable naming.

Robin flipped their eggs, and Phoenix dropped four slices of gluten-free bread into the toaster as she waited for his answer.

"I'm not ready for whatever this is between us to be over," he said. His voice had grown soft.

"Good," Phoenix said, as she mashed the avocado in a bowl with some garlic and salt. "That's good."

"But I'd still like to keep this just between us."

"Oh." Phoenix was thinking so hard about how she'd almost told Van after yoga the other day that she jumped when the toast popped up. She shook her head and said, "I prefer to keep things private. You know that," even though she could feel her heart sinking.

Phoenix could hear Robin retrieve plates from the cabinet but kept her eyes focused the act of spreading the avocado over the toast. He was beside her a moment later, two plates with two sets of perfectly cooked over-easy eggs. She slid the toast onto the plates, pretending that she was as unaffected by this conversation as she wanted to be.

Robin placed a hard kissed to her temple, not hiding the way he inhaled the scent of her hair. "I would especially like not to tell Van."

Phoenix chanced a glance upward to see his expression. The planes of his face wore the same calm, immoveable steadfastness she'd expected to see. But she did not expect him hook a finger under her chin and angle it up further. Robin brushed his thumb over her bottom lip, then lowered his mouth to hers. His kiss was gentle, firm, and made the tingles jangle through her limbs with excitement.

He pulled back and dropped another kiss to her forehead as the hand at her chin slid down to massage the place where her shoulder and neck connected. "And if we get to a point where Van needs to know, I'd like to be the one to tell her," Robin said, his lips still pressed against her forehead. It was as if just saying this had him fearing she might disappear.

Phoenix wasn't exactly happy about it, but she understood why he might need more time. Why having a relationship at all might be difficult for him after everything he'd been through. She could give him time.

CHAPTER 4

$\mathcal{B}$y the end of January, Robin had admitted to himself that this was not going to be a short-term affair, though Phoenix and he hadn't discussed the duration of their relationship in any terms other than travel plans through the spring.

They hadn't talked about much of anything, to tell the truth.

They barely had time to scrounge up food when they were together. They spent most of their time in bed, and while Robin appreciated that Phoenix was just as insatiable for his touch as he was for hers, he wanted Phoenix to know that he thought more of her as more than just a bed partner. Phoenix was one of the most intelligent people he'd ever met.

But he wasn't sure if she understood that he felt that way.

Robin also had zero clue what she wanted from him. He'd never seen her in a relationship, though he'd known she'd had them. Perhaps she conducted all her love affairs with the same discretion she used with him. They stayed out of the limelight as much as possible. Though Phoenix didn't tend to attract paparazzi as much when she was on her own, without Van, she was still cautious. Robin was the same. He'd find a few photographers trailing him every now and then, but mostly, unless his daughter was with him, they left him alone. It was Van and Bryant who attracted the most attention. Sometimes Clay even complained about the stupid photographers following him around, but somehow, Robin and Phoenix were able to fly mostly under the radar.

And Phoenix's Malibu home was in a gated community with enough security that the place was as secure as a medieval fortress. No one could spot them together there.

Except Van.

They'd had one short conversation on Robin's first visit to L.A. about how neither one of them wanted Van to know anything about what was going on between them. Phoenix had said that she didn't see any reason to tell anybody, that this was between them for now. Robin couldn't see any reason to ever tell his daughter.

Robin was quickly becoming obsessed with the feel of Phoenix's body beneath his. He looked forward to her texts and phone calls. He missed holding her on the nights when they were apart. But Robin couldn't see that this affair had any staying power.

After a few more weeks, months at most, the infatuation would fade eventually, and they would go back to spending time with companions in their respective age ranges. The idea didn't bother him. Robin Birch was not and never had been a foolish man. As much as he was going to get everything he could from this affair while it lasted, he could see that he and Phoenix were too mismatched to grow anything long term. By the time his campaign kicked off, he was certain this whole thing would be over.

That didn't keep him from wanting to explore the connection they had now. If losing two partners had taught Robin anything, it was to enjoy what he had while he had it, and as long as there was still little chance of Van finding out about their liaison, Robin was not above pushing Phoenix's boundaries.

It was dangerous, going out in public together, and he found himself turned on by the prospect of playing with the boundaries of propriety. The wanting, the desire, the fulfillment he was finding in Phoenix's arms, in her presence, held an air of the forbidden, and Robin was so used to being the steady, practical presence in everyone's life that he was enjoying the freedom in allowing himself to indulge in a little bit of well-deserved decadence.

But he was still too much of a chickenshit to ask Phoenix what she wanted, afraid she was going ask for commitment, for longevity, for telling Van, for going public. He couldn't give her any of those things, but he could give her more than orgasms. So his first act of non-sexual intimacy was to text her on a Wednesday night, two days before he expected her to show up on his doorstep. *What do you like to do for fun?*

Phoenix always answered her texts immediately. The only time he'd had to wait to hear back from her was if she was in yoga or working with her trainer. The rest of the time, he sometimes thought she had her answer typed before he'd even sent her his text, her replies were so swift. *My work is my fun.*

Work doesn't count.

But I love my job.

Robin couldn't help but chuckle at that. He thought that perhaps that was an understatement. Phoenix would probably never stop working if everybody else would let her, but surely, she had things she enjoyed outside of coordinating his daughter's career.

So do I, but I still have hobbies outside it.

Does yoga count?

Robin scrubbed his hand over his beard. The way Phoenix exercised, like it was her religion, or worse, her job, Robin wanted to say no, but he typed back, *Closer*, instead.

Well what are your hobbies, then?

Playing the piano for one.

And?

Robin hesitated. Mentioning the piano was safe. Most of America knew he'd been instrumental in introducing his daughter to music. Hell, he'd played the piano on the *Tonight Show* once—an experience he never wished to repeat if he could help it. Performing in the courtroom was one thing, but playing the piano on live television while his daughter sang was another thing altogether. He was better suited to living-room recitals when it came to music. For some reason, they hadn't been interested in his work for the historical society or the city council on the *Tonight Show*. A small-town lawyer's political ambitions were not nearly so interesting as the novelty of a man who could passably play the piano producing a musical genius.

He went with, *Tennis.*

When Phoenix responded with another *And?* He screwed up his courage and shared something nobody but Mary Beth had ever known.

And I've written four novels.

He could practically see Phoenix uncurling from whatever contortionist position she'd been sitting in as she typed back *What kind of novels?*

Robin felt his ears go pink. He enjoyed the writing process, but he'd never done anything with them. The four mystery novels he'd finished were mediocre at best. Though he'd been collecting them, waiting for Mary Beth to edit them for him over her summer break. But then everything had happened, and he'd lost Mary Beth. They'd been languishing on his hard drive since then.

He told Phoenix that they were mysteries, and she asked, *Can I read them?*

Do you like mysteries? Thrillers? The first one is a little dark.

It was about a serial killer and the lawyer who sought justice for the death of his wife outside the courtroom.

I have watched every serial killer documentary ever made. I'm practically an amateur detective. And I figure out whodunnit in almost every mystery I read by a quarter of the way through the book. Bring. Them. On.

Robin had typed that he would send them, then set his phone down to tidy around the house before sitting down to the piano before bed like he did most nights, only to find an insistent text from Phoenix asking what was taking him so damn long. So Robin trudged across the house to his study, booted up his laptop, and emailed Phoenix the first book with a short note that it was completely unedited and he hadn't looked at it for years.

She hadn't responded.

In fact, Robin barely heard from her over the next two days. She hadn't even reconfirmed her flight with him, and she loved reconfirming. It was what she did. Confirmed, reconfirmed, and then checked in once she was on board. That's how she did everything in her life.

But her car dropped her off right on time according to the itinerary she'd sent him at the beginning of the week when they'd made their weekend plans. He opened the front door for her, and on top of the phone and tablet that were ever present on her person, Phoenix also carried a thick stack of papers covered in both red and black ink.

She usually greeted him with a kiss and a teasing comment that had them disrobing each other on their journey to the bedroom, but this time, Phoenix stalked right passed him and into his study, where she moved his work out of the way and plopped her pile down on top of his desk like the office was hers and always had been.

"This should be a movie," she said, tapping the first page. "I mean, it's a good book, but I think it would make an even better screenplay. And you have to write it; I don't trust anybody else to do it justice. I made all the notes to make it easier in case you aren't familiar with screenplays."

Robin wasn't sure what to say. He'd seen Phoenix do this before, come in and take control of a situation, but she'd never done it to him. And definitely not in his study.

Robin rounded the desk to where Phoenix stood tapping the top of what Robin now knew was his printed manuscript. He closed his fingers over her shoulders and backed her into the desk with enough swiftness and pressure that she was forced to sit on top of the manuscript she had unceremoniously plopped down on his desk like she owned it. She'd shoved his weeks' worth of notes on the land-water dispute into a heap, and now her ass slid against the manuscript, wrinkling the pages until he'd pushed her so far back, she had to jut her elbows out behind her to keep herself from toppling over.

"Wha— Robin!" Her eyes were narrowed with outrage, even as her mouth gaped in surprise. "What are you doing?"

Robin dropped his hands to the desk, leaning over where she reclined and boxing her in. "I was going to ask you the same question."

"I—" she said, but as she focused in on the stiff set of his shoulders, and the grim line of his mouth, she went silent. After a minute of staring, Robin had trouble keeping his expression tense and disapproving. Eventually, Phoenix said, "I'm sorry," and glanced around her, noticing the disarray she'd made of his desk. "I didn't mean to—"

But Robin didn't let her finish. His lips crashed down onto hers, finding bliss after six days of deprivation. He molded his torso against hers while reaching one arm around her back to support her and push her more firmly against him.

Phoenix gave a cry of alarm that quickly quieted into a purr of approval as she relaxed into his embrace.

"I thought you were angry with me," she whispered against his lips.

"I am furious with you," he said and eased her all the way back, so she was laying on his desk.

Her brows furrowed in confusion as he kissed his way down her arm, over her fingers, before placing one hard kiss to the middle of her palm. Her hand smelled like honey. "Why?" she asked.

Robin didn't answer, but instead reached for the hem of her pencil skirt and pushed it up as far as it would go. Which wasn't nearly far enough.

"Robin," she said. "Are you really angry?"

He reached around to the slit at the back of her skirt, poised to rip the seam up the back. "How much time did you spend on that manuscript?" Robin had seen her amending her logs at night before bed. The woman tracked everything she did.

Her eyes went wide and sorrowful, like a puppy who'd been bopped on the nose for the first time and didn't understand what she'd done wrong.

When she didn't answer, Robin said, "How long, Phoenix?"

"Twenty-seven hours."

"I only sent you the book forty-eight hours ago."

Phoenix swallowed. "Sometimes I get a little wrapped up in my projects."

Robin knew his jaw was set at a stern angle and his eyes had turned flinty, but he couldn't help it. He knew her work ethic, and he knew what she'd been doing to herself.

"And what about your work for Van?"

Her brow uncreased as if she thought she realized why he was upset. "I don't neglect my duties."

"Phoenix," he said, his voice coming out as more of a growl than he meant it to.

She closed her eyes as if she were disappointed in herself, and he knew his voice was too hard and that there was nothing he could do about her working herself into the ground, but he could make sure she took the weekend off to enjoy herself.

Robin ripped her skirt, and Phoenix flipped the fuck out.

She screamed and her foot kicked out, one of her heels caught him in the knee, her nails dug into his arms before one hand swiped for his face at the same time one of her knees connected with his groin and Robin went down.

∾

Phoenix knew she was crying. Knew she had screamed, maybe she was still screaming. She couldn't even tell what was happening as she flew down the stairs on shaky legs; she wrenched one ankle and abandoned her shoes in the stairwell as she pulled herself along the bannister to where her apartment in Robin's house was and locked the door behind her as she collapsed on the floor in a heap.

She couldn't breathe. She was sobbing, and her ankle hurt, and her lungs wouldn't take in air. Oh God, she'd gotten away, and she was going to suffocate after saving herself.

Phoenix pinched her leg. She pinched it hard, pulling at the skin until all she could think about was the pain. Slowly, her breath evened out. The sobs came less frequently, and Phoenix had the presence of mind to wipe the tears from her cheeks.

"Oh God," she said out loud as she looked around the familiar apartment.

How had she even gotten here like this? She wasn't even sure what had happened.

She'd been so excited to talk to Robin about his book, about the millions of possibilities she saw with it. About the pure, raw potential of it that had consumed her for the last two days. She'd thought that maybe he'd be excited with her.

No. Phoenix had been certain of it.

How had she miscalculated so completely?

Not just about Robin's book, but about Robin himself? She'd always felt so safe around him, but upstairs, it had been like he'd been a different person. Aggressive. Scary.

She didn't know why he'd been angry, but he'd pinned her and ripped her skirt, and Phoenix had just reacted.

She reached beneath her, and her favorite navy-blue pencil skirt was split along the back seam, all the way up her ass.

And she'd left her overnight bag on the floor in the foyer.

Fuck.

She pulled herself to her feet and, with unsteady steps, made her way to the bedroom at the back of the apartment in search for any clothes she might have left here, but of course, there was nothing. Phoenix was far too thorough for that. She didn't need to leave anything behind, because she thought ahead for all contingencies, so she always packed exactly what she needed.

Except she didn't foresee her boyfriend— No, not boyfriend, Robin and she weren't in a relationship. They were clearly having a very inappropriate affair—or they had been—because she had never even entertained the idea that Robin Birch could be the kind of man who would overpower a woman for his own means.

Clearly, she had been wrong.

Phoenix's breath started to come too quickly again as her mind realized how narrowly her body had escaped being raped—again.

Holy fuck.

Fresh tears sprang to Phoenix's eyes as flashbacks to middle school flooded her. Her dark, quiet bedroom at her mom's house. The soft sound of footsteps in the hallway. The dim light from the kitchen momentarily illuminating a dark figure sneaking through her door and tiptoeing inside her room. Her stepbrother stretching out over her on her bed, pushing her shirt up and her pajama bottoms down.

Phoenix heard herself gasping again, unable to catch a

breath as she tried to shove the awful memories from her mind. She wouldn't relive that again. She'd worked so hard to push those sensations and fears out of her mind. Out of her being, and all it took was one near miss with a man and Phoenix felt like she was fourteen again. Scared and alone with no one to believe her.

Would anyone believe her about this?

Van wouldn't.

She wouldn't even believe that Phoenix had been sleeping with her dad, let alone that it had gone bad.

Then Phoenix heard pounding footsteps down the interior stairs, and the doorknob rattled as Robin tried to come in after her.

"Phoenix!" he yelled. "Phoenix, open the door."

"Go away!" she called, half hiding behind the bedroom door, as if that would protect her.

"I didn't mean to scare you," he said, and Phoenix heard his voice crack, but she couldn't let that fool her.

She fumbled for her phone in her blazer pocket. Thank God it was still there. She could call the police if she needed to. She could call the car service whenever she wanted. They could park in the back. She could make a break for it out the back entrance if he broke through the door.

"You tore my fucking skirt."

She heard a soft thump and imagined his forehead coming to rest against the door. "I was trying to be sexy." His voice sounded so defeated, Phoenix opened the bedroom door just a little further.

"You were angry with me."

"Fe . . ." He'd started making generous use of the nickname, and she'd found she liked it more so than when anyone else used it. Now it simultaneously made her heart melt and put her on her guard, because she didn't trust it. He was trying to melt her, to convince her to let him in so he could . . . Phoenix wouldn't let herself finish the thought.

She'd always felt safe in this apartment before. Had felt safe for having been offered the use of it instead of one of the many spare bedrooms upstairs. She should have just stayed in a hotel, with built-in security and plenty of anonymity, even if it meant being further from Van when they were in Kansas. She could have avoided all of this.

"I'm sorry," he said when she continued in her silence. "I was upset that you'd devote all your energy to something as silly as my book when you already have so much on your plate, and I showed it the wrong way. I was making a game of my frustration with you, and clearly that was the wrong move, but please, just let me in."

"No."

"I didn't mean to scare you, honey. I'm sorry."

"You goddamn pinned me on the desk and tried to tear my clothes off because you were pissed at me."

"I wasn't really angry," Robin's voice was pitiful. "I was only trying to prove a point, and I was wrong."

Phoenix cocked her head to the side. She wasn't sure she'd ever heard a man admit he was wrong before.

"What point were you trying to prove?" Because her mind could conjure a million different violent scenarios, but her imagination broke when she thought of Robin actually following through with any of them. She was going to break, and she didn't want to break. She didn't want to believe that he was capable of assaulting her, but her body still screamed that she was in danger.

"I'm sorry," he said again, and Phoenix could hear his forehead knock against the apartment door three times as she inched across the living room. "It was a stupid game, and I pushed it too far."

"Why?" She didn't like how small her voice was as she pressed her hand against the door, as if that might make sense of what was happening.

Robin sighed, and Phoenix imagined him sagging against the door. "You already barely sleep. Barely take any time for yourself. That you'd spent so much time on something as stupid as that damn book—"

"I liked the book," Phoenix said, suddenly defensive that he would call his own work stupid. She'd thought it was brilliant.

"And I appreciate that, but I don't like it when you get so wrapped up in what you're working on that you don't check in."

Phoenix frowned as she tried to recall anything out of the last two days that was out of the ordinary and realized she'd been so preoccupied with finishing her notes on Robin's manuscript before she arrived at his front door that she hadn't checked in with him. She hadn't told him she was getting on the plane, or that she'd landed safely. And usually she checked in at every leg of her journey. It was just what she did.

She wanted someone to know where she was since no one else knew about these weekend trips.

"So, you were worried about me?"

"Yes!" Another *thunk* sounded on the door, likely his forehead. She wished he'd stop that. He could hurt himself. "You work too much as it is, and I don't want you to exhaust yourself on my account."

Her hand on the door turned from a steadying pressure to a caress. "You tore my skirt."

A dry chuckle sounded from the other side of the door, and Phoenix got the impression that his whole weight rested against the wood that separated them. "I was annoyed and trying to turn it into a sexy role-play sort of scenario. It was too much, and I'm sorry."

"Oh," was all Phoenix could think to say. And when the silence lengthened between them, she added, "You scared me."

"I know. I'm sorry," Robin said. "But Phoenix, you have to know that I would never hurt you."

She dropped her forehead against the door as her heart broke in two. How many times had she heard that line before? How many times had he said the same thing as he covered her mouth with one hand and pulled down her pajama bottoms with the other?

"I have a hard time trusting men," she said, barely able to force her voice above a whisper.

Robin knocked his forehead against the door again and sighed.

"Stop that," she said, "You're going to hurt yourself."

"I deserve to be hurt," he said. "If I gave you any reason to believe you were in danger with me, I deserve to be hung, drawn, and quartered."

Phoenix turned the lock and pulled open the door, just far enough to peak outside. Robin braced himself with hands on either side of the doorframe. His head was bowed and his shoulders were hunched. He had a red splotch on his forehead and an errant lock of steel-gray hair fell over his right eye. The desperate and forlorn look in his silver eyes broke her heart in a whole new way. One that healed a little bit of the other breaking.

"That's a little extreme, don't you think?"

He shook his head, his lips rolled beneath his teeth, as his eyes roamed over her from head to toe. She wondered how awful she looked. She definitely had mascara streaked down her cheeks, and it wouldn't surprise her if her lipstick were smeared as well. Who the hell knew what her hair was doing. She'd worn it down, so it was probably a tangled mess.

"It's what I want to do to whoever hurt you."

"He's already in jail," Phoenix said.

"Because you put him there?"

She shook her head. She'd never had the guts to confront him publicly. Too many other people hadn't believed her for too long. "He got ten years for trafficking photos of minors on the internet."

Robin cursed. "Were you...?"

She shook her head. "Not of me. He'd moved on by the time I turned sixteen. Too old for him, I guess." She shrugged, even as her body started to tremble, just like she did every time she thought about it.

"Jesus fucking Christ, Fe. I had no idea."

She shrugged one shoulder again. "There's not much to know. My stepbrother is a vile human being, and he's got five more years in prison before I have to worry about him again."

"I hope somebody kills him."

Phoenix let out a noise that was half sob, half laugh. "It's a good possibility."

Robin stepped into the door, pushing it open a little wider, and reached one hand toward her. "Can I?"

She closed her eyes and gave a slight incline of her head.

Robin touched her with just the tips of his fingers at first, wiping away all trace of the wetness that was still running down her cheeks. Then he cupped her jaw and stared into her eyes. All she saw reflected back at her was kindness and devastation on her behalf. Then she saw the scratches on his neck and down his forearms. Scratches that were bleeding because she'd clawed him with nails she kept sharp and pointed in case she needed to use them as weapons.

Phoenix lost herself all over again.

She threw her arms around his waist and buried her face in his chest as she cried. "I'm sorry," she said over and over again as he held her and quietly shushed her.

Phoenix didn't know how long she cried. She didn't remember when they'd settled on the floor, but when she finally quieted, she was in Robin's lap, his shoulder was soaked, and he'd pulled the box of tissues off the side table. His hand ran up and down her spine in a steady rhythm.

And an exhausted calmness had stolen over her. "I'm sorry I scratched you."

"Don't be," he said.

"You have blood on your shirt."

"It'll wash out."

"I panicked."

"It's okay."

"I didn't mean to."

"I know. I didn't mean to either."

"I like the idea of games, in theory."

A rough laugh caught in his throat. "Really?"

"On the right occasion, a little bit of rough play and bodice ripping could be fun."

"Phoenix, you don't have t—"

"But we'd have to both agree to it first, okay? I need to know you're playing and not actually trying to punish me."

He nodded and pressed his nose into her hair. "Of course."

"And maybe we shouldn't try for another few weeks."

"Whatever you want."

Phoenix nestled down further into his embrace. "Is it alright if I just want to go to sleep?"

"Yes."

"Will you stay with me?"

Robin kissed the top of her head. "Always."

CHAPTER 5

*R*obin lay awake next to Phoenix for hours trying to wrap his mind around what had happened to her. And feeling like a prize idiot.

He deserved to be flogged. Because he had been annoyed with her, and he'd been letting her know it, even as he'd tried to seduce her. Where had he been going with that? It had been a game to him, seeing how far she would let him push her, but he didn't trust the place inside him where the idea had originated.

If he would have picked up on her panic and fear sooner, he would have stopped before he'd scared the life out of her.

Jesus Christ, he was the biggest prick.

He didn't deserve the place next to Phoenix in her bed. His desire for her proximity was more reflex than want, but he did not deserve to claim it. The only reason Robin was there was because she'd asked him to stay with her. Because she didn't want to be alone after he'd made her remember the abuse she'd suffered.

Robin expected her to phone her car service and be on a plane to L.A. come morning.

Whatever they'd had going on was over—or would be soon. And Robin wouldn't blame her in the slightest, despite her talk about play.

And he found himself weighed down by the knowledge more than he'd expected to be, like he'd been soaring on lightness Phoenix inspired in him and someone dropped a boulder on his back. He'd been telling himself this whole thing had just been about sex, but his annoyance at her not taking care of herself, his desire to murder her stepbrother, his own anger at himself for frightening her. It spoke of more than a casual fondness for a temporary lover.

The idea of her leaving him in the morning made him want to cling to her sleeping body, to beg her to forgive him, to stay with him. To not go back to L.A. ever again.

But he wouldn't. It wouldn't be fair to her.

A real relationship with her wouldn't be fair to Phoenix, ever. She deserved a man who could stay with her. One who could spend a lifetime with her. That was why this age gap nonsense was ridiculous. He was probably the same age as her father. If they started a life together, he would be geriatric before they even had a chance to get started. She'd still be in her prime, and Robin would be stooped and wrinkled, the way his own father had been at seventy.

This thing between them would have to end sooner or later, so it was just as well if Phoenix left him in the morning.

He must have dozed off at some point, because Robin awoke mid-morning. He was alone in the bed in the basement apartment, the spot where Phoenix had slept long gone cold. He yawned and prepared himself to find the rest of the house empty as well. Sitting up, Robin stretched and adjusted the pair of gray sweatpants he'd worn to sleep. Somehow, sleeping next to Phoenix in only his underwear hadn't seemed right after everything she'd confided in him. And after she'd asked him to stay with her, he'd wanted her to feel as comfortable as possible.

But, by the silence of the house as he ascended the back staircase up into the kitchen, Phoenix hadn't been comfortable enough to stay. He pulled back the checked curtain over the window at the back of the kitchen where a sliver of the driveway was visible between the skeletons of the lilac bushes and the corner of the garage. He craned his neck as if he could spot some evidence that the car service had been by to pick her up. Robin sighed and turned to fill the coffee pot.

As he reached for the glass canister of grounds in the cabinet, he thought he caught the whiff of pizza. There hadn't been pizza in his house for weeks. Possibly since Christmas. But as he measured out the grounds and flipped the maker on, the smell of pepperoni and marinara was too strong to be a coincidence.

Unless he was about to have an aneurysm or a stroke or something. Smelling phantom pizza at nine o'clock in the morning had to be a bad sign, and Robin did not appreciate the reminder of his mortality as he followed the scent through the living room and across the foyer to where his study was tucked under the front staircase.

The smell not only grew stronger as he approached, but he could make out the soft swish and shuffle of papers. So, someone had broken into his house, ordered a pizza, and was in his office sorting through his case files?

But even from the doorway, Robin could make out

Phoenix's flame red hair poking over the top of his desk. A Skittle's pizza box just visible on the floor to her right.

The mess of crumpled paper and spilled file folders that had covered his desk and littered the floor when he'd collected himself after Phoenix's crotch shot was significantly smaller than it had been the night before.

Robin stepped on the creaky floorboard so Phoenix would hear him approach. The sound of shifting paper paused, then resumed, her acknowledgement that she'd heard him.

"You know, some of those files are confidential. Especially the water dispute."

Phoenix shrugged. She wore the shirt he'd had on the night before and the yoga pants that had gotten lost in his bed on Christmas. The ones he'd been keeping as a trophy but had brought her to wear as a concession for the ripped skirt. "Then I guess it's a good thing I'm trustworthy."

Robin recognized the false lightness in her voice as what she used whenever she had to make a statement on Van's behalf. Her press voice. One meant to put people at ease at the same time it hid her true feelings. He rounded the side of the desk and knelt in front of her and covered her hands with his.

"Phoenix," he said. "You don't have to clean this up."

She didn't meet his eye. "It's my fault that everything's a mess."

Robin pulled the file folder from her grip, then shuffled the stack she'd been sorting together and set it aside. "It's not. I'm the one who behaved like a prick."

Her head shot up at that, her eyes a little wide, her mouth pulled into the barest hint of a smile. "I couldn't sleep this morning," she said. Robin recognized that shifting the conversation away from guilt and blame was both an apology and an acceptance of forgiveness.

"Because you were hungry?" he asked, nodding toward the half-eaten pizza.

"Partially." Phoenix lowered her gaze to the stacks of paper at her knees, and a lock of hair fell into her eyes. Phoenix didn't wear her hair down often. It was always in a neat, efficient updo so it didn't get in her way throughout her workday, but Robin loved the way the sunset red locks tumbled over her shoulders in slight waves. He especially liked how her hair was fluffed from sleep instead of its usual shiny slickness.

He reached out a hand and tucked the hair behind her ear. "And what was the other part?"

She shrugged again, and Robin wondered if she ever talked about herself with anyone. Robin had learned important things about her over the last few weeks. She always slept with one leg outside the covers. She measured every ingredient when she cooked, even if she was just making herself a salad. She liked oversized sweatshirts and fluffy socks in the evenings, but she really did like her structured clothes for working. She used exactly one tablespoon of coconut milk creamer in her coffee in the mornings, and even when Van wanted to order a pizza, Phoenix would eat one slice and switch to salad. He even knew a little about her family, her background, but when it came to what she was thinking? How she felt about her life? If she truly found her work fulfilling or if she worked so much because she was escaping something else? Robin still wasn't sure.

He did know that she wasn't magically healed by a night of sleeping in his arms. If nothing else, the pizza proved that point.

"Phoenix," he said.

"Just feeling insecure, I guess. It happens sometimes."

So that's what this was. Robin had never seen Phoenix vulnerable before last night. 'Powerhouse' was the word he normally associated with her. She was the kind of person who always got everything done. Most people complained about balancing fitness, career, family, sex life, but Phoenix gave the appearance of having it all figured it out. But perhaps all the regimentation, all the scheduling, was there for a reason, and Robin found himself wanting to know a little bit more about what that might be.

What could this beautiful, capable woman possibly have to feel insecure about? But he knew better than to voice that opinion aloud. Instead he asked, "What about?"

"I get antsy sometimes when I don't feel useful."

"Ah," was all Robin had the heart to say, probably because his heart was breaking. He supposed it made sense. Being shuffled between parents like she was a burden and a liability instead of a treasure, working in a field that demanded constant awareness and evolution. Then last night. He imagined she was exhausted, possibly afraid that he didn't want her anymore.

He had to stifle the urge to let out a morbid laugh at the idea, when he'd spent the whole night expecting her to be the one to not want him. Instead, he scooted closer to her, careful not to disturb the neat stacks of paper she'd made. "You don't have to be useful here," he said at the same time that he smoothed his fingers into her hair. She leaned into his touch, so he did it again and again until she crawled into his lap.

Phoenix crooked one hand around his neck, her thumb brushing back and forth over the base of this throat. He continued to trace his fingers through her hair, and Phoenix made the satisfied sound she usually made when he was spooning her in bed.

"I was afraid I might have scared you off with all my baggage," she said, and Robin tightened his hold on her. He wanted to crush her into the safety of his arms, to tell her that she should never be afraid, especially of him not wanting her. Even if he knew this strange relationship of theirs couldn't ever go anywhere, Robin had started to suspect that he might never stop wanting her.

"You're in a relationship with a man who's already lost two wives, and that hasn't scared you off. Why would yours scare me?"

Phoenix angled her head up to look at him, and offered him a soft, sympathetic smile. "Sometimes I forget that you're a widower."

A cold shot of pain sliced through Robin's chest. Not at being reminded of his wives or the loss of them, but at the idea that it was possible to forget. Robin could never forget, though a part of him wanted to forget the gut-wrenching finality of Mary Beth's sudden passing, and the slow, soul-rending powerlessness of watching Caroline waste away. The grief would linger with him always, a phantom always crouching in his shadow. Probably the same way the pain of what her stepbrother had done to her would stay with Phoenix.

"Have you ever lost someone that way?" he asked.

Phoenix snorted. "My mom's mom died when I was nine, but she and my mom didn't get along in the same ways that my mom and I don't get along." Phoenix's fingers crept up his neck in spider-light tickles until her fingers were buried in his hair. "I'm not sure I've ever loved anyone enough to miss them the way you must."

Robin was silent a moment, contemplating what a lonely life it was that Phoenix must lead to never have held anyone close enough to feel as if a part of her was missing when they were taken away. He took comfort in the feel of her nails in his hair as she relaxed into his arms. Uncurling a little and leaning into him rather than rolled in a ball against him.

"There are two people I could think of that losing would devastate me."

"Who?" He asked, foolishly thinking of himself. Wishing possibly more than he should.

"Van, of course," she said, and Robin nodded. He'd expected that one. "And Eve."

She fell silent as if she were contemplating the pain of those losses, and Robin asked, "Who is Eve?"

Phoenix shook herself from her dark musings and withdrew her fingers from his hair. She traced the line of his collarbone from shoulder to chest and only then seemed to become aware that he wasn't wearing a shirt. She looked down at her shirt, and a small smile played at her mouth as she realized that he wasn't wearing a shirt because she had stolen it.

"Eve is my mentor. She's worked in the film industry since she was my age. I met her when I was slush-pile reader. I brought a script straight to her office and told her it needed to be made into a movie, and she told me she liked my moxie."

"Did the movie get made?"

Phoenix snorted. "No. But she made me her assistant, and I worked for her for two years before Van came along. I still call her for advice sometimes, and we have brunch together once a month. She's kind of a surrogate mother."

Hatred for Phoenix's parents coursed through him. She had a mother and a stepmother and she was still forced to find her own mother figure. Brunch once a month was nice, he supposed. That was about all he saw Van these days, but she lived half a continent away, not in the same city. And even then, this woman was a business contact. A mentor. Perhaps she was also a friend, but Jesus Christ, Phoenix needed a family.

He knew that was what Van had become to her, but as much as Phoenix had become friends with Bryant and Bishop, she still held them at arm's length. She didn't seem to like Clay, which Robin hadn't understood before last night, but he supposed Clay's crush on Van was enough to make him suspect in her mind. But both Clay and his crush on his stepsister were harmless. They always had been.

Robin wasn't stupid, he'd noticed the way his stepson watched his daughter. Robin had drawn clear boundaries with Clay about his duties as an older brother when he'd married Clay's mother and brought him into the house, and Clay had taken Van's safety seriously from the beginning. He still did. Robin had had to talk him down from flying out to Los Angeles and pursuing vigilante justice when a stalker had broken into Van's condo in the fall.

Instead, Clay had flown down the next week to record an episode of *Pop Star*, Van's reality show, where they made it appear as though both Bryant and Clay had been visiting Van when the stalker had broken in. They hadn't been. Thankfully, nobody had been there. Van's security had chased him off in the attempt to apprehend him. Two days after the show had aired, the motherfucker who'd been threatening his daughter had been caught, and as much as Robin was thankful for Clay's fierce loyalty, he'd known the idea to force the issue on the TV show had been Phoenix's.

And he was thankful every day that this woman was in his daughter's life.

Robin only hoped that whatever they were doing here wouldn't ruin that relationship. Because as much as he wanted Phoenix to be a part of his family, she and Van needed each other more than either of them needed him.

Because he wasn't sure what else to do, Robin kissed the top of Phoenix's head, and she sighed into him as her hand splayed over his chest.

"You're the best man I know," she whispered into his skin, and Robin wasn't sure whether he'd been supposed to hear that. Though he felt as though he'd stepped into a hot, fresh shower on a cold winter morning with the way her words warmed his bones.

"I'm just an old man," he said.

Phoenix perked up then, shifting so that she straddled his hips, her arms wrapped around his neck. "You are not that old," she said.

"The mirror says different," he said, though he was only half joking.

Phoenix ran both hands through his gray hair, then traced his sideburns down into his silver beard. Her thumbs smoothed over his eyebrows, and he hadn't realized he'd been frowning until her fingers coaxed his forehead to relax.

"I don't know what the mirror's been showing you, but I see a gorgeous man who throws his sex appeal off in waves that you can feel from states away." It was Robin's turn to snort, and Phoenix bopped him on the nose with one blue, sharp-tipped fingernail. "Well, maybe not everyone finds your intensity attractive, but I do. It's not every man who can command the respect of an entire room, but also knows when to keep his mouth shut."

Robin thought about how he was often on the periphery of the strange little family his daughter had built up around them. He'd always felt like the equivalent of a parent watching the neighborhood kids at the park, always cast in the same benevolent father role he played at Christmas. Though he rarely spoke or corralled. It was Phoenix who kept everyone on schedule and in line. He was just there. Appreciated and invited, but somehow still just on the periphery, still lending his support.

One of the most important things he'd learned about showing love after Caroline had died was how important it was to just be there. He would never not be somewhere when Van asked him to be. But that Phoenix saw that part of him, admired it in him, was attracted to him, made Robin realize exactly how much she saw from behind her screens. When he met her eyes, he saw more than he'd been prepared to see. A tenderness and vulnerability that he didn't think was safe or smart, but fuck if he wasn't power-less to deny her.

His lips met hers in a hot kiss that meant more than he'd wanted it to, but even if it was just in this moment, Robin didn't know how to deny what he felt for this delicate woman who was somehow made of steel. He wanted her in his arms and in his life and could be selfish for just a little while longer.

~

All of Phoenix's work had been undone by the time she surfaced from under the haze of pleasure Robin's touch always pulled her into. They lay sprawled over a blanket of printer paper.

"I hope none of these were too important," she said pulling a crumpled, slightly damp sheet out from under her hip.

Robin shrugged and tossed the paper over his shoulder. "They were mostly notes on a case."

"An important case?" Phoenix asked. She didn't really know much about his work. It wasn't something that came up often. Robin was a lawyer in a small city in Western Kansas. She'd sort of assumed that he'd handled mostly small, Western-Kansas cases. But that was before she'd known him like this. Now she knew that she'd been unfair to him.

"This water dispute case will likely define my career, be a stepping stone for me into bigger and better things."

Phoenix didn't know what water disputes were like in the Midwest. In California, water was a big deal, and everybody was fighting over it all the time. But in Kansas? Everything was always so green during the warm months. Her eyes flicked to the window, where the bare branches of a deciduous tree Phoenix probably should have known the name of but didn't, stood brown and drab. And she shivered and snuggled deeper into Robin's arms. Having seasons was still something she wasn't used to. It was such a stark change, getting on the plane in L.A. and getting off the plane in Kansas.

"Who's the dispute between?" Phoenix asked. "I always think of the Supreme Court when I think of water rights."

"That's when it's states arguing over who gets what. My

case is between a rancher and large grain farmer, arguing who gets what percentage of the water that runs through both their properties."

"And who are you representing?" she asked.

"The cattle rancher."

"Do you think you'll win?"

Robin's kissed a line over her bare shoulder. "I wouldn't have taken the case if I didn't think I could."

"And what's the significance if you win?" Phoenix asked. "Why would it make your career?"

"Because it would set a precedent for more responsible water usage, particularly for grain farmers in arid climates."

Phoenix wasn't sure she'd call Western Kansas arid, but what did she know? She'd lived next to the ocean her entire life.

"Will you at least look over the notes I made about turning your novel into a screenplay? I want to show it to Eve."

"If I can find the pages in all this mess," he said and kissed up her jaw.

Phoenix smiled a satisfied smile, and finally felt herself go drowsy with satisfaction and lack of sleep as Robin kept kissing her neck. "Don't worry," she said. "I always make copies."

CHAPTER 6

The local historical society meeting had lasted an hour longer than it needed to that evening, and the only thing that masked the loud rumble of Robin's stomach was the scuff and scrape of the chairs around the conference table as everyone stood.

"Henry's?" John asked him as they gathered their things.

"Please," Robin said, as he closed his folders into his messenger bag. He used to carry a briefcase, the nice one in a fawn leather his father had purchased for him upon his graduation from law school. But the briefcase had started to show its age after twenty-five years of use and Van had gifted him a new bag for Christmas two years ago that helped protect his laptop as well. Which was something he'd needed. He'd dented his last computer, letting it rattle around inside his briefcase with everything else he carried, even with a protective sleeve.

Still, there were times where Robin felt out of place among his colleagues in this small town. His suits were better quality, tailored to hug his still-fit physique while the rest of the men in the room were either so skinny that their collars hung loose around their necks or had paunches straining the buttons at middles. Then throw in the cross-body messenger bag, the Italian loafers, and the watch Van had given him after her first big paycheck—well, Robin felt like he didn't quite fit in with this group anymore. Like he was destined for bigger and better than maybe just what running for mayor of Wellville might imply.

That had been his plan for the last two decades. First the city council, then mayor for two years, then the state senate for ten. But he was already five years behind his goal, and he was restless. He'd already been on the city council for eight years. What more did he have to offer as mayor? The idea felt redundant, like treading water, and it wouldn't even come with the redeeming, roll-up-your-sleeves-and-help-restore-windows-in-a-historic-building-on-the-weekends diversion like his position on the board of the historical society did.

The statewide organization had asked if he was interested in taking on an officer's role. Namely, they wanted him to act as presumptive president, making him president during the 2020 term—at which point he planned to be actively running for office. He wasn't entirely certain, but he couldn't imagine that that wouldn't be a conflict of interest.

"You heard the news then," John asked as they were seated at their usual table at Henry's. It was a slightly upscale steakhouse downtown—the closest Wellville got to fine dining. Frank, the other part of their friend group, the manager of the main bank in town, was already waiting for them, having beat them there from his board of trustees meetings.

"That Carlisle isn't running for reelection next year?" Frank said. The bastard had already eaten half the bread basket.

Robin snagged a slice before the glutton ate it all. There were three reasons Robin came to Henry's. They under-charged on good Scotch, their fresh-baked bread rivaled his grandmother's, and the only place you'd find better steak was if you butchered the damn cow yourself.

"Not just that Carlisle isn't running for reelection," Robin said, as he spread butter on his slice of bread. "But that they don't have anybody to run instead."

They were speaking about the long-time Kansas repre-sentative to the House in Washington D.C. He was essen-tially retiring, and the Republican Party didn't have anyone in the queue to take his place.

"There hasn't been a Democratic rep from this district in more than sixty years," John said.

Rebecca, their usual server, set down a glass of ice water and whiskey in front of both Robin and John. She'd been flashing Robin an extra-warm smile for months now, and he'd always brushed it off as a woman who was interested in his near fame and far, far too young for him. But as he looked at her now, he realized she was probably the same age as Phoenix.

Robin's stomach clenched at the thought. Both at the reminder that he was sleeping with someone young enough to be his daughter and also because he hadn't seen Phoenix in more than two weeks. Between his upcoming case and her award season commitments, they hadn't been able to make time for each other recently.

He ached for her in ways he hadn't expected. Yes, his body wanted hers, but he found himself missing the ability to reach for her hand, the way she always scraped her nails over his forearm as she brushed past him in the kitchen. The way she microwaved her coffee six times because she couldn't drink it unless it was scalding her tongue. Or the way she texted him at precisely the same time every day when they were apart. He didn't like admitting how much he missed her. Then he'd have to admit how he actually felt about her, and that was something he couldn't ever allow himself. Phoenix definitely did not deserve the consequences.

"But there hasn't been a candidate as strong as Birch in that time," Frank said to John; then he grinned at Robin. "And no one with near your name recognition either."

Robin took a quick sip of the whiskey. The top shelf Scotch he preferred, neat. "As long as we leave Van out of it."

Rebecca was back with a new basket of bread but didn't stay to take their order, though from the interested tilt of her head, Robin suspected she'd heard Van's name.

"Not entirely out of the campaign, surely," John said. He'd raised his own glass. Some cheap American swill. Robin could see his campaign manager's spirits sinking like the Titanic.

"Yes, entirely. My potential political career has nothing to do with my daughter."

"But most of the country already knows who you are," John said. "We should capitalize on that."

"As long as it's an avenue to introducing voters to what I stand for, then sure. But we're not trotting my daughter out like a circus pony to mesmerize people into voting for me."

John frowned into his drink. He hadn't reached for a slice of bread. Good. He was taking his pre-diabetes diagnosis seriously. Robin would need him healthy if they were really going to do this.

"Perhaps she could sing the national anthem when we announce your candidacy?"

"We can discuss it" was all Robin would say. He knew if he asked Van, she would say yes, but as proud of he was of his daughter's success, the last thing Robin wanted to do was use her to get elected. Sure, that voters would recognize him from her reality show wouldn't hurt, but he hoped it made them more apt to listen to him. To vote for blue in a traditionally red district. But he had worked his whole life to get this point. Maybe it was his own ego getting in the way, but if Robin was going to join the House of Representatives, he wanted it to be because of what he stood for, what he could do for the people of Kansas, not because his daughter was a household name.

Robin adored Van. He loved how fearless she was. He admired that part of her, even if there were times, like when she'd moved to L.A. on her own, that it had made him nervous as hell. But that had all worked out. Van was doing well. Clay's business was growing every month. He was finally putting the guilt of how he'd failed Mary Beth behind him, and life was moving on. He had the chance to do something for himself.

And Robin was going to take it.

CHAPTER 7

*P*hoenix hadn't seen Robin for almost a month. He'd kissed her and put her on the plane back to L.A. after that horrible night back in February, and they'd been so busy with individual projects and accommodating Van's schedule that they couldn't spare a weekend away. When Robin finally arrived on her doorstep at ten o'clock on a Friday night near the end of March, she didn't let him leave her bed for almost twenty-four hours.

God, she had missed him. She'd missed the feel of his garden-calloused fingertips skimming over her skin. She missed the feel of his lips on her lips, her jaw, her neck, her shoulder, and lower. She missed his quiet confidence, his mischievous eyebrow raises, the way he looked at her like she was a treat he didn't deserve. She even missed how fucking bossy he was.

That was a part of him that Phoenix hadn't expected. The bossy, stubborn part of him that he kept under wraps. She'd always seen him as a man of few words and a large presence. She'd always noticed his manner, and his face, if she was honest with herself. She'd always thought he was dead gorgeous and his graying hair only enhanced his inherent attractiveness.

Back when they'd met, he'd just been Van's married Dad. Phoenix had never thought of him as old or off-limits, even after he'd become a widower again. It was more like she'd just never thought of him until one day he'd reminded her to take care of herself, and then he'd walked into her field of vision all crisp and clear and beautiful, and she hadn't been able to stop thinking of him.

She'd had some time to examine their relationship since Christmas, how neither one of them had shown their peculiarities to the other yet, how he hadn't known that she might not recognize play. That she hadn't figured out how all his pieces fit together quite yet. That he was part mother hen, part stubborn asshole, and part force of nature, she saw, but those weren't who Robin was as a whole.

Over the past few weeks apart they'd texted a lot, but not the constant exchange of thoughts Phoenix wanted to have. She'd had multiple devices at her fingertips for so long that no one even thought twice about her texting during a meeting. They just assumed that Phoenix was quietly and efficiently putting out a fire that no one else wanted to even know about, much less deal with. And most of the time, that was exactly what Phoenix was doing. If she happened to be sneaking in lascivious texts to her boyfriend, then so what?

No.

Not boyfriend.

Lover.

Robin was not her boyfriend. They were carrying on a secret affair. It might even be illicit. It definitely wasn't something they could tell other people about. It was entirely the wrong time to be fending off a media shit storm about Phoenix dating Van's father. It wouldn't be as big as the one that was threatening to break to the public any day now, the way Van and Bishop were carrying on. When the world found out that Van and Bryant had never really been together and that Van Birch was now dating her manager? Phoenix didn't want to think about it, because she already knew she wouldn't sleep for weeks, and she definitely wouldn't be able to sneak away to Kansas for a weekend to escape into Robin's bed for a little respite from the piranhas waiting to devour Van piece by piece.

But Phoenix would do it for Van. And she knew Robin would understand. That was one of the biggest things they had in common. They were both one-hundred percent there to support Van. But if Phoenix didn't have to deal with the media circus regarding her own relationship, she didn't want to. Not yet anyway. Not after he'd given that speech about keeping it quiet the last time he'd visited her in L.A.

But Phoenix could see the practicality behind keeping whatever they were under warps for now. Would she like to call him her boyfriend? Absolutely.

She just wasn't sure where Robin stood on the issue, and despite his texts and his phone calls and his dedication to flying to see her multiple times since this whole thing had started, she had a feeling that he was even more commitment-phobic than she was. And more spooked by their age gap than he would ever admit to her out loud.

But good lord, after nearly a month apart, they'd spent a full twenty-four hours in bed. They'd only left to get food and drink so they didn't run out of energy for all the naughty touching they had to make up for. Phoenix thought that maybe she was falling a little bit in love with him when he brought her coffee in bed Sunday morning and suggested they get out of the house.

"Where would you like to go?" she asked.

He sat on the bed next to her with his own cup of coffee. He wore only his boxer briefs, and Phoenix couldn't help that her left hand reached out to trace the contours of his abdomen. He'd leaned out over the last few weeks, his muscles closer to the surface than they had been before. She suspected he was doing it to impress her, and she was not going to object in the slightest. He was already the most attractive man she'd ever seen naked, and if he wanted more muscles for her, she would let him build them.

His stomach twitched as if she'd tickled him, and Phoenix smiled into her coffee as he covered her hand with his and squeezed. "If I don't get you out of this house, I'm afraid you might do me in."

"From too much sex?" she asked.

"Yes."

"That's not possible."

"But it is possible to be so sore I won't be able to think straight during my hearing on Monday."

Phoenix waggled her eyebrows. "If you're looking for an apology, you're going to be disappointed."

Then Robin's stomach growled, loud and long and empty sounding. He'd basically eaten their entire giant sushi order by himself last night. Phoenix had only sampled one of each of the rolls they'd ordered, and he'd inhaled the rest.

"See," he said. "Too much exertion and not enough fuel could break a man at my age."

Phoenix rolled her eyes. "You look so broken."

But she tossed the duvet back and slid out of bed all the

same. She needed a shower, and she wouldn't mind a meal that wasn't takeout for a change.

Phoenix wound up taking him to her usual brunch spot, because it was discreet and exclusive, and as long as she was indulging in Robin, why not delight in her other favorite indulgence. Phoenix didn't usually eat regular bread. It was an extravagance she had learned she couldn't afford and not show up on the cover of tabloids with an arrow pointing toward her abdomen and endless pregnancy speculation A croissant or two at her favorite bistro every now and then was acceptable however.

Phoenix was a little nervous that the paparazzi might be out since she and Van did sometimes come here together on Sundays, but as Robin opened the door for her, no one even seemed to notice them. She still didn't dare take his hand. And because they both knew the stakes, he didn't grab for it.

That didn't stop him from tapping his foot against hers after they sat down, or his fingers from brushing hers when he handed her the drink menu. Or from teasing her about not being able to take the heat from his ultra-spicy Bloody Mary and having to down her entire first mimosa to tame her taste buds.

When he was still laughing at her as she took a healthy sip of her second mimosa the second their server delivered it, she kicked him with her pointy heel under the table.

"I don't like spicy food, okay?"

"You're such a California girl," he laughed. "Avocado and cilantro all the way."

Phoenix rolled her eyes, but she had ordered a slice of avocado toast with mango cilantro jam on it to go with her giant butter croissant and eggs, while the dish Robin had ordered always came dusted with crushed red pepper flakes.

She attempted to kick his shin again, but Robin caught her ankle before she connected and started running his finger up the inside of her calf. If they were trying to keep their relationship a secret, they were doing a terrible job of it. Phoenix found herself not caring when the playful look in Robin's eye turned heated. She was just thinking that she might prefer to have Robin for breakfast after all when a husky feminine voice said, "Phoenix, darling, I haven't seen you in weeks."

Robin dropped her leg and sat up straight as Phoenix hopped to her feet to place a kiss on either side of Eve's cheeks, which was how she preferred to be greeted.

"Eve, it's so lovely to see you."

"Same, darling. Where have you been lately? You're even more impossible to pin down than usual."

"Same with Van," Phoenix said.

"Yes, Vanessa does keep you on the run. Where is the dear girl? Is she here?" Eve was tall and thin with smooth blonde hair Phoenix had never seen down. She peered over the tables looking for Van's shorter form, but then her eyes landed on Robin, and her lips curled into a smile Phoenix could only describe as 'interested.' Very interested.

"Van is on her own this morning," Phoenix said. "Have you met her father, Robin?"

Robin stood then and offered his hand. "Robin Birch," he said.

Eve placed her hand in his, not to shake, but the way a lady might who expected her knuckles to be kissed. "Eve de Silva."

Robin squeezed her hand and stepped back to motion to the table, and Phoenix was impressed by how smoothly he was dealing with Eve's blatant scrutiny. "Would you like to join us?"

Eve raised her eyebrows, as if she was also impressed, but said, "Unfortunately I am here with a business companion, but I am curious how you managed to lure our Phoenix away from her technology this morning."

Her eyes flickered between the two of them, and Phoenix knew she had to have seen him teasing her. She just hoped the tablecloth had blocked most of leg fondling.

"I'm working on a screenplay," Robin said, "And Phoenix offered to give me some advice, given her history."

It was Phoenix's turn to raise her eyebrows. Robin had said he'd been reviewing her notes, but that he'd actually started working on the screenplay was news to Phoenix. He'd made it sound like his caseload was taking all his time. And he certainly hadn't asked Phoenix for her advice.

Eve opened her clutch and handed Robin her card. "Send it to me when you're done with it. I would be happy to critique it for you."

That was a generous offer. Eve never sought out new manuscripts. She was already drowning in more than she could handle.

"Thank you," Robin said.

Eve only nodded and turned to Phoenix; she wrapped an arm around Phoenix's shoulders. "When you tire of him dear, send him my way, will you?"

Then she stepped back and said, "Enjoy your meal," to them both and swept away in a flutter of her breezy yellow blouse.

"So, that's Eve?" Robin asked after they had taken their seats again.

"That's Eve." Phoenix couldn't help her wide grin. "And

she *likes* you."

"I had the impression she'd like to eat me for lunch," Robin said with a laugh.

"What makes you think I won't?"

Robin's answer was a sly grin as he settled his napkin into his lap. He said, "Because you know I'd eat you first," as the server set their food down in front of them, and Phoenix felt her toes curl. There was definitely a promise in that statement.

Later that week, Robin shared a file with Phoenix. She got the notification while she was in a meeting at the television network. Curious, she clicked it open anyway. The note he'd left with it read, *I wasn't completely lying, anyway.*

In the document, Phoenix found the very beginning of Robin's screenplay.

She minimized and flipped back to her meeting notes on her tablet. They had already planned out most of the upcoming season, so a large portion of her work was done. She was only taking notes as they haggled over the filming schedule so that Phoenix knew where Van had to be when, and to make sure that filming didn't coincide with any of the things Van liked to keep completely private, like her training sessions and her time with Bishop.

The cameras were only allowed to follow her for four hours a week outside the scripted episodes. Most of that ended up being filler material, but it was still an energy drain on all of them when they were constantly playing everything up.

The reality show had been Phoenix's idea, and Eve had helped her pitch it to the network. Eve still carried an executive producer title, even if Phoenix did most of the actual work. *Pop Star* had been what had allowed Phoenix to buy the house in Malibu. To set up a fund for girls who'd been abused by family members like she had and create her reputation as a powerhouse in both the music and television industries.

Phoenix loved the empire she'd created for Van. She tended to it like the most attentive gardener to a rose garden. She allowed herself, just for a second, to feel unstoppable.

Her phone buzzed on the table. She glanced at it and saw that it was from Robin. She nestled the phone against her tablet screen and clicked the message.

Take off your clothes was all it said.

Phoenix rolled her eyes and tapped back. *I'm in a meeting. Get out of it.*

She checked her watch. It was almost four o'clock, which meant in Kansas, it was almost six.

I'll be done in an hour. I can consider your ridiculous demands then.

Instead of words, Robin texted her a picture. Of him. In bed. Shirtless.

She was so busy staring at Robin's bare torso on her phone screen that she missed what date and time Rob had just asked her about, and she'd had to ask him to repeat the question while she flipped back to the calendar app on her tablet.

Another text came in from Robin as the meeting proceeded, and Phoenix turned the phone to silent so it would stop buzzing every time Robin texted, since he seemed set on whatever his agenda was. But as she minimized the volume control, Phoenix got an eyeful of exactly what his agenda was and felt herself go red as she minimized the conversation before anyone could see.

Robin Birch was sexting her.

And it was actually kind of really hot.

I am still in a meeting, she texted back.

I already told you to get out of it.

And do what? Take my clothes off in the bathroom? No thank you.

I need you, Fe. This was accompanied by another, somehow even more explicit picture. Phoenix had received dick pics before. Hell, some of them had even been fun mutual texting situations, but none of them had made her squirm in her seat the way Robin's cock encircled by his long fingers was doing to her now. God, she wanted to sink down onto that length and then bite him for teasing her. But it was only Tuesday, and Phoenix wouldn't see him and be able to scold him for his unpredictable misbehaving until Friday.

Robin. Stop.

The next text was a picture of his face. Phoenix knew that face. It was the one he made when he was trying not to come, and she had to bite her lip.

She was starting to think he was possibly intoxicated. It didn't matter that he was actually turning her on with all his teasing.

Well, I'm still in a meeting, so until you learn to time your shenanigans after working hours for both of us, I'm afraid you're on your own.

Then she turned her phone off and set it aside. Just the knowledge that Robin was in his bed, naked, thinking of her as he pleasured himself had Phoenix's concentration on the fritz. And Phoenix didn't haven't trouble concentrating. She was able to concentrate on multiple things at once. She had to; she basically controlled the lives of two people.

But she had to ask questions. Phoenix didn't ask questions. She was almost always the one telling people how it was done.

When she wrapped up, she was so flustered and annoyed that she turned her phone on to tell Robin off only to find a photo montage of him getting off, and Phoenix spent the whole ride home plotting her revenge.

Robin cracked open a beer and settled into his desk to work on the screenplay he'd started earlier, because he was committed now. He'd shared it with Phoenix, and he knew she would hound him until it was finished, and probably critique it as she went. He shook his head as he sipped his beer. He'd wonder what he'd gotten himself into, but he knew. With the trial. With Phoenix. With the campaign. Then add the screenplay on top of that. He knew exactly what he was doing with work and the campaign. What he hadn't bargained on was how all-consuming Phoenix would become. Robin should have known. He hadn't spent six months denying his attraction for nothing. He'd had a hunch it would turn into this impossible situation. Where he couldn't get her out of his mind, where he couldn't get enough of the feel of her body. Where he would find himself longing for her company, not just in bed, but her distracted conversation at dinner. The way she bumped his hip out of the way so she could take over the vanity mirror in his bathroom as she got ready in the mornings. How he'd had to start working out more because finishing the food off her plate had caused him to gain almost ten pounds in January, despite having more sex than he'd had since his early twenties.

And all of it would be good. It would be fantastic, if it were any other woman on earth. Well—it could be better if the woman was closer to his own age, but a woman twenty-five years his junior who also happened to be his daughter's best friend and business partner was a disaster waiting to happen. For multiple reasons.

Robin could feel it looming. It had been almost a whole season. The first hints of spring were sprouting up through the frozen ground. Winter was slowly losing ground to a verdant green spring, and Robin knew that this relationship should have ended already. Maybe that was why he'd pulled the stunt he did earlier. To push her in some way, whether it was away or it was into thinking he was no better than a nineteen-year-old boy. Jesus, what had he been thinking sexting her and sending her cum shots?

Yeah.

He'd done that.

Robin rubbed his hand over his beard, half ashamed, half proud of his little stunt this afternoon. She'd been annoyed, but he knew she'd also been turned on. Knowing Phoenix, she was probably more pissed than anything, and a part of him was awaiting her return volley. Since she was fire to her very core, he expected to be set aflame.

It had been radio silence for the past few hours. Though that had been part of the fun, because he knew the usual Tuesday evening routine was yoga and smoothies with Van. But that was fine. He could be patient.

He tapped a few lines into his new manuscript. Deleted a few more. He reread the first chapter of his first novel. Then the second. Then he flipped through the screenwriting book he'd just finished reading, and just when he'd opened a second bottle of beer—something he never did on a weeknight—cracked his knuckles, and prepared to finish the opening scene, his phone chimed.

It took him a second to make sense of what he was seeing, then the purple vibrator came into focus against the blue and white pattern of the comforter on Phoenix's bed. And just as he was about to ask if she was going to use that, or if she already had, a new text came in.

If any of this ends up on the internet or in the hands of anybody who isn't you, I will destroy you so completely, you'll only have a chance to be sorry as the wind sweeps your ashes away into a damn field of cow turds. Got it?

Ashes and cow pies. Got it.

Then he sat back in his office chair, his beer in one hand, his phone in the other.

A photo came next, a selfie, hair still up from yoga, focused just low enough to show that she was topless with her arm crossed over her breasts, but not low enough to see what her arm didn't cover. Then there was a shot of her lower half, her legs crossed to preserve her modesty, but it showed off the bare curve of her hip and the smooth skin of her upper thighs.

Robin loved the skin on her legs. The smooth softness over developed muscles. The silken feel against his lips, the tight grip of them around his hips as he nestled inside her.

He felt himself stirring to life, even though his release earlier had been fucking intense.

Phoenix's next message read, *Oh, and before I continue. There's one rule for this little show.*

What's that?

You're not allowed to touch yourself.

Tease

Do you agree?

I accept your terms. Proceed.

She sent him a photo of herself flipping him off, but she did nothing to hide her nakedness, and he could see her clearly, seated on the edge of her bed. One breast was exposed, her legs slightly parted, but all that was in focus was her aggrieved expression and her middle finger.

So maybe he'd grovel a little bit.

You're gorgeous.

He was rewarded with a photo of her torso taken from above as she reclined on the bed. Full breasts and long, thin waist with just the flare of hips. Then another photo, the same vantage point, but lower, showing off the thin strip of red that disappeared between the *V* of her closed thighs, and Robin groaned.

She was definitely pissed if she was teasing him this hard, but he found that he could get behind this kind of anger as the next shot was of her hand squeezed down into that V. Then there was one of the vibrator resting against her belly, and Robin swallowed hard as he saw where she was going with this, and he wanted so badly to see her do this. To be there to watch her come apart as she pleasured herself.

You still keeping your hands off yourself?

Yes, ma'am. And he was. He'd put his beer down, but he'd kept his hands away from where his erection was growing painful against the zipper in his jeans.

Then, instead of another text, a video chat from Phoenix took over his screen. But instead of her face, the phone looked down on her from her bedside table. Robin could see the tip of her chin, her slender shoulders, both breasts, and he could trace where her arm should be disappearing between her legs if the angle had been wide enough for him to see.

It took a moment for him to make sense of the sounds he was hearing, but when he did, he sat forward in his chair.

Holy shit.

The buzz of the vibrator whined, and Phoenix made satisfied, breathy pants as her body writhed.

"Jesus Christ," he said, and Robin could practically hear Phoenix smile as she undulated into her toy. God, he wished he could see what she was doing with it, but that, he thought, was part of the punishment she was dishing out.

He was seeing just enough to haunt him for the rest of the week. She knew he'd have a constant hard-on until they were together again, and it was clear that she did not care.

"You're killin' me, Fe." he said.

She hummed, then sighed. "That's kind of the idea, old man."

He groaned and considered joining her as his free hand strayed toward his belt, but she anticipated him, tilting her face onto the screen. "The 'no-touching' rule still applies."

Was she watching him as she pleasured herself?

Robin cursed and ran his hand through his beard, then his hair as he sat on the edge of his seat. Phoenix only let out a self-assured giggle followed by a soft moan. Her body moved more urgently. Robin knew she was getting close, and he'd never been so jealous of a damn toy.

Her moans were growing higher pitched, and the bed creaked beneath her, and Robin felt like he was going to explode if she didn't come soon.

"Jesus, Fe," he croaked. And that seemed to be the last little push she needed to send her over the edge because her body seized, then a long sigh of a moan escaped her mouth as she rode out the waves of her orgasm.

"Fuck." It was the only thing he could think to say. His dick ached, and he wanted to jump through the phone and land on top of her and cover her with kisses while he told her how perfect she was.

Phoenix stilled and snatched her phone off her night-stand and held it over her flushed face. "What did you say?" she asked, her voice still breathless, but also urgent.

"I didn't say anything."

Phoenix narrowed her peacock-blue eyes at him. "Yes, you did. You just said I was—"

"Perfect," Robin finished for her. He hadn't meant to say that aloud. But the self-satisfied smile that spread over Phoenix's lips pleased him more than he wanted to admit.

"That's the opposite of how you're supposed to feel right now," she said, but her scold fell short. "You're supposed to be frustrated and turned on and pissed at me for teasing you."

"Oh, I am all of those things," he said, letting some of his sexual frustration spill into his voice. And he was satisfied to see heat flash in her eyes. "But I will never get tired of watching you come."

Her entire being softened at his words, and he had a feeling that she was perhaps taking his words a little too seriously, but in the moment, he didn't care. He never would get tired of watching her overcome with sensation. And as long as he could justify it, Robin wanted to be the one who gave it to her.

"Want to do it together this time?" she asked, and he heard the vibrator switch back on.

She didn't need to ask him twice.

CHAPTER 8

*R*obin's mind had been completely shot the last few weeks. He'd gone through the motions at work, been working on the preliminary steps toward starting his campaign. He'd answered phone calls, talked to his daughter, met with clients. Paid the bills. He'd eaten, exercised, all that bullshit, but the whole time he'd only wanted to get back to Phoenix.

They'd been able to see each other most weekends, and it had gotten to the point where Robin turned off his phone and ignored his email and devoted all his time to the woman he was slowly becoming obsessed with. When they weren't together, they'd started video chatting every night. He had a whole gallery now of salacious photos he and Phoenix had sent to one another.

He was sitting in his home office, scrolling through them, growing aroused and contemplating shooting Phoenix a text to see if she was home and ready to add to the gallery when his phone buzzed to life in his hand. John's name flashed across the screen, and Robin cursed. The man seemed to think he could call Robin whenever he liked now. But good lord, it was almost nine o'clock on a Thursday night. Surely Robin deserved a little time off.

He answered with an annoyed, "Yup."

"Am I interrupting something?" John asked.

"Not yet." There might have been more of a growl to his voice than was polite to use with his best friend, but Robin hadn't always been reasonable when it came to the women in his life. He'd been so obsessed with Caroline that he'd had to remove himself from the house for days at a time so he could focus enough to pass the bar, and they'd still ended up with Van. And he and Mary Beth had decided to get married largely because they couldn't stay out of each other's beds and didn't like leaving the kids alone at night. And Robin had missed living with someone. He'd long ago stopped looking for signs of Caroline around the house, and instead found her legacy in Van, but there were still times when he would expect to find Mary Beth's discarded candy wrappers or her bras hanging in the laundry room. He missed tripping over her muddy boots. It had taken him a year to donate the wide-brimmed hat she'd worn while gardening. He'd let it hang on its hook by the back door for months after her passing, as if she might walk back in and reclaim it any moment. Sometimes he still brushed his fingers over the hook as he left the house, his own little altar to his second wife.

"Good," John said. "I was trying to catch you before you went dark for the weekend."

Robin gritted his teeth. He'd been hoping nobody had really noticed that his weekends had been quiet, but no such luck.

"What can I do for you, John?"

"I take it your lady friend is on her way over?"

Robin's heart stuttered, and he struggled to draw in enough breath to say, "Excuse me?"

"Well, that's what I called to speak with you about, actually."

John sounded nervous. Good. He was venturing into dangerous territory. Robin only waited as John cleared his throat a few times then said. "Well, Frank and I. We've figured for a while that the reason you don't take calls on the weekends is because you have a new lady in your life, and we're concerned."

"If that were the case, I would think my two best friends would be encouraging me. When someone who's been widowed finds the courage to move on, it's generally considered a good thing."

"Yes, but when you're moving on with a twenty-eight-year-old waitress, we're allowed to become concerned."

Robin actually held the phone back to look at it. His brain couldn't put the two pieces together. He was sure they could mistake Phoenix for a lot of things, but a member of the service industry definitely was not one of them.

"What do you mean, 'waitress'?"

"Look. We get it," John said, and Robin could practically hear the blush creeping up his friend's face as his voice rose slightly. "Rebecca is an attractive woman, and we can't fault you for getting back in the game, but we just wonder if you've given any thought to what it looks like," John cleared his throat. "On a professional level."

"You mean, you think dating a woman half my age might make me look bad to voters."

"I, um—yes." John said. "I don't want to tell you how to

live your life—but honestly Robin we all have kids the same age as she is."

The only thing that kept Robin's temper leashed was him rolling his lips between his teeth and thinking about how embarrassed Phoenix would be if she knew people thought of her as his mid-life crisis.

"I'm not sleeping with Rebecca."

"Oh. Really?"

"Yes, really. Jesus, John."

"Oh. Well, alright then. I didn't really think of you as the younger woman sort of man." John chuckled in relief. "Of course, no one could blame you if you were. You're single and in decent shape, but a woman closer to your own age would be more appropriate, and you would have thought of that."

"More appropriate for what?"

John cleared his throat again and Robin let him squirm. "Just, in general. You know. A better fit as a partner."

"Mary Beth was nine years younger than me."

"Yes, but Mary Beth was in her thirties when you met. She had a son. You two made sense. Someone like Mary Beth would be perfect."

"Perfect for me or perfect for the campaign?" Robin asked.

John sighed. "I'm sorry. The campaign is all I think about. I just don't want to see you hurt again, Robin. You've been through so much, and well, someone that young is likely about the wrong things dating a man old enough to be her father, is all I'm saying."

"Look," Robin said, pulling up his best diplomatic court-room voice to hide the rage bubbling inside him. "I appreciate that you're concerned about me, but my love life never has been and never will be any of your business."

"But if it affec—"

"It will not affect the campaign in any negative way. Now, if you don't mind, I am expecting company, and I'd like to not scare her."

"I didn't mean to upset you, really."

"I know. I understand you're only trying to be thorough, but there are some things that are off-limits, and this is one of them."

"I understand," John said, sounding chastised. "Have a good weekend, Robin."

The second Robin hung up, Phoenix's video call connected. She was wearing something blue and silky that set off her hair and enhanced her eyes. The creamy skin of her breasts was overflowing the décolletage, and Robin's first instinct was to growl as his arousal surged beneath his still simmering anger.

"I am going to tear that to ribbons when I get to L.A. tomorrow."

Phoenix raised her eyebrows even as her mouth hitched into a smirk. "You promise?" Then she pulled at the tie that was holding the lingerie up. The silky blue fabric fell away, and Robin forgot all about John and the campaign and everything except for the sight of the woman in front of him.

CHAPTER 9

"*Y*ou have been acting weird all day," Van said as they plopped onto the sofa in Phoenix's apartment in the basement of Van's childhood home. "Was it just because Clay was around?"

"I'd only give a damn about Clay if he were trying to touch you, in which case I would eviscerate him, but since he isn't, I won't."

"Then what's got you in a mood?"

Phoenix shrugged. Part of it was the hangover from the party at Tessa's to celebrate Van's birthday the night before. But an even bigger part of it was that Robin had acted as though Phoenix didn't exist ever since they'd landed in Kansas yesterday afternoon. She had expected it to some extent. They had agreed a long time ago that they needed to keep their relationship secret, especially from Van. But that was Christmas Eve, and now it was the beginning of June, and they hadn't slowed down one minute.

If anything, Phoenix thought this weekend would have

been a good opportunity to start easing their friends and family into the idea of them together as a couple, because Phoenix wasn't sure she was capable of not fawning all over him when they were in the same space. Normally she couldn't help but touch him, but Robin's attitude toward her had been nothing short of cold. He'd not accompanied them to the club last night—not that he had gone out much since Mary Beth had died, but still. She'd thought that maybe he'd go out for Van's birthday. Instead, he'd begged off after dinner to return to his big empty house all by himself without even a significant glance in Phoenix's direction.

When the limo had dropped them off after their night of whiskey and dancing, Phoenix had contemplated going up to his room, but after she'd texted him from Tessa's that she missed him and his response had been a rather condescending *Enjoy a night with your friends, Fe.* She decided that he didn't deserve her body.

She'd stumbled down into her apartment, and that's basically where she'd been ever since. She'd even made Van squeeze into the apartment's tiny living room for their Skype call with their trainer. It wasn't quite enough space for them both to do burpees, but they'd shoved the sofa into the corner and made it work.

Van was super cranky too. Bishop hadn't come with them for this trip, since he was competing in some sort of surfer competition this weekend, and Phoenix could tell Van was annoyed he'd chosen surfing over going to Kansas with his girlfriend on her birthday.

But Van didn't complain about men—well, most men. She'd complained that Clay had yet another girlfriend tagging along with him at Tessa's and how it was stupid of him to come if he wasn't even going to drink. Phoenix just rolled her eyes.

If Phoenix didn't find Clay's feelings for Van so suspect —he was obsessed with her only because he'd never figured out how to sleep with her, and the moment he had what he wanted, he'd break Van's heart—she'd tell them to sleep together and get the tension over with. But Phoenix knew better than that. Van had loved Clay since she was fourteen. That her crush had become her stepbrother the next year had been maddeningly inconvenient since Clay had spent his youth policing Van's sex life while he'd done whatever he pleased. He was still a man-whore who sneered at Van and Bryant—who was supposedly his best friend—and at Bishop.

Phoenix was actually relieved Bishop hadn't come with them. He was a top-notch manager, but he also had a superiority complex, and purposefully baited both Bryant and Clay. It was easier with Bryant, since Bishop was one of the few people on the planet who knew Van and Bryant's public relationship was a farce. Not even Clay knew that there was nothing more between Van and Bryant than friendship.

Phoenix would feel sorry for him if she didn't find him such a monumental asshole.

"I just don't want to film tonight," Phoenix said.

Van groaned. "Fuck, I forgot. The birthday party."

They were filming Van's family birthday party in Robin's dining room that night. It was a show, of course, with a birthday cake and presents, like she was turning seven instead of twenty-five. But one of the big parts of the Van Birch brand was portraying Van as an all-American Midwestern girl at heart, which meant all-American Midwestern birthdays.

Phoenix only had an hour before she had to be upstairs overseeing the decorations.

She wondered if Robin would still avoid her when she was covering his dining room with flowers and cheesy banners.

"Have you heard from Bryant today?" Phoenix asked.

He'd probably drunk more than any of them, which wasn't something she was necessarily worried about. Bryant could hold his liquor, but he'd been distant with Phoenix over the last year, and she just wanted to make sure he made it to the filming.

Van shrugged. "He and Clay had an appointment with a potential remodel at noon, and he texted me this morning to ask if I wanted him to bring me something from the donut shop for my birthday. When I told him I'd hit my calorie limit for the week in whiskey last night, he offered to beat up Stark for us."

Phoenix grinned. There were days when she felt like beating Stark, their trainer, up herself, but not today. "How's he doing?"

Phoenix really wanted to know. They hadn't hung out together in ages, and Bryant's behavior had felt off recently. They might not be super close like he and Van were, but Phoenix still considered him a friend—part of her extended family even.

Van rolled her eyes. "He's been mopey for ages, but he won't talk to me about it. He likes to pretend he doesn't have a sex life, but you and I both know he's probably been hooking up with a hotter guy than either of us could land."

Phoenix nodded. Back before this thing with Robin, when she'd been in the market for the occasional hook-up, she and Bryant had always hung out at the bar, playing each other's wingman. And he always ended up with the hotter guy. Which she supposed was only fair. He was one of the most beautiful people she'd ever met.

"It's not easy on him," Phoenix said. "If someone sees him out with someone who isn't you—man or woman—he's going to be a villain. You're so well-loved in this crazy country, he's going to be dealing with harassment both on- and offline, rude questions from reporters, probably even death threats."

Van groaned and buried her face in her hands. She and Phoenix had had this conversation before. Phoenix had never been super comfortable with the whole fake relation-ship scam, but she was not above exploiting it for her own purposes. Because Van and Bryant did have chemistry—and they truly loved each other, even if they didn't love each other in that way, their affection translated well on film. And Phoenix had chosen the right interviews, the right scenes on the reality show, the right photo-ops for the paparazzi to really sell them as the current IT couple. She even approved of their couple name, which was VanBryant, though there was a developing subsect of VanBishop ship-pers who had been giving her trouble.

Keeping Van and Bishop's budding relationship out of the press was getting harder and harder to do. The two were virtually inseparable. It was one reason why Phoenix had been able to keep up her affair with Robin undetected. Van had been too distracted by Bishop to notice. It was both a blessing and a curse, because the longer things with Robin went on, the more Phoenix wanted to tell Van about what a fucking fox her father was, even if Phoenix could not frame it like that.

But she wanted to. If Robin weren't Van's father, she

would absolutely soliloquize about his body and how perfectly he seemed to just get her, but Phoenix couldn't tell Van any of that without totally grossing her out.

That didn't change how desperately Phoenix wanted to tell her best friend about the man in her life, and maybe, just maybe, if Van weren't constantly climbing on her manager, she would have already noticed that Phoenix was falling in love.

Phoenix sat up straighter as Van weighed out loud for the millionth time the pros and cons of maintaining her charade with Bryant. Phoenix was able to shut down her own line of thought. The "L" word was dangerous territory.

She didn't want to admit how much she cared about Robin, even to herself. He was becoming the thing she looked forward to most out of each day. Their texts. The sexts, the phone sex, the way he would bring her a glass of wine in the evenings or wake her up with kisses and coffee. She loved his body, his drive, the way he could sometimes be kind of an asshole when he didn't get his way, and the way he could be tender with her just after he'd fucked her brains out.

". . . and sometimes I think, what if I got Bryant and Bishop together in the same bed? I mean, I wouldn't mind two guys, and Bry's bi, but I just don't know if Bishop would go for it, you know?"

Phoenix choked on her own saliva as she tuned back into Van's babbling. "What?" She said between coughs.

Van cackled. "I knew you weren't listening." She clutched her stomach as she fell back into the arm of the sofa laughing. "I was prepared to go to extremely explicit lengths to get your attention."

Phoenix pinched the bridge of her nose, attempting to

banish the idea of her best friend in the middle of a three-some from her head. She and Van talked about sex all the time, but in more abstract ways. "I love you, and you have all the three-ways you want, but that might be too much for me."

"I always knew you were a prude," Van accused.

Phoenix kicked at her friend, and Van only cackled louder. "You can do whatever you like behind closed doors. I am simply happy keeping my encounters to one partner, that's all."

Van sat up, waggling her eyebrows. "Is this where you tell me about the guy you've been hiding from me? Because I am so dying to know."

Phoenix could do nothing to hide her blush. She wasn't going to tell Van about Robin now, not when Robin hadn't even looked at her in the last thirty-six hours. No texts, no promising glances, nothing.

"You're blushing!" Van said. "Oh my God, you have to tell me who he is. It is a guy, right? Have you discovered a new facet of your sexuality? Because I support you if you have."

"He's no one," Phoenix said, but she couldn't keep the smile off her face. It was growing too wide.

"Oh, right, no one. Absolutely."

"Ok, so he's not no one, he's someone," Phoenix said. "He could be someone special, I think. But he's very private."

Van nodded as she screwed her face into a wince. "The fame thing is causing you trouble too?"

"No." Phoenix shook her head. "It's just—" Phoenix had been going to call it new, but she didn't think five months of clandestine meetings really counted as new. "We're just taking it slowish, and we're not quite ready to share just yet."

Van's features twisted in the other direction, more skeptical amusement than anything else. "Right. Well, I'm dying to know who's giving you the tingles these days." Van waggled her fingers.

Phoenix blushed again. She hadn't thought about the tingles in ages. There was no need to use her sixth sense when she was having regular sex, and Robin's touch never failed to set her on fire.

"Soon," Phoenix said. "I think it'll be soon." She just hoped that wasn't wishful thinking.

Van gave her a too-knowing look, and Phoenix wondered if her friend already knew somehow.

Robin couldn't sleep.

The house was too quiet.

He'd told Phoenix the day before they'd arrived that it was important to him that they keep their relationship from Van over her birthday. That he wasn't going to ruin her birthday by telling her. They'd been video chatting, and Phoenix's response had been, "But we are going to tell her eventually, right?"

Robin felt guilty about pinning it all on his daughter. It wasn't a lie that he didn't want to tell her over her birthday. Van's birthday should be all about her. But it would be a lie if Robin denied that John's words had been reverberating through his head for the last few weeks. That voters wouldn't like that he was dating someone so much younger than he was.

Then he would tell himself that he was being ridiculous. The election wasn't for another sixteen months. The whole world could change in sixteen months. And as true as that was, Robin was almost ready to file his paperwork. Rumors were starting to flow that he was going to run. And they were doing most of the work to ready his campaign kickoff this summer, because he was going to spend most of his time on the water rights trial. Then in January, he was going to announce his candidacy, and they'd be off.

So really, it was already on him.

And Phoenix was so private. Did he really want to drag her into that? She'd become an object of scrutiny instead of the woman behind the scenes.

He was laying on his bed, and he realized he'd never answered her. Phoenix's face was visible where his phone screen lay propped on his nightstand. He'd cleaned himself discreetly with a tissue, but he still felt stickiness between his fingers and drying in the hair on his belly. He needed to shower. Part of him still felt like a dirty old man, a voyeur of the worst kind, despite the fact that he'd been the one to initiate the long-distance sex. And he couldn't help it, watching Phoenix ride her vibrator while calling out his name and coming undone never failed to bring him to his figurative knees. He didn't deserve her, and his daughter didn't deserve to be betrayed by him, not in this way.

"We'll talk about it," he said as a way of postponing the conversation. He didn't miss the dimples that appeared between her eyebrows then, but she hadn't pushed it. She'd been trying to push it more often lately. But she'd never outright said she'd wanted to tell Van. Robin could see her yearning for that step, which would legitimize them as a couple.

It was one he couldn't give to her.

Part of him wanted to. To ask her to move in with him,

to ask her to split her time between Kansas and L.A. as best as she could. To never leave him. But he wouldn't. He couldn't.

Van didn't deserve the scandal their relationship would stir up, and he certainly wasn't going to put his daughter in that position. And just the thought of Phoenix being Van's stepmother was so ludicrous, Robin couldn't even allow himself to entertain the idea.

The public would be a whole other story.

He didn't want to make a spectacle of Phoenix or himself, and that's exactly what they'd be.

Then earlier that night, he'd overheard Van and Phoenix talking. He'd gone down to see if he could catch Phoenix alone, for admittedly selfish reasons, but he'd heard Phoenix telling Van that she'd been seeing someone. *Someone special* she'd said, and Robin's blood had run cold.

He'd let this affair go on too long. It wasn't anything other than selfishness on his part. It had felt good to feel wanted. And by someone so young and so beautiful was gratifying to his ego.

But she couldn't care about him, not the way she'd been implying to Van that she did.

That he couldn't allow.

Robin sat up in bed and threw the covers off. He couldn't allow it to go any further, and he couldn't wait any longer to tell her.

She was asleep. Phoenix had gone to bed early, complaining about a lingering headache, and they were leaving for L.A. again tomorrow afternoon. If he was going to speak to her in person before next weekend, this was his only chance.

Stealing downstairs in the middle of the night was not

easy. Whichever staircase he used was loud and creaky, but he chose the front stairs, because they were further from Van's bedroom, but then he had to sneak through a dark house to make his way to the basement stairwell.

Phoenix had left her door unlocked, which he took as a good sign after he'd done his best to ignore her the past few days. Her bedroom door was ajar, and Robin allowed it to swing open slowly so the creak would alert her to his presence. He had always been hesitant to creep into her room, afraid it would remind her of her worthless stepbrother, but Robin was equally desperate in his need to be near her and his need to make sure she knew they could never be more than this.

He sat on the edge of her bed. There was just enough light from the nightlight in the hall to highlight her red hair, splayed in a corona around her head, her own crown of flames. Her eyes were closed, so he caressed her cheek with his knuckles. She let out a soft hum and her lips parted on a sigh.

"Wake up, Fe."

"Robin?" She propped herself up on her elbows with a yawn, the sheet slipping to tease him with the sight of just the tops of her breasts. "What are you doing here?"

Her voice was low and sleepy, and her hair held the extra volume from being splayed out over her pillow.

He'd come down to explain to her why he'd stayed away, why he had to continue keeping his distance. Forever.

But she was so deliciously sleep rumpled. He knew her body would be warm and pliant, and he couldn't leave her without one final taste.

He closed his mouth over hers, and Phoenix fell back

against the pillows with a whimper, practically pulling Robin on top of her. He loved it when she told him what she wanted, and he was powerless to deny her. Robin had missed touching her. Seeing her the past two days and not embracing her, not taking her into his arms and kissing her, not wrapping his arms around her in front of everyone and claiming her as his own had been a special kind of torture.

He ground his erection into her mound through the blankets, and the way Phoenix writhed beneath him satisfied him in a place so deep that he didn't dare to touch it. Instead he stood and shucked his boxer briefs to the floor, then ripped the comforter off Phoenix, revealing her naked body.

She stretched into a languid spread of arms and legs, inviting him to join her. Wordlessly, he climbed between her legs, and teased her by gliding the head of his cock over her wet folds until she whined his name.

He slid inside her, and he'd meant to fuck her out of his system, but his body slowed so he was thrusting into her in long, sensual strokes. And when Phoenix exposed her throat to him, Robin covered her neck and shoulder with long, sucking kisses until she was mewling beneath him and urging him with her hips to move faster.

Her legs wrapped around his hips, taking him deeper, her nails bit into his shoulders, and he had to grit his teeth to keep from roaring his pleasure as her body tensed beneath him in the way that meant she was coming, and his release barreled through him.

Robin wasn't sure how long he lay draped over her, but at some point, she tapped him on the shoulder, and he rolled to the side. She disappeared into the bathroom and

Robin rearranged the sheets so the bed wouldn't be a mess when she came back. It was the least he could do.

She sashayed back into the room, swaying her hips like she had to work for his attention. She didn't. Robin would be aware of every move she made whenever he was in her presence for the rest of eternity. She dropped down next to him in the bed, snuggled into his chest, which he also found himself powerless to deny, and said, "It really sucked, having you ignore me for the last two days."

"I know," he said, but Robin couldn't bring himself to apologize.

"We should talk about that," Phoenix said. "Because I am not going to just let you ignore me and then sneak into my bed whenever you want."

Robin tamped down the surge of pride he had in her for standing up for herself. "You shouldn't" was all he said. The less actual talking they did about this, the better. There were a few hard lines he was just realizing he wouldn't cross, and Phoenix wouldn't stay once she knew what they were. So he just said, "I can't tell Van about us."

"You can't or you don't want to?" Phoenix asked.

"I won't," he said. He'd expected Phoenix to struggle out of his arms and kick him out, but she only cocked her head to the side to try to see him in the dark.

"And what if I tell her what we've been up to."

"You won't."

Her brow creased, and Robin wanted to kiss it away, but his daughter was more important to him than anything. Phoenix knew that. It had just been him and Van for so long. He had to protect her. And the fact that Phoenix didn't get along with his stepson had been bothering him lately.

He couldn't be with someone who despised one of his children, no matter how much she loved the other one. Because Clay was his. He didn't care if he hadn't even met Clay until he was fifteen, Robin considered himself Clay's father. He used that frustration to keep going, keep pushing Phoenix until she understood what he was in her bedroom to do.

"I've never kept a secret from her for this long. I normally tell her everything."

"But you won't tell her this."

"How do you know?"

"The same reason I won't." She angled her head again, and Robin did kiss her brow this time. "Because you don't want to hurt her any more than I do."

"I want to tell her," Phoenix said. "She's only going to be angrier the longer we keep it from her, and she has enough secrets in her life."

"It won't hurt her if there's nothing to tell her," Robin said, and Phoenix jerked in his arms.

"Oh." Again, Robin had expected her to squirm away. He wanted her to get angry. To kick him out of her room and throw one of her sharp three-inch heels at the back of his head. He wanted her to be upset that he was ending this—whatever it was between them. Anything but this calm acceptance.

"Does this have anything to do with the rumors of you running for that House seat?"

Robin ground his teeth together. "Phoenix—"

"No, don't answer that question. It's enough to know that you're ashamed enough of me that you don't want to tell Van. Why would you want to embarrass yourself in front of the entire nation?"

"Phoenix." He couldn't say anything else. He was ashamed of himself, because yes, he couldn't let their relationship go public for exactly those reasons. But also because he'd already let this obsession go on too long. She was starting to believe it was love—and Robin couldn't let it become love. Anyone he loved was doomed. And he couldn't do that to her.

"But you are running?"

"Yes." He didn't know why, but her betrayed stare hurt more than anything she could have said in anger. Was she upset that he hadn't told her about his plans?

"You should probably go then." Her voice was flat, void of all emotion, and Robin would have definitely preferred the shoe throwing. He wanted one last taste of her fire.

"Fe—" he started, but she cut him off.

"Don't, okay. It was fun while it lasted, but it was always unrealistic. You and me, wasn't it."

It wasn't a question, and Robin stood, swiping his boxers up off the floor and sliding them on. "We were never suited for a public relationship," he said, and she let out an annoyed scoffing sound that implied she didn't agree, and Robin felt so much relief, he almost wanted to apologize if he hurt her. But he wouldn't. He wanted her angry. If she was mad at him, she wouldn't be sad.

"It would have been embarrassing," he said. "To be seen holding your hand in public. All the speculation. All the gossip."

A pillow connected with his chest. Good.

"Get out," she said through ground teeth.

"I can't afford that type of publicity, not with the year I have coming. The trial. The campaign."

Another pillow flew past his head.

"Get the fuck out," she said again. Robin turned on his heel and left without a second glance. As he shut the door behind him, he heard her mutter, "You're such a fucking selfish bastard."

Good. That's what Phoenix should think, because that was exactly what he was.

CHAPTER 10

*P*hoenix had spent the last few weeks vacillating between being so angry she could punch a hole in the wall (she stuck to her heavy bag instead) and feeling so nauseous that she had been actually throwing up. The only other time in her life that she had thrown up because she'd been upset was after her stepbrother had left her room each night.

That was what had driven her to buy the pregnancy test. Because she was upset that Robin had ended things, but she wasn't that upset. She was devastated, obviously. She loved him, and the stupid bastard loved her. She knew he did. He was just too stubborn to admit it to himself, so he was hiding behind every excuse he could think of. Sure, he had some hefty life changes coming up, and it would have been nice if he had talked to her about running for office, but still. Half the men in Congress were married to people significantly younger than they were. Phoenix would hardly be an outlier. Though she wasn't sure how she felt about being a political wife. But that was skipping about sixteen million steps since

1. She and Robin weren't currently together.

2. She had barely allowed herself to think the words "boyfriend" or "girlfriend' before

they'd broken up.

And

3. Robin couldn't even bring himself to tell his daughter about them, let alone entertain

the idea of marrying Phoenix.

And the more Phoenix thought about it, the more she was convinced Van wouldn't give a damn that her best friend had fallen in love with her father as long as both of them were happy, because as self-centered as she could be sometimes, Van was a genuinely good person.

It was Robin who was the bastard.

And now he was going to be a father. Again. And Phoenix had no idea how to tell him.

It had to have been that night when he'd come down to her room. Because they hadn't had sex for more than a week before that because she'd had a UTI after the marathon session they'd had two weeks before. And she should have made him use a condom, warned him that the antibiotics could mess with her birth control, but she'd been so worried about how he'd been ignoring her that she'd been goddamn grateful that he was paying her any attention at all.

That was why Phoenix didn't do relationships. Because they made you vulnerable, and she didn't want to vie for a man's attention ever. She didn't need to. Men should be begging for the privilege of touching her, not be fucking embarrassed to be seen with her in public.

What a fucking piss-poor excuse. He was such a fucking coward. And he was not going to take Phoenix's news well.

She was going to keep the baby. There was no doubt in her mind about that. Even as she still sat on the toilet staring at the positive pregnancy test in her hand, trying to wrap her mind around her new reality. She knew she was absolutely keeping this baby. She didn't know if she'd ever have another opportunity to have a baby, and she definitely knew she wouldn't find a better partner.

Not that he would want to have anything to do with the child. With the way he'd treated her last time, Phoenix tried to tell herself that he would be indifferent, but she knew that was a lie. Robin loved his children too well to not be a father to the child she was carrying—though she could see him reacting badly initially. Wanting her to terminate. Wanting her to make it go away so he wouldn't have to deal with it or deal with her.

But once she refused.

It would hurt to share a child with him, but she wasn't going to let that stop her from being a good mother.

She snapped a photo of the pregnancy test before she tossed it in the trash, thinking that the best way to tell Robin—when she was ready—might be to just text the photo to him, and let it speak for itself.

She had just washed her hands when she saw headlights outside her house. The gated and guarded community Phoenix lived in didn't have much in the way of neighborhood traffic. And sure, the beach was crowded with all the houses too close together for her taste, but a car in her driveway after midnight had to be Van.

Sure enough, when Phoenix peeked out the living room

window, it was one of the black cars from the service they used.

Van fell out of the car. Then stumbled up the walk. The driver was out and trying to help her, but Phoenix heard Van shriek at him not to touch her as she tripped over her own feet on the way up the porch steps. Which was odd. The driver looked like Mills, and he was Phoenix's favorite driver because he never sold their itinerary to the paps. Van thought he was the best driver they had, and she baked him cookies at Christmas.

Phoenix's fingers fumbled on the door latch, not able to get it open fast enough to get to Van. Something was wrong with her friend. Horribly, terrifyingly wrong.

The door gave way just in time for Van to collapse into Phoenix's arms, sobbing and trembling.

"What happened?" Phoenix asked the driver, who stood on the walk, wringing his hands.

"I'm not sure, Ms. Lambert. I got an alert to pick Ms. Birch up from her condo, and Mr. Bishop was there." The driver rang his hands some more. "It looked like they'd been fighting. He didn't want to let her leave, but I got her in the car, and the only thing she would say was your name, so I brought her here."

"Thank you, Mills." Phoenix said. "I can take care of this."

"May I?" he asked, gesturing to the porch steps. Phoenix nodded, and he strode up, careful not to stand too close to Van, and whispered in Phoenix's ear. "I believe he hurt her. There are bruises on her wrists."

Phoenix pulled back the sleeve of Van's leather jacket and could see the dusty ring of purple on her skin.

She was going to kill Henry Bishop. The second she got

Van taken care of, the bastard was dead. Phoenix would claw his fucking eyes out.

"Do you mind waiting?" Phoenix asked. "We might need a ride to the hospital. Maybe the police station."

He nodded. "I can wait as long as you need."

"Thank you, Mills." He retreated before she thought to ask him to keep quiet. "Oh and—"

"Not a word, Ms. Lambert. I would never." A sad smile tugged down the corners of his kind eyes, and Phoenix decided he deserved a lot more than cookies this Christmas.

It took the rest of the night to sort out what had happened and to get Van taken care of. She'd called the hospital ahead of time, and they'd taken them in a delivery entrance and seen to them in a private room. The police had come, of course, and it was only as Phoenix held Van's hand as she recounted the events to the detective that Phoenix realized how much she wanted to kill Bishop. She'd known the second she'd seen the bruises on Van's wrists that he'd raped her, but to hear the details, to watch the person she loved most in the entire world break down like she was doing now. It killed Phoenix on the inside.

When Van posed in her underwear for pictures that showed off all the bruising on her arms, on her hips and thighs, Phoenix actually had to excuse herself to throw up. Van had struggled, and he hadn't been nice about it. He might as well have punched her in the face for how roughly he'd treated her.

They didn't get back to Phoenix's house until after dawn. They had given Van a sedative to help her sleep, but despite Phoenix's exhaustion, she couldn't do more than doze.

Instead, she sent Mills to Van's condo to pack some of

Van's things and to let in the locksmith so that Bishop couldn't get back in with his keys.

She made herself eat a bowl of cereal, because she knew she needed the energy. The baby needed the energy.

Eventually, Phoenix acknowledged that she needed to call Robin. Not about the pregnancy. That could wait. He needed to know what had happened. Phoenix was sure he'd be on the first plane out of Kansas, and once he was in L.A. and Van was on the mend, they could talk about the baby then.

But she stalled. How did someone tell a man that his daughter had been abused by the person she was in a relationship with? Someone they had all trusted?

Phoenix did yoga, showered and dressed, taking her time with her hair and makeup. It was one of the only things of value her mother had taught her, that it was always easier to do hard things when you were at your best. Her mother's advice, of course, had limited itself to appearance, but Phoenix found calm in the daily routine. Her nausea even ebbed somewhat.

Then she spent the next five hours on the phone with what felt like every person she'd ever met in Los Angeles. She spoke to their lawyers, to the police again. She spoke to Eve and to the record label. She fielded calls from journalists, who she basically told to leave them the fuck alone and wait for their official statement—which Phoenix wasn't going to make until Van was ready.

But as she picked up her phone to dial Robin, Van's phone rang from where it was charging on the kitchen counter. Phoenix hurried to it. She'd been monitoring it, just in case, for the police investigation, but it was Robin's number, and Phoenix almost cried with relief.

"Robin," she said as she picked up.

"Phoenix?"

"Yes. I have Van's phone while she's asleep."

There was a pause, and Phoenix could hear voices in the background and sounds like he was at a construction site. Maybe he was visiting Clay?

"Is she okay?" he asked.

Phoenix shook her head as tears welled. She hadn't expected to cry, but she couldn't choke back the burning in her throat. "Something went down last night with Bishop."

"What happened?" Robin's voice was like steel, and Phoenix had to swipe at her eyes. She knew what that hard, metallic tone meant. He was feeling too much, and he was having to shut it down.

"He assaulted her. Physically and sexually."

Robin let out a long string of curses and threats, and Phoenix was glad there was 1500 miles between the two men, because she knew he'd probably follow through with some of them.

When he calmed down, Phoenix caught him up with the rest of their night.

"I want to talk to her," he said.

Phoenix peeked into the spare bedroom where Van was still out.

"I don't want to wake her."

"I need you to check if she's awake. Now."

"She's exhausted and hurting, and this sleep is the only relief she's going to get from that for a long time. I'll have her ca—"

A crash interrupted her sentence, and Phoenix cringed at the phone. "Where are you?" she asked. "Is everyone okay?"

Robin sighed. "That was Clay's neighbors moving some debris off a car."

"Debris? What's going on, Robin?"

Another pause, and Phoenix heard Clay's voice in the background saying something.

"There was a tornado here last night, Fe. A bad one."

"Is everyone okay?"

"I'm fine. We haven't gotten a hold of Bryant yet. Clay isn't hurt, but he lost his house, along with about half the town."

"Holy shit. I haven't seen the news yet."

"We only just got cell signal back."

"But you're not hurt?" Phoenix asked again. She couldn't help it. She needed to make sure.

"I have some shingles to replace, but I'm fine. I'm more worried about Van," he said.

"Right," Phoenix nodded, then felt silly. She didn't know what to do with all the things she was feeling right now. But she understood why he wanted to speak to his daughter. "I'll see if I can wake her up."

Van was stirring when Phoenix gave her the phone, then left to give her some privacy. Phoenix immediately started the process of arranging the travel to Kansas, and then she steeled herself and checked the news. Phoenix has been so busy doing damage control, she hadn't had a chance to actually check in on what everyone was saying. It was bad, and Phoenix was almost grateful. At least she was able to distract herself the rest of the day by managing the media shit storm while Van rested.

Two things kept her from breaking down that day. One was knowing she had to be strong for Van, and the other was the life she now had to keep safe from monsters and natural disasters. And she would do it, even if it killed her.

Robin played piano for Van until she was practically falling asleep on the bench. She'd insisted on working tornado relief all day, and she'd smiled and taken photos with fans. But she was still wearing a long-sleeved shirt on 95-degree July day, and Robin understood why. Bruises peeked out below her sleeves if she moved too quickly. That had been rare. She walked as if her entire body was sore, and the second she wasn't talking to a fan, her face fell. He wondered if his daughter was still in shock, but she'd assured him she had daily sessions scheduled with her therapist and that she would be fine.

He hadn't been able to stop hugging her. He didn't like letting go of her either. It had been Robin's worst fear for her when she'd moved out to L.A. When she'd been living in that shithole they'd rented for her in that awful part of town. That someone would follow her home one night and there would be no one there to protect her. But she'd been fine then. Hungry sometimes, but safe. And now, in her million-dollar condo, alone with her boyfriend—ex-boyfriend—she'd been violated.

Robin would kill him if Bryant and Clay didn't get to it first. But he didn't show any of that to his daughter. He wouldn't. He would give her nothing but support.

And after the taco bar Phoenix had ordered had been cleared away, Van had asked to play piano with him. She'd done more singing than playing tonight, but that was fine. It was how they'd always dealt with their grief. It had been how they'd bonded after Caroline had died, and again when they'd lost Mary Beth.

Robin would play for her until his fingers bled. He'd already known his wrists would be stiff in the morning and his fingers might be sore. But he would take all that pain and more, he'd take everything for Van if he could.

When she'd slumped against his shoulder, he'd wrapped his arms around her and held her until she pushed back out of his embrace. "Thank you, Dad," she said, then dragged herself up the stairs. Robin stared at the keyboard for a moment before shutting the guard over the keys. He drummed his knuckles on the lid, then went into the kitchen, where a bottle of whiskey was calling his name.

He hadn't bothered with his favorite rocks glass and had gone straight for the shot glass. He was under no pretense as to the purpose of the whiskey tonight. This was not to sip as he worked at his desk. Tonight, it was to erase some of this unbearable pressure on his chest. This fucking helplessness.

He'd knocked back one shot and was filling the second when Phoenix emerged from the basement staircase. She'd changed into her yoga clothes, a blue and pink sports bra with matching tights that he didn't allow himself to look at too closely.

Robin hadn't stopped wanting her when he'd ended their affair, but he couldn't think about that now. He pulled a second shot glass from the cabinet, filled it, and held it out to her.

She took it, and toasted wordlessly, but when Robin knocked his back, Phoenix only set hers on the counter. He'd never known Phoenix turn down whiskey or wine. Like a stupid lovesick puppy, he'd stocked up on both of her favorite brands over the spring. He still had a whole case of her favorite red in his wine cellar. He hadn't been able to touch it in the last six weeks.

When Robin's shot glass hit the counter, she pushed hers towards him, and he knocked that one back too. Phoenix took both shot glasses and set them in the sink. Then she re-corked the bottle and stood on her tiptoes to hide it away in the cabinet over the refrigerator. When she was through, she turned around and locked her sparking blue eyes on him.

"How are you doing?" she asked.

Robin wasn't sure what Phoenix saw in his eyes; he'd tried to show nothing, but whatever he'd let show through had her flinging her arms around his shoulders and pulling him close.

In all the chaos in his head, holding Phoenix was the one thing that made sense, so he wrapped his arms around her so tightly, she probably couldn't breathe.

"Thank you for taking care of Van."

"Always," Phoenix said.

Robin didn't have the words to express how good it felt to hold her, how comforting it was to have her near when both his children's worlds had been destroyed in one night. When his lips fell to hers, it was the most natural impulse in the world to him.

He'd half expected her to push him away, but she leaned into the kiss as if it was what she needed too. Her fingers tangled in his hair, the sharp tips of her nails biting into his scalp in a familiar way that woke his body from the denial he'd been living in during these last few weeks apart. The heat between them was inescapable, and losing himself in Phoenix was serenity in the midst of the storm.

Without words, Phoenix led him down to her bedroom, undressed them both and laid him back on the bed. He let her take the lead. Watching her pleasure wash over her as she rode him filled in an emptiness that had threatened to swallow him whole, and when they'd caught their breath, he'd said, "This isn't over yet. You and me."

Phoenix had collapsed on top of him, kissed his shoulder and said, "Not even close."

As much as Robin wanted to stay in her bed for the rest of the night, being there with both Van and Clay in the house made him uncomfortable. He didn't like the idea of Van or Clay spotting him trying to sneak up from Phoenix's apartment come morning. And he wanted to check on Van.

He kissed Phoenix on the forehead and disentangled himself from her. Then stole upstairs to check Van's room. She wasn't in her bed, and Robin's heart almost stopped beating. Surely she couldn't have sneaked out while he'd been downstairs?

He crept to Clay's bedroom at the other end of the hall. When he poked his nose through the door, the bedside lamp was still on, and Van lay curled up on Clay's chest. Clay had one arm wrapped around Van, another thrown over the pillow, but his eyes were open, and his expression when he met Robin's gaze was part defiance, part protectiveness. Robin only nodded and backed out.

He didn't trust Van with many people, even fewer after the last few days, but Phoenix and Clay were at the top of a very short list.

CHAPTER 11

*K*eeping her pregnancy a secret was more difficult than Phoenix anticipated. Not that she necessarily wanted to keep it a secret, but what with organizing the rebuilding effort and keeping up with Van's commitments from before the incident and keeping on top of the constant social media catastrophe that was The Van Birch Incident, as it was being called. . . And it was even more difficult when she couldn't call on Bishop for backup. He'd always been better at speaking to the media on Van's behalf. Phoenix was better at the background stuff.

Plus, the constantly keeping reporters at bay had her wanting a drink at the end of the day. She'd never noticed how available alcohol had been before. Robin kept opening bottles of wine for her in the evenings, and she could only pretend to drink for so long before

1. Someone noticed her pouring her wine into the fern in the kitchen window.

2. The fern died of alcohol poisoning.

And the fundraiser at Tessa's? Having to deal with

celebrities sober? Torture. Bryant didn't make it easy on her either. He kept pulling her over to the bar and demanding she take a shot with him. She didn't have the heart to tell him she'd kept her lips closed on the bottle when they'd done shots in the limo on their way in, so it only looked like she'd had something.

But Bryant was such a good time when he was tipsy, less inhibited, funny even, and Phoenix hadn't hung out with him in so long that she let him pull her to the bar three times, even if it did interrupt her from speaking to someone important.

"Bryant, that was the governor," Phoenix whined, but it was only half-hearted.

"Oh shit, really?" Bryant checked back over his shoulder. He hadn't even noticed who Phoenix and Robin had been chatting with; he'd only grabbed Phoenix by the hand and said, "I need to borrow Fe. We have an appointment at the bar for shots," in his tipsy half-slur that meant he'd had a few already. "Madam Governor, you wanna do a shot with us?" he called.

The governor raised her glass of diet soda and shook her head with a smile. Phoenix caught Robin's eye. He only raised a playful eyebrow at her, his way of encouraging her to have a little fun.

Bryant called for two shots of Jameson once they hit the bar, but Phoenix caught the bartender's eye and held up a finger for one. Either the bartender was psychic or just really good at her job, but she set a shot of soda down in front Phoenix. Bryant didn't notice, even when they toasted to the night—again.

"You look hot," he said, eying her from head to toe.

She'd worn a dove-gray sheath dress that made her hair

look like flame. Conservative, but sexy. She was running the show tonight, after all.

"You hitting on me, Wilder?"

Bryant's eyes turned sad for a second, before he pasted on a silly grin and leaned over the bar. "Nah. Just thinking about old times. We should totally find you a movie star to hook up with tonight though. What are you thinking? Action star or . . ." Bryant scanned the crowd. "Fuck, there's that long-haired dude from that band. I don't remember his name, but I have it on good authority…" Bryant didn't finish his sentence but held his hands an ever-increasing distance apart while waggling his eyebrows.

Phoenix slapped him on the arm. "Stop being an ass. I'm working tonight."

"You're always working," Bryant said. "Doesn't mean you can't have a good time."

Phoenix rolled her eyes. "I'm going to go back to the house and go straight to bed, because I am exhausted." It wasn't a lie. If there were a horizontal surface handy that wasn't likely covered in something disgusting, Phoenix would be asleep in less time than it took her to close her eyes. "That doesn't mean we can't find someone for you tonight, though. Maybe you could hook up with," Phoenix mimicked Bryant's hand gesture about the rock star, but Bryant didn't laugh like she thought he would.

Instead he gripped the edge of the bar so tightly, his knuckles turned white. "Van's coming home with me tonight," Bryant said, and Phoenix didn't understand the flinty tone in Bryant's voice.

"I know," she said. Phoenix had probably known Van was planning to spend the night at Bryant's tonight before Bryant had. She knew where Van was and who she was with at all times. Not just because the security team also reported to her, but because Phoenix planned Van's life. She knew about Van's hair-brained idea that being in a real relationship with Bryant would magically fix all her problems. She didn't listen to Phoenix's advice, so Phoenix had decided to let the two of them figure out on their own that they weren't meant for each other like that.

But Phoenix had never seen Bryant like this. His shoulders slouched in defeat; his jaw clenched in anger. She rested her hand on his elbow. "Hey, is everything okay?"

He shrugged her off, forcing a smile and signaling the bartender for another drink. "Everything's fine."

Everything was clearly not fine. Phoenix had the hunch that maybe things hadn't been for a while, but she and Bryant had never been call-each-other-on-the-phone-and-chat buddies. That didn't mean she cared about him any less.

"You can talk to me, you know."

Bryant pivoted to face her, his eyes so full of agony that Phoenix actually thought he might share something, but that was the exact moment that Clay's girlfriend thrust herself between them at the bar. "I can't find Clay. Have you seen him?" she asked Bryant.

Bryant shook his head and looked away as the bartender delivered his next shot.

"You know what," Phoenix said. "I need to find Van. Why don't we look together?" Amber looked at Phoenix like she'd forgotten to wear pink on Wednesday but reluctantly followed her anyway.

It didn't take them long to find Van and Clay. It might have been better if the two of them hadn't been making out in a dark hallway, but at least Amber had made Clay leave immediately, and the rest of the night had gone smoothly. Phoenix had pretended to take one more shot with Bryant, hoping to find out what was bothering him, but he'd only mumbled something unintelligible about a bookstore and pulled Van onto to the dance floor.

Robin had taken Phoenix home not long after, and Phoenix fell asleep curled in her lover's arms, just grateful for the time with him. Being in Robin's house, seeing him every day, sleeping with him every night was almost like they were in a real relationship. Van had been spending most of her nights at Bryant's, and Clay, thankfully, was either out with his dog or moping in his bedroom and didn't venture downstairs much in the evening. That left Phoenix plenty of time to spend time with Robin.

They had dinner together most nights. He would open a bottle of expensive red wine, and Phoenix would pour her glass bit by bit into the potted plant when he wasn't looking, and they spent the evening discussing their problems. He was always most concerned with Van and checking in with the security team, finding out what threats had been levied that day and what Phoenix and Butch were doing to protect Van. After they'd finished that debriefing and put Butch on speaker phone, he would relax somewhat, but still, Phoenix could tell that Robin was not managing the stress well.

The trial date for his water rights case was set for early October. It had been pushed back after the tornado—everything had been. But he didn't expect to close before Christmas, and Phoenix knew he was worried about it. She couldn't blame him. With everything else that was going on, a stressful court case was exactly the opposite of what he needed. At least Phoenix spent her day concentrating on the things that directly affected her family. But Robin had to completely switch gears, and he spent an hour each night venting about how frustrated he was with it all.

Partially because of that, and because pregnancy had made her horny as hell, Phoenix found herself bringing Robin lunch on a sunny Tuesday. It was hot as hell outside, and the silk lining of her dress stuck to her sweaty skin. It was only eleven thirty, but Phoenix was starving. She'd grabbed sandwiches from a place down the street, the one she knew made Robin's favorite roast beef and horseradish and had the sweet spicy pickles he liked.

Adam, Robin's assistant, was packing his messenger bag when she came in. They'd interacted over the phone and through email many times, but they'd never met face to face. Phoenix had the errant thought that Adam was the kind of man she should be attracted to. He was tall and lean, about her age, and had perfectly styled short, black hair with square black glasses and a square jaw to match. He was dressed more casually than Robin's customary suits, but the business casual look suited him, like he could hop on a bike and ride across the city without even breaking a sweat or ruining his clothes.

He noticed her as he slung his bag over his shoulder and froze, his eyes bulging, just a little bit as he realized who had just shut the suite door behind her.

He blinked and almost tripped over the foot of his desk, as he stepped forward to greet her. "Ms. Lambert," he said. A blush stole over his cheeks as he found his balance and offered her his hand.

Phoenix shifted her lunch bags to her left hand and grasped his hand in a firm grip. "Please, it's Phoenix. It's so nice to meet you in person, Adam."

"L-likewise. Mr. Birch is in a meeting with his campaign

manager. He should be done in a few minutes. I can let him know you're here before I go."

"If you don't mind. We have some business we need to discuss."

It wasn't exactly a lie, though that business had shifted from touching base about what was happening with the lawyers in L.A. to curiosity about the campaign manager. There had been rumors for months about Robin running for Congress, and he'd more or less admitted it to her in June, but she hadn't heard a thing about it since she'd been in Wellville.

Adam called Robin through the intercom built into the phone system. "Phoenix Lambert is here to see you."

"Thank you, Adam. Tell her she can come on in. Enjoy your lunch."

Adam gave Phoenix a sheepish smile as he hung up the phone. "Go on in," Adam said, then crossed the small front room to open the door to Robin's office for her. Phoenix didn't miss the slight pink tinge to his cheeks as she thanked him again.

Robin and his companion both stood as Phoenix entered. Robin buttoned his suit coat and took the bags from Phoenix's hands, a content, yet curious smile on his face. As his friend approached where they stood by the door, Robin stepped closer to Phoenix, almost too close. "John, this is Phoenix Lambert, Van's business partner. Phoenix this is John Gardner. He's a good friend of mine."

"And Robin's campaign manager, I hear," Phoenix said as she shook this man's hand. He was about Robin's age. Shorter and rounder and older looking, more tired than Robin, but in a grandfatherly sort of way. He struck

Phoenix as kind and capable, and he didn't stare at her boobs, so she thought she might be able to like him.

John grinned and puffed up. "Robin Birch belongs in Congress."

Phoenix raised her eyebrows. "I have no doubt he'd make a stellar representative." She glanced at Robin, who had the good sense to look ever-so-slightly abashed.

John also glanced to Robin, then back to Phoenix. His expression never faltered, but she thought she saw a gleam of comprehension in his eye for just a moment before he nodded at Phoenix. "It was nice to meet you, Ms. Lambert. I'm sure you have business to attend to. Robin, I'll call you later."

"Bye, John," Robin said, already angled toward the work-table where he'd set the food earlier and set about unpacking it. Until John shut the suite door behind him, and then Robin corralled Phoenix toward his office door, shutting it and backing her into it.

"This is a surprise," he said, nuzzling his nose over her neck.

"I'll say. A bid for Congress, who knew?" Phoenix said.

"We only started putting the team together. Do you think it's a bad idea?"

"No, I think you'd be brilliant at it. Just surprised. You haven't mentioned it since that night." She let the part about him being a complete asshole be implied. To his credit, he didn't back down.

"I always meant to get into politics eventually."

Robin raised his head to meet her eyes, she saw heat and desire, and just the barest hint of vulnerability. She wrapped her arms around his neck and pulled him in for a light kiss on the lips. "It makes sense." And it did, only Phoenix dreaded what it would mean when he was living on the East Coast and she was back to living in L.A. most of the time.

But maybe she was thinking too far ahead. The election wouldn't be for another year. It was anybody's guess what would happen between then and now. And Phoenix hadn't even told him about the baby yet. She'd had half a mind to do it now, to ply him with roast beef and spicy pickles and tell him he was going to be a father and that despite all the bullshit they were wading through now, she was excited—ecstatic even. Their nursery theme was going to be gender neutral. Whales, she'd already decided, but she would let him suggest names if he wanted.

Instead, Robin pressed Phoenix into the door with his body as his lips brushed over her jaw. "Did you have urgent business or . . .?" he asked, and she could hear the plea in his voice that told her he just needed a break. Which was fine. They had plenty of time to talk about the baby.

"I missed you, but I can probably come up with something if you'd like to work."

"I'd rather not," Robin's voice was gruff, hard.

"Good, because I've always wanted to go down on you in your office." Then she pulled him in for a hard kiss.

Robin sighed against her lips, brushing his tongue out to meet hers as his hands landed on her hips and squeezed. Phoenix managed to shove him out of his jacket. Then, with a rub of her cheek over his bearded chin, she grasped his tie and pulled him around his desk and pushed him back into his leather desk chair.

He grinned as she leaned over him. "Are you feeling bossy today?"

"I'm feeling bossy every day, Birch." She kissed him once more, then concentrated her attention on his fly. His suit was a light gray today, made out of a breathable fabric that was soft and cool beneath Phoenix's fingertips as she traced the ridge behind his zipper.

He barely breathed as Phoenix loosened his black leather belt and undid his fly. He wore gray boxer briefs beneath, and Phoenix pushed his white shirt tails out of her way as she pulled the fabric down just enough to expose him.

His cock was hard and ready, and Robin groaned as Phoenix wrapped her fingers around him and squeezed. She hadn't necessarily planned this part of her visit, but she had fantasized about this before. About doing this, here, with the danger of someone walking in on them at any moment. Phoenix stroked Robin's length twice, before licking her lips and swirling her tongue over the tip.

Robin's hips shifted forward in his chair, and Phoenix settled more firmly on her knees so she could take him in. She loved the salty, earthy taste of him. Every part of him was delicious, and Phoenix felt her core pulse with need as Robin cupped the back of her head, angling himself deeper into her throat.

She hummed around him, and Robin cursed. Before she knew what was happening, Robin had hoisted her up onto his desk. "Now it's my turn," he said against her lips.

Her skirt was already hiked high enough to allow her to spread her legs. Robin stepped between, grasped the string of her thong between his hands and ripped. Phoenix's insides fluttered at the knowledge that he wanted her so badly he'd shredded her underwear.

He was inside her a second later, hot and hard. She squeezed her legs around his waist, still wearing her nude heels. Robin growled as she flexed her inner muscles around him, then he braced his arms over her on the desk and drove into her so hard, the blotter beneath her ass slipped. Robin sent one hand to her hips to stabilize them and kept driving.

Phoenix used his tie to pull his lips to hers, and the second his hot breath mingled with hers, Phoenix felt herself fall, hard and long, like a shooting star flaming in orbit for eternity. She came to the ground at the feel of Robin spending inside her, the hard pulse of heat that represented his pleasure. She wrapped her legs more tightly around him, not wanting to lose his skin on hers just yet.

Robin ran his nose over hers when she met his eyes. His smile was lazy and contented, but also warned that he'd only just gotten started. That he wanted more. As much as Phoenix would love that, her stomach was nearing empty. She'd learned these last few weeks that if she went too long between meals, that was when the nausea really got to her.

Luckily, Robin's stomach growled then too.

They both grinned. "Come on," she said, patting his shoulder. "I brought you sandwiches."

Robin pushed off the desk, pressing a kiss just below her ear. "We'll finish this tonight?"

"You promise?"

Robin's response was a frustrated growl and a hard peck to her lips.

Thirty minutes later, when Adam returned from his lunch break, Phoenix and Robin sat at the work table discussing the latest developments in the downtown rebuilding, namely the Colorado developer who had purchased an old warehouse and was turning it into luxury apartments against the historical society's wishes, despite the warehouse not being on the historical register. They were sipping their waters and picking at the last of the chips with the door to the office open, like they'd just had a regular lunch.

Phoenix smiled to herself as she left, remembering the pieces of her underwear that were now hidden in Robin's pocket.

CHAPTER 12

*P*hoenix devoted every spare moment over the next two weeks to taking care of Robin. The tension in his shoulders did seem less noticeable for her trouble. There wasn't much opportunity to meet him at the office, but in the evenings, she would make him eat dinner, get a glass of wine or two down his throat, then take him to bed where he took out his frustrations on her body. She had exactly zero complaints. Her body loved the attention. About the only thing she didn't do was tell Robin about the pregnancy.

Phoenix knew she couldn't keep it a secret for much longer. By her calculations, she'd been around five or six weeks when they'd come to Kansas, and she had an appointment with a local OB/GYN this next week. She'd be ten or so weeks then. The online due date calculators told her she was due on Valentine's Day, so waiting for Christmas to tell Robin about the the pregnancy, when his stress load had leveled off, was ridiculous. She'd probably be showing by the time his trial started. She wasn't sure when she was going to fit it in, but she wanted to trust that, like when she got the tingles about a man, she'd get a signal from her body or her intuition or whatever about when to tell the man she loved that she was going to have his baby.

She'd felt the pull a few times, to blurt out the truth, when they'd been in bed together. Aside from the fact that he still insisted on hiding their relationship from everyone, Phoenix felt very much like he was taking their affair more seriously this time around. It was as if the weeks apart hard sharpened his regard for her. He'd admitted to missing her when they'd been apart, and he'd started holding Phoenix as they slept.

Not that they'd never cuddled before. It was just that when they had, it had been winter, and Robin's house was old and drafty and cold. In the summer, it was a little too humid and a little too warm, but that hadn't stopped them from winding their limbs together and ignoring sweating skin to hold each other throughout the night.

Sometimes Phoenix woke up to him stroking his hand over her stomach as if he already knew.

She would pretend that he did know, that he was imagining the family they would grow together. The life they would build. It was such a satisfying daydream that Phoenix liked to pretend that it was real.

To escape the chaos of the rebuilding effort, Phoenix had started spending most of her days in the back of a local bakery and bookstore. She had chosen the bookstore for her own devious reasons, but Revival Coffee and Books had the added bonus of being only three buildings away from Robin's office, and he could meet her for lunch without arousing suspicion. Or at least too much suspicion. The paparazzi were fierce in Wellville at the moment, but they'd never had much of a thing for Robin. He was just Van's dad.

But Phoenix was popular enough—though there were times she regretted it—from making herself into a character on Van's reality show that sometimes she had a few photographers on her tail. That was part of the reason why Revival was so perfect. Minnie, the adorable single-mom owner, had hidden a conference table in the exact center of her used book stacks that couldn't be seen from the front window, or even the coffee counter. It was the perfect hiding place, and just secluded enough from the shop's regular business that Phoenix could use it as her office with little to no interruption.

And it was the perfect excuse to get cozy with Minneapolis Halvarson. Not only did Phoenix not know any other women with children, Phoenix had a few theories that Minnie was behind Bryant's moodiness. At first Phoenix had thought it was because Minnie had had a baby with another man. But then on her second morning working at Revival, Minnie had introduced Phoenix to Malcolm. Phoenix had to literally bite her tongue to keep from asking the woman if Bryant knew the kid was his. She had never seen such a strong resemblance between father and child. Malcolm was basically a mini Bryant. But Phoenix didn't want to frighten her new friend off.

Because, of course, Phoenix had googled her. Minnie Halvarson was a fucking heiress who seemed to be hiding out in Kansas because she'd caused a scandal on the East Coast when she'd accused a lacrosse player of assaulting her at a party. Minnie had basically been bullied out of New York, and Phoenix did not blame her for choosing a quiet little town to take refuge in.

Phoenix wouldn't have stuck around to be made a fool of either. She hadn't. The day that she'd convinced her parents to let her finish high school with her dad in the Bay Area had been the most triumphant day of Phoenix's life— closely followed by helping Van land her recording contract.

Phoenix was basically obsessed with what had happened between Minnie and Bryant. She needed to solve the mystery of how Bryant didn't know he had a kid and how Minnie had ended up with Rocco. Sure, he was hot in a gruff-silent-type-with-muscles sort of way, and the couple times Phoenix had met him, it was clear he loved Malcolm like he was his own, but Phoenix wondered how many people actually believed Rocco was Malcolm's biological father.

It had taken Phoenix two weeks of slow prodding for Minnie to explain that Rocco had been her childhood friend, and how they'd grown up together, both the bastard children to abandoned mistresses. Minnie's father had recognized her after her mother had died. Rocco's father never had. But he'd made a life for himself, put himself through school, and after college, Minnie had moved here to be with him. The baby had come along not long after. "We've decided we're better off friends than lovers," Minnie finished, pulling Malcolm up into her lap to keep him from pulling on Phoenix's computer cords.

"And that's the whole story?" Phoenix asked.

Minnie's pale pink cheeks turned red, and she angled her head down so that her diaphanous blonde hair hid her eyes. "That's everything."

Phoenix wasn't buying it, of course. She was trying not to look too hard at Malcolm, who had blue eyes the exact color of Bryant's. A forehead the same shape as Bryant's. Hair the same color as Bryant's. And Rocco was Latinx. Phoenix had a working theory about Minnie breaking up with Bryant because she didn't want to be in the spotlight, but was that before or after she found out she was pregnant? And why hadn't Bryant ever said anything? Did Van know? Did Minnie know about Van when she and Bryant hooked up? Phoenix had *so many questions*.

"But you still live with him?" was the only one Phoenix asked, congratulating herself on only being a little nosy.

"Separate bedrooms," Minnie said, flushing deeper red. "It works for us."

Phoenix was even more skeptical now. "It didn't work out very well on *Friends*." Phoenix said, and Minnie rolled her eyes.

Then she cocked her head to the side and gave Phoenix a knowing little grin that looked sinister juxtaposed against her still-red cheeks. "Now that I've spilled my tea, it's time for you to spill yours."

Phoenix pulled the nearest iPad into her lap and focused on the blank screen. Minnie hadn't even started to spill, but Phoenix said, "I don't know what you mean."

"So, that handsome silver-haired man who buys you lunch every day is just Van Birch's father."

Phoenix felt her own cheeks heat. "He's a friend. And an attorney. He's consulting on . . . everything that's going on."

"Uh-huh." Minnie waggled her eyebrows at Phoenix. "And the fact that he stares at you all moony-eyed and you light up like a Christmas tree whenever he's around is just because of the consulting."

Phoenix bit her lip, trying not to smile. "He doesn't look

at me all moony-eyed," she said, and when Minnie's smile widened, Phoenix asked, "Does he?"

Minnie giggled, and Phoenix couldn't help but join her. "He is so over the moon about you. He'd probably be able to pluck it out of the sky and give it to you if you asked."

Phoenix buried her face in her hands and let herself feel the joy in that statement. That Robin had enough affection for her that someone else could see it was one of the best things she'd heard, and also painful. Sometimes Phoenix had trouble convincing herself that what was happening with Robin was real, outside of the very real consequences, of course. She only just stopped herself from covering her abdomen with her hand. That would be a dead giveaway to a mother like Minnie.

"Nobody knows," Phoenix said, peeking out from beneath her fingers.

Minnie's face went slack with surprise. "Not even Van?"

"Especially not Van, God, can you imagine? 'Hey Van, I know we've been best friends for years, and you entrusted me with your money and your career, and I know your boyfriend just betrayed you in the worst way possible, but I just wanted to let you know that I've been banging your dad for the last few months. Just in case you needed to develop any more trust issues.'"

Minnie shrugged. "I don't know, I feel like it would probably get worse the longer you let it go. Especially if it's really been months already."

"Since Christmas," Phoenix said.

Minnie covered Malcolm's ears and cursed. "That's longer than any relationship I've ever had. And you've been keeping it a secret this whole time?"

Phoenix squirmed in her seat. "I wanted to go public. We

actually split about it for a few weeks because he was adamant that he wouldn't ever tell Van about our relationship. But then the thing with Bishop and the tornado and we just—"

"Didn't want to pretend you didn't love each other when everything else was falling apart?" Minnie asked.

"Yeah. At least, I didn't. I'm not exactly sure how he feels."

"I am. He loves you, and he's terrified because he's already lost two wives, AND you're his daughter's best friend. He's probably going bonkers."

Phoenix chewed her lip. She'd not let herself think those words, but it did make a lot of sense for the way Robin insisted so hard on secrecy. If he didn't let them go public, there was less legitimacy to the relationship and therefore less to lose. Frustration still bloomed in her chest if she thought about it for too long. Phoenix wanted to be worth losing.

Silence fell as Minnie rocked Malcolm to sleep in her chair. Phoenix was so lost in her thoughts that she nearly jumped when Minnie asked, "Were Van and Henry Bishop really a thing?"

Phoenix had been expecting that question. She was surprised Minnie hadn't asked it sooner. "Yes," Phoenix said. "But if you tell anyone that, I will sue you and deny everything."

Minnie grinned and mimed locking her lips and throwing away the key. Then furrowed her brows and asked, "But what about—"

"Bryant Wilder?" Phoenix asked.

Minnie's eye twitched, and Phoenix wanted to jump on it, and ask Minnie exactly how much she knew about

Bryant Wilder. Address? Middle name? If there was a birth mark on his butt cheek?

"Everyone knows that he and Van have been together for years. Since high school."

Phoenix shrugged one shoulder. "Do they? Or do they just believe the image we've sold them?"

Minnie nodded, biting her lip. And Phoenix wanted to shout, "Gotcha!" and force the other woman to fess, but before she could figure out how to coax a confession from Minnie, the iPad in Phoenix's lap dinged with a notification. So did the tablet on the table and both her phones.

Only certain people had access to accounts she had attached to each device. She unlocked the iPad, and when she read the email she found waiting for her there, her heart sank and her stomach churned her tuna sandwich and coconut-milk latte hard enough that she had to take deep breaths until she was sure she wasn't going to be sick.

Only vaguely did she register Minnie asking her if she was alright.

"I need Robin. Now." The words were enough to turn the tide on her nausea, and Phoenix made a dash for the bathroom.

When she returned, it was to find Robin standing next to her conference table, a strained look on his face. "Are you alright? Minnie said something made you sick?"

Phoenix didn't have the energy to talk. She only held up the email from Bishop. Claiming that if they didn't drop the assault charges against him, he'd release a sex tape of him and Van.

Robin's face turned stony. "Did you know about this?" he asked.

"I don't think Van knows about it," Phoenix said.

Robin's frown deepened. The start of a sneer curled at the corner of his lips. "Do you think she'd tell you?"

Phoenix had to sit down; the world was spinning around her, and Robin's intensity wasn't helping. If she wasn't careful, Phoenix was going to puke all over Minnie's pretty Persian rug.

"Are you alright?" he asked, focusing in on her as she sank into her chair.

"I'm overwhelmed," she said, which was absolutely true. It was the perfect opportunity to tell him about the pregnancy, but absolutely the worst timing in the world.

"Is that all?" he asked. "You've been impossible to wake up in the mornings lately." He cupped her jaw, his thumb straying over the curve of her cheek, and Phoenix crashed so hard into his love that she didn't think she'd be able to get out again.

"I'm going to the doctor tomorrow. Don't worry about me."

His grim set of his lips told her he was going to do nothing *but* worry about her until she told him what the doctor said. "Let me know how it goes. If I'm wearing you out, I'd like to know." The soft smile he gave her was so tender and teasing that Phoenix almost did tell him. She wanted to so badly. She needed to get this secret out of her soon, or she was going to explode.

"You're not what's wearing me out. It's all this." She motioned toward the conference table where all her things were laid out. "And no, I don't think Van would consent to be filmed. We don't talk about everything, but we have talked about how the risk of something like that going public is too high, and she's told me multiple times that she's never wanted to take that chance."

Phoenix couldn't help but recall how many compromising photos Robin had of her. She'd absolutely trusted him with them when she'd sent them, but the consequences if they went public were really only starting to hit her.

"So if Bishop does have something, it was likely filmed without her knowledge," Robin said.

Phoenix nodded.

"That's another assault charge. You'll call the team in L.A.?" he asked.

"Right now."

He stood. "I need to call the P.I."

Phoenix jerked. "What P.I.?"

"The one I hired the second Bishop was released. I don't trust him."

"Neither do I, but do you really think we need a private investigator?"

"I'm not taking any chances with Van's safety."

"Neither am I," Phoenix said, wounded that he thought she would do so.

Robin knelt in front of her. "That wasn't an accusation, Fe." When Phoenix only set her jaw against him, he cupped her chin with both hands. "I'm sorry I didn't tell you about the P.I. With all of this and the tornado and the trial coming up, I barely know what day of the week it is."

She closed her eyes and nodded. She was too vulnerable right now, and it didn't feel right. She didn't want him to be so tender to her right now. She was going to dissolve into tears if she wasn't careful.

Robin's lips landed on her forehead, then her nose, then her lips. They were short, chaste kisses, but they were still public kisses. Any number of people could stumble through the stacks at any moment. And it was so at odds with the man who had told her only months ago that he would be embarrassed to be seen holding her hand in public that she started to really let herself hope that they'd be able to pull a life out of this whole debacle.

"We'll get through this," he said as he stood. "Forward me that email."

Phoenix nodded. He placed a final kiss on her forehead and had his cell phone out of his pocket before he'd even left her hearing.

She had the email forwarded with two taps of her stylus, and then she called their legal team in L.A. to report the blackmail and see how they should handle it.

The rest of day felt like she was living under water. Van had been sequestering herself away in her room every night to work on her album. While Phoenix had heard Van's acoustic guitar, she was afraid what Van was really doing was working herself up over social media. But things had been hard enough between them over the last six months. Bishop and Robin had somehow torn them apart, and Phoenix didn't know what to do about it.

She left Revival when it closed at six and had a text from Robin that he was working late, so Phoenix set up shop in the office of her apartment at Robin's house and worked until midnight. Even then, she only went to bed because she was nodding off at her desk.

She'd probably been in bed about an hour when Robin slid under the covers beside her, placing a kiss to her temple as he spooned her from behind.

"You're late," she said.

"I know," he said. "I'm trying not to make a habit of it."

"Did you eat at least?" she asked.

"I grabbed a sandwich before the place on the corner closed."

"I could have brought you dinner," Phoenix said.

Robin chuckled and squeezed her closer. "Then I would have ended up having you for dinner, and I would have had to stay late tomorrow night too."

"Hmm." Phoenix said as sleep began to claim her again. "We should do that sometime soon."

She didn't hear Robin's response.

CHAPTER 13

$\mathcal{R}$obin thought that if one more thing got dropped on his plate, it was possible he was going to explode. He wanted to kill Bishop, hide Van in a (ventilated) bank vault, whisk Phoenix away to the south of France for a month-long vacation, and disappear from public life altogether.

John still wanted to talk strategy every second of the goddamn day. Every time Robin turned around, the water rights case was demanding another hour of his time on top of the nine a day he was already putting in. Then there was the ridiculous developer from Colorado who was trying to use the tornado rebuilding as an excuse to "redevelop" downtown Wellville by bringing in national chains and transforming some of the empty historic buildings into luxury lofts, and despite Robin telling the historical society over and over again that he didn't have time to deal with the asshole, the proposals kept landing on Robin's desk. They wanted him to find a legal reason why they shouldn't let him in. Robin had just reminded the historical society president that he wasn't on the town council anymore and couldn't do a damn thing. He'd ended by telling them to book an appointment with his assistant and quoting them his rate per billing hour before hanging up.

It was out of character.

Robin had always prided himself on being diplomatic in everything. He knew the reason the historical society kept coming to him was because he'd always made them a priority before, but it was like they didn't understand that his whole life felt like it was unraveling. His daughter was falling apart; his son wasn't doing much better. The biggest case of his career, the one that was going to lend him the credibility to jump straight to the US House was looming. It was a case he *had* to win. Every time Robin thought about the campaign, it was like someone had pulled his tie so tight, he couldn't breathe. And then he'd get a call from L.A., from the P.I. or the lawyers he'd been consulting with for Van's case, and he'd feel like someone had stabbed him in the gut. He'd even been studying up on California law in what little spare time he had and had contacted The Bar there to find out what sort of residency restrictions there were about sitting for the exam. Not that he didn't trust the lawyers to seek justice for his daughter, but Robin didn't trust them not to give up if the wrong sort of pressure came their way. And fucking Bishop was the kind of man who would know how to exert that pressure.

Tonight, Robin had worked until after midnight, taken a nap in Phoenix's bed, then snuck back up to his room. Van had fallen asleep with her lamp still on, and Robin had sneaked in and switched it off. She'd looked so peaceful in her sleep, like all of this wretchedness wasn't actually happening to her. If Robin could take it away from her, he would. If he could make it so that none of this had ever happened to her, even at his own expense, he would exchange his own well-being for hers in a heartbeat. All he could do now was try to contain the damage. He made a mental note to make time for her in the next couple of days. They hadn't played the piano together since she first came home, and that wasn't fair to her.

He checked in on Clay too, who was asleep, his dog at his feet. Pebbles perked her ears towards the door. "Just me, girl. Thanks for keeping him safe," Robin whispered as he retreated. The dog sighed, and Robin smiled. She understood how difficult it was being the one who was responsible for everybody else. Clay had been distant recently, ever since he'd seen Robin and Phoenix emerging from the basement the week before. Neither Phoenix nor Clay had brought up how their secret was partially out, and Robin hadn't had the brain space to bring it up. He didn't think Clay would say anything to anyone, but there was no love lost between Clay and Phoenix, so it was only a matter of time before the two were forced to work out their differences.

He'd barely had a chance to blink his eyes closed before his alarm was going off and it was time to head into the office all over again. He texted Van, who was already out on her run, about making time for them to play the piano and grabbed a cup of coffee and a piece of toast on his way out the door.

He'd spent his whole day on the phone with the counsel for the other party in the water rights case. With his client.

With the P.I. With the lawyers from Los Angeles. He worked right though his usual lunch time and texted Phoenix to apologize that he'd gotten caught up in work. She'd told him not to worry, she was waiting on her doctor, but twenty minutes later, a huge assortment of Thai food arrived at his office, and he texted her a thank you that she didn't respond to until almost five o'clock with a simple, "You don't have to thank me." That came in right as Adam sent back a request for an appointment from the secretary at the historical society to meet with Robin about officially consulting on Historic Downtown developments.

"Can you tell them to please call Roberts instead," Robin asked over the intercom. "I don't have any time in my schedule for this shit right now. But don't use those words."

Adam chuckled. "Sure thing, boss."

"And grab some of Thai food before you go. I think Phoenix ordered the entire menu."

Adam hadn't needed telling twice, and Robin saw him with two bags full on his way out the door a few minutes later.

Robin left the office at six, carrying the weeks' worth of Thai Food with him. He was looking forward to an evening with Phoenix. They could relax, open a bottle of wine and talk about something that wasn't his case or The Incident. They could just be themselves for a little while.

Phoenix had become a sort of haven over the last few weeks. She represented safety and reprieve. She was so eager and levelheaded, always thinking five steps ahead of everyone else, always quick to come up with solutions to everyone's problems. She was also soothing and limber and welcoming.

In the weeks they'd spent apart, he hadn't tried to contact her once. They hadn't even needed to see one another for *Pop Star*. He'd missed the physical part of being intimate with someone, longed for the sound of her voice, and if asked under oath if he'd made use of some of the pictures he'd saved from their sexting for personal reasons, he'd probably have to plead the fifth. But it wasn't his fault that nothing else did it for him anymore. He'd only wanted Phoenix.

None of that, however, had made him waver in his conviction that they were better off apart. He still thought that the whole premise of their relationship was bound to bring them nothing but pain. And by the time his campaign started in January, they could not be together anymore. But that day when Van and Phoenix had arrived in Wellville after the tornado, it had felt so good to hold Phoenix. He hadn't had enough emotional energy left to continue to resist her.

Robin had wanted nothing more than to sink all of his trouble into her since the moment he'd seen her, and he'd known how futile it would be to resist. They hadn't had much of a conversation about what the terms of their relationship were this time around, only that they wouldn't put labels on anything while Phoenix was staying in Wellville and that it was still best if they kept it under wraps. With everything else that was going on, Phoenix had agreed that she didn't want to add the revelation to Van's burdens.

Clay knew. He had to have suspected before he'd caught them coming up from the basement together the other day. He'd been home consistently, while Van spent at least half her week at Bryant's house. It was hard to ignore the creaking stairs in the middle of the night or how Phoenix and he shared a bottle of wine in the kitchen most nights.

Clay hadn't said anything yet, but he'd been watching Robin with a strange expression lately. He'd have to address it soon, but for tonight, Robin was going to focus on Phoenix. Something was going on with her, and despite the fact that she was one of the healthiest people he knew, he'd been harboring an anxiety about her doctor's appointment today. That she hadn't immediately texted him an update worried him.

He dropped the food off in the kitchen when he arrived home and let Pebbles out into the backyard because he wasn't sure if Clay and Van had made it back home from the construction site yet. He loosened his tie on his way up the stairs and changed from his suit into a pair of jeans and a more casual shirt. He thought about athletic shorts and a T-shirt and going for a run, but he didn't want to have to shower and change again, wasting time when he could be spending the entire evening with Phoenix.

When he descended into the kitchen, she was there picking through the leftovers from his lunch. She held out one of the hand-thrown plates Van had picked out as a teenager. "I took the rest of the drunken noodles," she said, showing him the plate full of noodles and tofu and basil.

"Go for it," he said. "I'm after the sweet chili noodles, myself."

Phoenix held the half-empty box out to him. He'd eaten that and a whole order of money bags for lunch along with the bottle of Perrier that had been delivered with the food. He went straight for the bottle of Pinot Noir on top of the refrigerator instead and poured himself and Phoenix a glass as she nuked her food in the microwave.

She wore his favorite dress of hers. A navy sheath dress that showed off her toned arms and ample breasts. Whenever he saw her in it, he wanted to smooth his hand down her shoulders, over her breasts, across her waist and over her hips until he found the hem. Then he wanted to fold the skirt up her slim thighs until he could reach for the flame-colored strip of hair between her legs.

It had been too long since a woman had driven him this wild, and he tried not to think about what that meant for him as a man. Because Caroline had been his first true love, and she was irreplaceable, but the feelings he had for Phoenix rivaled his feelings for his first wife. He couldn't spend too much time thinking about how he'd never been fair to Mary Beth. He'd loved her in his own way. He was coming to realize that he'd held a lot of himself back from her because he'd been afraid to commit to someone as fully as he had with Caroline, but if he let himself dwell on it, guilt over how she'd picked up on it and wanted a divorce would bowl him over. Then guilt of how, if she'd left for work from their house instead of from Clay's house, she wouldn't have been in that wreck threatened to overcome him, and he didn't have time to linger in grief and self-recrimination.

Someday it would catch up with him. Robin knew that. But after the water rights trial. After some of the immediacy with this awfulness with Van had passed. Then he could unpack everything he was feeling about his wives and his losses and what that meant for him and his future. Without Phoenix.

Robin still wasn't sure he'd ever be able to tell Van about their affair, even though they'd been together, for all intents and purposes, for the better part of a year.

And despite his reluctance to tell Van about their relationship, Robin also didn't want to let Phoenix go. Not anymore. Not even though he knew he had to. She was the only thing that made any sense in his life right now.

"How did your doctor's appointment go?" he asked.

"Fine," was all she said, and he frowned as they traded places in front of the microwave. She grabbed herself a can of La Croix from the refrigerator and shoved the glass of wine to the far edge of the breakfast bar with a wrinkle of her nose.

"Nothing's wrong?" he asked. It wasn't like Phoenix to reject wine.

"Everything's fine," she said and shoved a wad of noodles into her mouth with her chopsticks that was so big her cheeks bulged.

"Hungry?"

"Starving."

"Did you eat lunch?"

"Just a croissant. I was too nervous."

"Why?"

Phoenix swallowed and shoveled more noodles into her mouth, washing it down with a swig of her fizzy lime water. "Promise you won't freak out?"

Robin snagged a single noodle with his chopsticks. "That depends on what's going on."

Phoenix set her ever-present phone on the breakfast bar between them, and with a few clicks, a blurry black-and-white image appeared on the screen. She angled the phone toward him, and Robin picked it up to examine more closely even as the noodles in his stomach turned to stone.

"What is this?" he asked, though it was obviously a sonogram. There was even an arrow pointing to a gummy-bear shape framed in black that said, "Baby."

"I'm exactly ten weeks, as of today."

Robin's mind immediately rejected the idea that the child was his. There was no way. They'd used condoms, and then birth control. And he was too old to have another child. And Jesus. John would have a heart attack.

"How?"

"I had a UTI around Van's birthday. The doctor thinks the antibiotics interfered with my birth control."

Robin recalled the night they'd spent together in June and swallowed. "You're sure it's mine?" he asked and immediately felt like shit for asking when Phoenix's cheeks colored.

"I haven't been with anyone else for a year, Robin. It's pretty likely."

"I can't," were the only words he could form as he downed his glass of wine and remembered all the wine they'd shared over the last few weeks.

"How long have you known? Have you been drinking all this time?"

Phoenix shook her head, then motioned toward the fern beside her. "Haven't you noticed how sad your houseplant has been looking lately?"

"You've been feeding it wine?"

"And the occasional shot of whiskey."

Robin chuckled despite himself. He'd had no idea. He'd noticed how tired she'd been, but he'd been completely oblivious to her condition. "How long have you known?"

Phoenix chewed her lip. "I took a test about five minutes before Van showed up at my door after everything went down with Bishop."

He felt himself sober as the impossibility of the situation washed over him again. Phoenix was pregnant. Pregnant. He couldn't even start to fathom what he should do with the information. "So there hasn't been much time for you to process everything?"

Phoenix shook her head.

"Then you haven't decided if you're keeping it?" he asked and didn't fail to notice the way Phoenix scowled at the hopeful question in his voice.

"There was never a question that I was keeping this baby."

"Fine," Robin said, and rubbed his hands over his jeans.

"But you'd prefer if I had an abortion," she said, pointedly.

"Jesus, Fe. I don't even know right now." He was battling too many emotions to put into words. A part of him, one that was perhaps too loud, was proud of his own virility. He and Caroline had tried for children for years before she'd gotten sick. And ostensibly he'd understood that their inability to conceive after Van had more to do with Caroline's ovarian cancer than his own fertility, but there was still a loud and proud part of him that wanted to crow about his own potency.

Another part of him, one that felt dark and slimy and just as powerful as the first part, didn't want to think about how Phoenix being pregnant would necessarily and quickly bring their affair into a very public relationship. She was already nearing the end of her first trimester. She would start showing in the next few weeks, and he'd have to explain to the entire goddamn world that he'd been fucking a woman his daughter's age.

He just didn't know if he could.

"Take your time," she said, but he recognized the crispness in her voice that meant she wasn't impressed with his reaction.

"I will take my time," he said. "This…" Robin tapped the phone screen, and the image zoomed in on the blurry gummy bear like splotch. "It's unexpected."

Phoenix shrugged and resumed eating her noodles.

He ran a hand through his hair as he picked up Phoenix's phone and examined the image of the baby. His baby. "Jesus Christ, I should be waiting for Van to have babies, not having children of my own."

"It wasn't like I was trying to get pregnant, but now that it's happened, I want to do this. I might never have another chance."

Robin stared at the ceiling and was vaguely aware of Phoenix taking his basically untouched dinner to the sink and refilling his wine glass. She sat down beside him again and slid her phone back in front of her as she switched off the screen.

"If it helps, I'm not exactly ready to go public with all this either, but it's going to come out eventually."

Robin could only nod. "I'm going to need a few days to wrap my mind around it," he said.

Phoenix nodded and pulled her wine glass closer to her again. She didn't sip from it, just spun it between her thumb and forefinger. Robin could feel her pulling away, pulling into herself, protecting herself from his lukewarm reaction, but he didn't know what to do about it. This scenario was surreal, and he didn't think he could make anything better for her by pretending to be ecstatic.

He was fifty-three years old for Chrissake. He didn't

want to have another child. What sort of father would he be to be in his seventies when they graduated high school? Would he even be around to see them graduate college, fall in love, start a family? A father should be there for that. Should be active and involved the way he'd been for Van. He didn't know if he had that sort of energy anymore.

He squeezed Phoenix's shoulder, and she gave him a reluctant, watery smile. He knew he couldn't let her do this on her own. He'd always loved being a father and remembered how desperately he'd mourned the pregnancies Caroline had lost. How he and Caroline had only grown closer in their grief. Phoenix's family was a fucking mess. No one had ever been there for her, so he would work on being square with everything, because it was the responsible thing to do for her sake. Robin knew it was only a matter of time before he warmed to the idea.

Before he had a chance to tell her as much, Clay stormed into the kitchen, demanding to know where Bishop was. "Did you know they were dating?"

Phoenix set down the glass of wine she'd been idly spinning "Of course I knew they were dating. But I'd want to rip his balls off even if they hadn't been."

Clay rushed at her, and Robin almost stood to protect her, but he trusted his son, even if he was having a breakdown. "Then why haven't you?" Clay asked.

Phoenix stood, getting right in Clay's face. "Because it would only make things worse for Van, you prick."

Robin reached for her then, not wanting her to be any more upset than she already was. "Fe." She slapped his hand off her hip, and Robin realized he wasn't helping.

"Don't you dare make this harder on her than it already

is. You put on your protective big brother pants whenever it suits you, but the rest of the time, you treat Van like dirt. I don't care how much she loves you, I will squash you like the little roach of a man you are if you hurt her again."

Robin blanched. He couldn't help but feel like some of those words were meant for him as well.

"What I want to know is why you aren't crushing Henry Bishop?"

Phoenix glared at Clay then slapped her phone on the counter. Robin already knew which message he would find on the screen, and he watched the horror dawn over Clay's face as understanding set in.

"He has a fucking sex tape?"

Phoenix inhaled slowly through her nose. "I'm not taking the chance that he's bluffing. Not right now."

Clay frowned at Robin. "You knew about this?"

Robin chewed the inside of his lip. He hated that he always had to be the voice of reason. Sometimes Robin wanted to be the one to throw a temper tantrum like Clay was doing or just simmer and burn like Phoenix always did. But Robin always had to be the level-headed one. The one that kept the peace. There were times when he didn't want to be the parent anymore. And the prospect of starting all over made Robin's blood run cold.

He didn't have the patience to mitigate a fight between these two at the moment, so he did his best to appear unconcerned. Maybe if he pretended, he'd actually start to feel that way. "Phoenix mentioned it. I think it's best to play on the side of caution until the legal system bows out completely."

"What does Van say?" Clay asked.

Phoenix took her phone back from Clay. "I haven't told

her about his threats yet. I'm not certain she even knows about the tape."

Robin and Phoenix both jumped as the butt of Clay's hand hit the countertop. "She doesn't know about it?"

He and Phoenix had discussed that part already, and Robin had had just as hard a time leashing his anger as Clay was. Only Robin had called his P.I. and had him start looking into that too.

"I'm not sure," Phoenix said. She stepped up into Clay and poked him in the chest. "And if you fucking say anything, I'll have your balls in a vice for sure. So don't go mouthing off about it before I have all the details."

Clay's face turned red with frustration, and Robin understood. He wanted Bishop's blood too. "He can't get away with this."

"It's a waiting game," Robin said, letting his lawyer brain take over. "We can't do anything unless he makes a move, and he won't while he's still under investigation. We've informed the police, but we can't even get a restraining order right now, not unless we have proof of violent intent."

Clay gritted his teeth, and Robin knew Clay wanted to point to the fortress the house had become, with the guards and the fence and the death threats, but the important thing was that none of those threats had come from Bishop. And even if he was spurring on the social media trolls, that wasn't enough.

"The police are idiots. She showed me the bruises. There is no way—no way that was consensual."

Phoenix squeaked and took a step back. "She showed you the bruises? When?"

"The first night she was back. She needed to talk, so," Clay shrugged. "I listened."

"Oh," was all Phoenix said, and Robin could feel the sadness, the disappointment in herself radiating off of her.

"Does anybody else know about his threats?" Clay asked.

"We've talked to the lawyers in L.A.," Robin said. "They're ready with a lawsuit if he releases the tape."

"And we have a P.I. sniffing around in case there's a reason why they won't prosecute."

Robin hadn't been planning on mentioning the P.I., but he let it go. He and Phoenix had bigger things to argue about. Just, usually, the fewer people who knew about a private investigator, the more likely it was that things stayed more, well, private.

"You mean like Bishop bribing the DA?" Clay jumped to the worst-case scenario, but both Robin and Phoenix answered in the affirmative because it was a possibility.

Clay looked between him and Phoenix; his attention shifted as he noticed the open bottle of wine. The two glasses. The two of them sitting so close. Robin scrubbed at his beard. The last thing he wanted to do was to be forced into talking about his relationship with Phoenix. Not right now. Not in front of Phoenix. Not when she'd just told him she was pregnant. Jesus. He couldn't even begin to wrap his mind around what kind of scandal that would cause.

"Does Van know?"

Robin gave a discrete shake of his head, but Phoenix said, "About the P.I.? She knows we're looking into things. The private investigator was implied."

Clay didn't break eye contact with Robin, but Robin wasn't going to give Clay anything else. Robin didn't have any answers.

"You need to tell her. The sooner the better." Then Clay

glared at Phoenix. "You need to tell her about the tape. She deserves to know. About everything."

"I really fucking hate him sometimes," Phoenix growled as Clay stormed off.

"He's just concerned about Van," Robin said. Exhaustion washed over him so completely that he didn't have any fight left for anyone.

"He wants in her pants the same way he always has."

"Clay cares about Van."

Phoenix snorted.

"You don't think so?"

"Clay reminds me a lot of my stepbrother sometimes."

The little hairs on the back of Robin's neck stood up. "He never…"

"No. He's never followed through, but that doesn't mean the potential isn't there," Phoenix said.

Robin relaxed somewhat. "Clay's been in love with Van since he was sixteen. It hasn't been easy for him."

Phoenix rolled her eyes this time and pushed her wine glass toward him. "The smell is making me nauseous."

Then she left him alone at the breakfast bar for the first since they'd reunited.

When he knocked on her bedroom door a few hours later and asked if he could join her, she gave a sleepy shrug and said, "Sure."

But when Robin tried to spoon her, she shimmied to the other side of the bed. This he was familiar with. But he'd learned better than to press a woman when she was angry but not talking. She was probably disappointed in Robin's reaction to the pregnancy, but he wouldn't apologize. She'd had a month or more to acclimate. Robin had been broadsided tonight. He didn't want her to feel alone, because he was there for her, but if she refused his attention, that was her own fault.

Robin tossed and turned late into the night until he finally fell asleep late enough that he woke in Phoenix's bed alone and had to sneak up the back staircase in a house full of people already getting ready for their days.

CHAPTER 14

*P*hoenix had armed herself with roast beef sandwiches again. Well not for her. Just about the only thing she wanted to eat these days was turkey sandwiches with tomato and spicy mustard. She might be able to eat that for breakfast lunch and dinner and be happy. Normally the spicy mustard would have made her tongue burn, but now she craved it. She'd ordered Robin his roast beef and his spicy pickles and decided to bring him lunch again. He wasn't eating like he should be, and maybe, just maybe, if they could enjoy a repeat of what had happened last time, they could put the awkwardness of last night behind them.

Phoenix wasn't unreasonable. She understood that the man had a lot on his plate and that the pregnancy was a surprise. She wanted to let him know that yeah, maybe she was disappointed that he wasn't ecstatic out of the gate, but she still wanted him. Still wanted to do this *with* him.

So she plastered a smile on her face and walked into his building, even though her heart was hammering like mad.

~

John had been hemming and hawing on speakerphone for fifteen minutes now, and Robin was losing his patience. There was only so much talk about how he should present himself on social media over the next few months that he could take.

"While we're showing you with your sleeves rolled up talking to everyday Kansans, we should probably start thinking about how to introduce the concept of your lady friend."

Robin's heart skipped a beat. "I don't know what you mean," Robin said.

"Oh, so Phoenix Lambert isn't the woman you've been mooning over for the last nine months?"

"I haven't been mooning," Robin said, but he angled his desk chair toward the window so he could see Revival's storefront. Because that's where Phoenix would be right now, working on six different devices. He still wasn't sure how she got anything done. A smile stole over his lips for just a moment before the dread that had been threatening to overwhelm him all day took over.

Phoenix was pregnant.

Pregnant.

Robin still didn't even know what to do with that.

"But you have been seeing Phoenix?" John asked.

"I seem to remember having a conversation about how my love life was none of your business."

"And I remember telling you that dating someone half your age was bad for your image."

"Still none of your business."

"It is my business if you don't want to be seen as a predator. Maybe ten years ago you could have pulled off a relationship like this without anyone batting an eye, but these days, you have to be more careful."

Robin looked back at the ceiling. He really didn't want to have this conversation. "John."

"I think if we introduce her early and maybe you guys start talking about getting married, start talking about kids, it'll make you look like the family man you are instead of a letch."

"Jesus, John."

"What? Tell me I'm wrong."

Robin shook his head. He couldn't marry Phoenix. That had never been on the table. "Just leave Phoenix out of the campaign planning okay?"

"People are going to want to know about the woman in your life. A good-looking single guy, running for office. Every damn reporter is going to ask."

"I'm a widower," Robin said. "There is no woman in my life. I've done that. There is not going to be a new marriage, no more kids. I'm going to be there for the people of Kansas like I always have been for Van and Clay, and that's how we're going to run it."

"If you're sure," John said, but he sounded anything but.

"I'm sure." A rustle of paper sounded behind Robin. Adam wasn't due back for another hour, so he rotated his chair to face his office door. Phoenix stood there in a peacock-blue dress with her hair around her shoulders, clutching a white paper sack and looking like she could breathe fire.

Robin's heart sank. He couldn't even feel his lips as he said, "Look, John, I've got to go," then hung up the phone without waiting for a reply.

"Phoenix," Robin said, pushing back from his desk and crossing the room.

She fisted her hands around the deli bag, but Robin could still see them trembling as he approached. "Look, that wasn't what—"

"I knew you didn't want the baby," Phoenix said over him. "But I was pretty sure you still wanted me, at least."

"Phoenix," he said again, not ashamed of the note of pleading that crept into his voice.

"I hope you enjoyed it while it lasted," she said, then dropped the sandwich bag on the floor as Robin reached for her. "Have fun in Washington. I'll bet you can find an intern even younger than me to screw."

And before Robin could move, she was out the door. He could see her walking on the sidewalk below his office windows with her head held high just a few seconds later. Dread and panic had turned Robin's entire body leaden. He couldn't move to chase after her.

Phoenix had been avoiding Robin for three days. It wasn't easy when they lived in the same house, but she'd already been making plans to rectify that. Finding an apartment in a town currently going through a housing shortage was proving even more difficult than Phoenix had expected, but that was fine. Phoenix never backed down from a challenge.

She'd been tempted to flee back to L.A., but Phoenix didn't want to leave Van or cancel her movie night with Minnie. Plus, leaving would be like letting Robin know that he'd won. That he'd used her and broken her when he tossed her aside. But Phoenix was not going to give him that power. That was one of the first things Eve had taught her about the industry. People could only hurt you if you gave them the power to hurt you, and Phoenix was above that. She'd lulled herself into restless sleep every night by stroking her belly and telling her baby that they were in this together, and nothing was going to stop them.

It was just about the only thing that had given Phoenix comfort the last three days.

Only there had been a pink smear on the toilet paper when Phoenix woke up that morning. And another, darker one the second time Phoenix had gone to the bathroom, and she was doing her best not to panic. Spotting in the first trimester could be normal. It didn't necessarily mean anything. When she called the doctor, she'd said the same thing, but she scheduled Phoenix in for a blood test just to be safe. They could compare the results to blood they'd drawn a few days before and see if Phoenix's levels were rising or falling. And she offered to do another ultrasound for Phoenix's peace of mind.

The ultrasound had not been promising. The baby was supposed to be a little over ten weeks, and they should have been able to detect a heartbeat. The doctor hadn't been encouraging but wanted to wait for the blood work before she came to any conclusions.

As day turned into evening, the spotting turned bright red and regular. The cramps were beginning to hurt, and Phoenix wanted to curl into a ball around her heating pad in her bed and weep until she fell asleep. Instead, she was waiting for Minnie to arrive for movie night and practicing how to smile.

Robin had kept his distance the last few days. He'd still come down and slept with her every night, but she hadn't let him do more than stroke her hair and tell her how beautiful she was. Phoenix knew he was trying to be conciliatory, that he wanted her to comfort him as he came to terms with the reality of her pregnancy. But he'd also been staying late at the office every day that week until today, leaving them zero opportunity to talk about anything. Not that she would have listened to him anyway.

Phoenix opened a bottle of wine for Minnie and Van to split. Robin came in the back door at the same time Phoenix's phone rang; she didn't even spare him a glance. Because of course he came home early tonight. He was probably hoping to speak to her and explain once again why she shouldn't be pissed about what he'd said to his campaign manager, like in the zillion texts and voicemails he'd left her over the last three days. The future congressman was going to be disappointed. Phoenix had already called in the pizza, Van was writing a song for once, and Minnie should arrive any moment. Phoenix didn't have the time to spare for him.

Instead, she answered her phone as she pulled glasses down from the cabinet, pretending she couldn't feel Robin's eyes on the back of her head. She listened almost outside her body as the doctor told her the results of her bloodwork. That her numbers were falling, that her progesterone hadn't been all that strong to begin with, and when Phoenix decided to try again, she should start with progesterone supplements. When the doctor asked if Phoenix would like to schedule a D&C, Phoenix said yes and booked it for the following day. If she was going to have a miscarriage, she wanted it to be over as soon as possible. She would make Robin drive her. It was the least he could do.

Then, Phoenix poured herself a glass of wine and swallowed it like she was chugging beer at a frat party. Robin was immediately at her side, pulling the glass out of her hand. "Hey now," he said. "You shouldn't be drinking."

Phoenix glared. "I just found out I'm having a miscarriage, so I will get as drunk as I like, thank you very much."

Robin stepped away and handed her back the glass. As she finished a second helping of wine, he rubbed her shoulders and whispered in her ear that he was sorry, that everything was going to be okay. Like he actually cared.

"Well, you got what you wanted. No baby and no mistress to deal with during your campaign," she said. "But you will be driving me to my appointment tomorrow."

"Whatever you want," Robin said. He tried to embrace her from behind, but Phoenix shrugged him off. He whispered, "I'm sorry, Fe," at the same time the doorbell rang.

"What I want," she started as she turned to face him. She would not let herself be affected by the doleful repentance in his eyes, the true concern. "Is for you to answer the door while I go upstairs and make sure your stepson isn't taking advantage of Van, because they were supposed to be working on a song together, and I haven't heard guitars for more than ten minutes."

Phoenix marched straight up the stairs and to the closed door of Clay's room. She heard a moan and the creak of a bed. If she ever planned to stay in this house again—which she didn't—Phoenix would see that Robin did something to make the place more soundproof, but old and drafty like it was, if you were paying attention, it was impossible to keep secrets.

Phoenix pounded on the door, said something that was probably rude, and retreated before she had to confront Clay or Van. She just couldn't yet. She could hear Robin greeting Minnie at the front door, and he sounded so kind and so charming with her that tears pricked at Phoenix's eyes.

How could he be like that with someone he barely knew, and when Phoenix needed his support, he didn't have anything but distance and denial with a side of *but I still want to fuck you?*

She ducked into the bathroom and allowed a few tears to fall down her cheeks before dashing them away, dabbing at her eyeliner, then plastering a smile on her face and making her way down the stairs to meet her guest. She could deal with her grief later. When she had some privacy.

CHAPTER 15

*R*obin disappeared into his study to give the girls privacy. To give Phoenix space.

He felt awful. Robin hadn't been thrilled about the pregnancy, but he'd been warming up to the idea. There was still work to do on reconciling his public and private lives. He imagined Phoenix's belly growing round, and watching her pace around her beach house in the fluffy white robe, their baby in her arms. Robin could imagine the contentment he'd feel in that scene. It was a hell of a contrast to what he'd been feeling the last few months, and he'd been seeking out solace in the fantasy. As if he could leave everything behind and just escape into Phoenix's world.

The truth was, the stolen moments Robin spent with Phoenix were the only ones where anything made any sense. And now he'd lost her too. As selfish as it was, he'd wanted to keep her and their relationship exactly as it had been forever. He'd only said what he'd said to John to buy himself some time to figure everything out with her. Robin wanted Phoenix to be his special salacious secret while they went about the rest of their lives independently. He wanted Phoenix to be the place he could come back to for peace and reverie. She'd go back to L.A. eventually; he'd be spending half the year in Washington DC once he won the election. But sometimes they could have whatever dark intimacy it was that had developed between them. It wasn't anybody else's business.

Robin knew that arrangement wasn't fair to her, and it wasn't possible long term, but that didn't change that it was true. He'd been trying to work his mind around the pregnancy question. How if he'd wanted to keep Phoenix, that it would mean going public with their relationship and acknowledging the baby. And what a disaster that would mean for his career. What the added stress would mean for Van. Would his daughter be able to forgive him?

He hadn't wanted to do it, but he hadn't wanted Phoenix to lose the baby either. He and Caroline had experienced enough losses that he knew how excruciating that could be, both physically and emotionally. Robin didn't want to leave her to deal with the pain alone, but what could he do if she refused to talk to him?

Perhaps Phoenix would confide in Van if she wouldn't talk to him. He didn't want Van to know, but thinking of Phoenix, hurting with no one to turn to, he found himself not caring so much if Van found out. He had a better relationship with his daughter than he'd given them credit for. Van might be upset with him for a few weeks, but they'd get through it. They always had.

John would figure out how to deal too. Phoenix was a master at spinning perspective for the media. She probably already had a spreadsheet dedicated to what his campaign meant for their relationship.

And just like that, it was as if the months-old obstruction fell away.

Robin didn't care. He just wanted Phoenix to be happy. He'd do just about anything to erase the misery he'd seen Phoenix wearing on her shoulders the last few days. And the utter devastation on her face as she'd guzzled that wine? Robin never wanted to see her like that again.

He'd been about to slip into the living room and discretely pull Phoenix aside when his phone rang, the familiar number of the county jail popping up on the screen. He contemplated not answering it. He really didn't want to work tonight, especially not some petty case that he'd have to sandwich in hearings for around the water trial.

But the part of him that was still a struggling new lawyer in town who was paying back his dad for the down payment on this house and supporting his young bride and new daughter wouldn't let him not answer these Friday-night calls.

"Robin Birch," he answered the phone.

"Hey, Robin." Clay's voice sounded gruff and humble. "Something went down at The Fox."

Henry Bishop had gone down at The Fox. By all accounts, he'd gone down twice. And Robin found he didn't give a damn that Clay and Bryant were facing assault and battery charges. Had Robin been there, he might have been arrested right along with the boys, and he wouldn't have been sorry about that either.

When Robin was let into the conference room, both Clay and Bryant had scraped knuckles; both looked defiant and surly still, as if they only needed to be in the same room as Bishop again to finish what they'd started.

Robin wanted to tell them that the police would never release them while they continued to look unrepentant, but he didn't. He only sat down across from them, pulled out his pen, looked them both in the eyes and said, "Tell me what he did to provoke you."

It took hours to smooth out all the details and find out how unjust Bishop was, what charges he was pressing, what their bail would be, and when they could be released.

It had been years since Robin had pulled an all-nighter, but it was nine o'clock the next morning before Clay and Bryant were released, and of course the entire film crew had arrived to pick up on the drama. He wondered if that was Phoenix's doing, but when he tried to make eye contact with her, Phoenix averted her gaze and focused on what was happening between Clay, Bryant, and Van. Robin hadn't missed the way Clay had opened his arms, ready to receive Van, only for her to run to Bryant instead. Cameras or no, Clay never could keep his jealousy to himself. After their conversation the other night, about the hurtful things Clay had said to Van as a teenager, Robin thought he understood a little bit more about how deeply Clay cared for his daughter. It didn't excuse the slut-shaming he'd done, but that was up to Van to forgive.

To distract Clay, Robin clasped a hand on his shoulder and suggested they all go out to breakfast. They should have just enough time before he had to get Phoenix to her appointment.

Clay shrugged Robin's hand off. "We need to get to work."

Phoenix inserted herself between Clay and Robin, and she had a fiery gleam in her eye that replaced the dull grief that she'd been passing off as exhaustion whenever he checked in with her.

"It's okay. I spoke with Marie, and she called all the foremen. They have you covered for the morning."

Clay's jaw ticked as he said, "I could have handled that."

Robin's instincts railed at him to step between Clay and Phoenix, to protect them from one another, but he also knew that would only make Phoenix angrier with him than she already was.

"No, you couldn't have," Phoenix said as she stepped into Clay's face. "Because you let an asshole bait you into getting arrested."

Robin laid a warning hand on Phoenix's shoulder as Clay stepped up to her until they were toe-to-toe. At least she didn't shrug him off like Clay had.

"At least I've always seen that motherfucker for what he was. If you'd have listened to me last Christmas when I told you that man was bad news, none of this would have happened."

Phoenix dug her forefinger into Clay's shoulder, jabbing him with her pointed nail over and over again as she said, "Don't you dare put this on me. Bishop's actions are on him and him alone. And you are no better than he is, so stay away from Van."

Clay swatted her hand aside like it was nothing more than a mosquito buzzing in his ear, and Robin took a step closer to Phoenix. Not that he thought they'd actually hurt one another. He did want them to get through whatever this mutual dislike was, but he would stop this if it became any more heated.

"What does that mean?" Clay asked.

"You think I don't know what was going on last night? While you and Van were in your room 'writing a song?'"

Robin looked to Clay then. Pink stained his cheeks, but he still held his fists clenched, his shoulders back, his jaw clenched. "That's none of your business."

Phoenix made a sound like an angry cat. "I will never let Van fall victim to another predator. Never. So you can take your teenage need to prove how manly you are and shove it up your ass."

Phoenix's hand twitched at her side, and Robin was afraid she'd take a swipe at Clay the way she'd done at him that night he'd frightened her. He placed his other hand on her shoulder and squeezed. "Phoenix, Clay isn't a threat to Van."

Phoenix rotated out of his hold as if his touch physically pained her. "You didn't see it then either." She adjusted her jacket, and her eyes turned dull again as she focused in on Robin's shoulders instead of meeting his eyes. "I'll be waiting in the car. In case you've forgotten, we have an appointment."

He wanted to tell her that he hadn't forgotten, but as he watched her leave the building, Robin feared he had a lot more to fix with Phoenix then he'd originally thought.

He held back, talking to the county commissioner while Van and Phoenix had a whispered argument outside the front door, with Butch standing close by, the cameras still hovering. When Van got into a car with Butch, and the cameras surrounded a frowning Phoenix as she stood in the morning sunlight, her arms crossed over her chest as she watched Van drive away.

She wore the blue sheath dress that was his favorite under her blazer. The nude heels had to be hurting her feet by now, but she just watched the car drive away as the wind whipped the hair out behind her in a red plume.

Robin excused himself with a handshake and stopped only when he was standing too close to Phoenix, heedless of the cameras. "Shall we?" he asked, offering his hand.

Phoenix turned her scowl on him, scanning him from head to toe with disapproval. "I suppose it's close enough."

She did allow him to help her into the car, but Robin couldn't tell if she was performing for the cameras or if she was just used to the treatment. When Robin was buckled behind the wheel of his BMW, he asked, "Did you want to go home and change into more comfortable clothes?"

"I put a bag in your trunk last night. Let's just go and get this over with. I've already bled through half a pack of pads."

"Are you feeling alright?" he asked. He knew she wasn't, but her not talking to him was killing him. That Phoenix was avoiding him felt like someone was slowly smothering him, and if he couldn't coax her into trusting him, he had started considering the drastic measures he would be willing to take to keep her.

"I have killer cramps, I'm losing a baby that I wanted, and the man I love couldn't give a shit, so I'd say I'm doing just fine thank you."

She straightened the hem on her skirt and looked out the window like he was supposed to just start the car and chauffeur her to her appointment. But her words echoed through him like he was the Grand Canyon. He'd known how she felt, but she'd never said it before, and he'd never allowed himself to think about it. But Phoenix loved him, and Robin wanted that love desperately.

"Are we going to the hospital or women's clinic?"

"The clinic."

Robin drove around the corner and out of sight of the cameras, then said. "I care, Fe. I care about you, I care about what you're going through, and I'm sorry you're hurting."

"But are you?" she said as she whipped her angry blue gaze on him. "It's your baby too, Robin. I can't seem to detect an ounce of regret on your part."

"I haven't had a chance to decide how I feel," he said through ground teeth. "Everything's been happening so quickly. Between the trial and the tornado and everything with Van, I haven't had time to think, and I've barely been sleeping—" Phoenix huffed, and he knew she was thinking of all the nights they'd stayed up too late screwing. But what she didn't understand was that those were the only nights he got any sleep. Falling asleep next to her, exhausted and satiated, was the only time his mind shut off enough for him to do anything more than doze. "And even the best of us get overwhelmed."

"I'm sorry that months of regular fucking resulted in an unplanned pregnancy that you don't have time to deal with while you play big-time lawyer and plan your run for Congress, but it's been a pretty fucking big deal to me for a while now."

It wasn't a long drive to the clinic from the police station. They were only a few blocks away and already the clinic was in sight, just a stoplight and a left turn away, just across the street from where his dad's auto shop had been, before it had been torn down to make space for a cardiovascular clinic. "I'm not unaffected by all of this. Was I prepared for a pregnancy? No. But I was prepared to follow your lead."

He saw Phoenix shaking her head out of the corner of her eyes as he pulled into a parking space near the front of the women's clinic. "I am so sick of being the least important thing on your to-do list. What we had shouldn't have been an afterthought. We shouldn't have been something you had to make excuses about or denied your involvement with. Our baby shouldn't have been just one more weight on the scale of your stressors. We should have tipped the whole damn thing in our favor, but instead we were an inconvenience. This is all just..." She motioned down the length of her body. "I'm so over it. Just done."

Robin didn't argue with her. He was too exhausted to put up a fight. He had nothing to say in his defense. He was devastated by how everything around him felt like it was falling apart and there was nothing he could do to pick up the pieces. If Phoenix wanted space, it was probably better for everyone if Robin gave her space.

He grabbed Phoenix's bag from his trunk. He waited with her after she checked in, both of them with enough notifications on their phones to keep them busy until she was called back. Though the tension between them hadn't faded. He wanted her to look at him to acknowledge that he was here for her now, when it counted, but Phoenix wouldn't.

He told himself that if anger was what she needed to get through this, he'd let her have it. He'd let her be angry at him, but he couldn't shake the feeling that what he was doing was giving up.

"Would you like me to go with you?" he asked, standing as she did.

Phoenix shook her head. "I'd rather do this alone."

"I'm here if you change your mind," he said.

"I won't be gone long." Phoenix took a deep breath and disappeared into the back of the clinic.

A nurse pushed her through the door in a wheelchair a little over an hour later. She'd changed into leggings and one of her thin, off-the-shoulder T-shirts. She looked pale and exhausted, but otherwise fine. Robin took the bag that sat in her lap and placed a kiss on the top of her head. She didn't respond.

"I'll bring the car around," he said, though he wasn't sure if he was talking to the nurse or to Phoenix.

It was the nurse who responded, "We'll meet you outside."

Phoenix brushed off his help on the transition from the chair to the car and buckled herself in with a fierceness that had him bracing for a fight once he was settled in behind the wheel. Instead, Phoenix pulled out her phone, now connected to a spare battery, and said, "Has your P.I. found out anything about the sex tape?"

Robin paused before pulling out into traffic. "You want to talk about the sex tape?" He couldn't hide his incredulousness.

"Why not? We need to figure out how we're going to handle this, preferably today."

"I haven't heard from him yet today. But I can call him when we get back to the house."

"Good. I'd like to go to Van with a strategy in place later on today."

"Do you think it's wise to tell her?"

"Yes," Phoenix's tone brooked no room for argument. "It's ultimately up to her what she wants to do about it, but I'd like to make sure we have as many facts as possible."

"You should rest, Phoenix."

"I'm fine."

"You were up all night, and you just had surgery."

"I planned to take a nap, not that it's any of your business."

"Fe," he said. Robin couldn't look at her with the busy Saturday morning traffic swelling around them, but he could see her staring at her phone screen out of the corner of his eye.

Her stomach growled, and he pulled into the nearest drive-through. Now that he thought about it, he was starving.

"What are you doing?" she asked when the car stopped, and she peeled her eyes away from her phone.

"Buying you lunch."

"No."

"Do you want whatever excuse for a salad they have here, or do you want a double bacon cheeseburger with fries like I'm getting?"

Phoenix glared at him for a minute before her hunger won out. "The burger, but no bacon for me."

"Fair enough."

"And I'm Venmo-ing you the money for my lunch."

"I want to buy you lunch, Fe. It's the least I can do."

Phoenix was already tapping away, and a few seconds later he felt his own phone buzz in his pocket, and it was their turn to order, so he didn't argue. At least she was going to eat something with heft to it. He glanced at her again; she was too pale. She could likely use the iron from the beef.

Robin picked at his fries as he drove. And in the ten minutes it took to get back to the house, Phoenix had devoured her entire meal, but she hadn't said another word to him. Her eyes had never left her phone's screen, and when they got back to the house, she went straight to the basement.

Robin didn't see her again for a week. By then the sex tape was out, John had pestered Robin to death, and Van was all over the news and social media. The paparazzi had him trapped in his own home, and his water rights trial was due to start soon. There were more important things to think about than how his affair with Phoenix had crashed and burned.

Then Van was kidnapped, and Robin's world stopped entirely. His daughter had been abducted from the middle of one of the busiest blocks in the town, and though she'd only been missing for a matter of hours, Robin's whole world had stopped. That it had been Bishop behind the offense—again, had both ignited his undying ire and activated his mother hen instincts. The only time he left his daughter's side was when he vacated to make space for Phoenix, who still wouldn't even look at him. But then Van was on the mend, and the trial started, and Robin tried to concentrate on his work.

Nothing really distracted him, and trudging through the legal intricacies of his practice began to feel like hiking through a mud pit. Each day left him so dissatisfied and exhausted that he almost stopped noticing that they'd passed, empty and quiet. Then Clay and Bryant had emerged from the basement staircase into the kitchen hauling a mattress between them; the only thing Robin could concentrate on was the way his stomach burned away at the same time it felt like someone was strangling him.

"What's going on?" he asked.

The two men looked from one to the other before Clay said, "Phoenix asked us to bring her bed from here to her new place. She said the replacement will be delivered in a few days."

"Her new place?"

"You didn't know?" Bryant asked.

Robin shook his head. Phoenix had moved out, and he hadn't even noticed?

"She rented an apartment downtown. We thought you knew."

Robin scrubbed his hands through his hair. Jesus. He hadn't meant to make her feel so uncomfortable that she couldn't even stay in the same house as him.

"She didn't say anything." When they just stood there, holding a mattress between them in his kitchen, Robin rolled his eyes. "Don't let me hold you up. Get the woman her bed, by all means."

He wanted to text her. To ask her why the hell she was being so stubborn, but he knew that wouldn't go over well.

Robin didn't have time to deal with it all. If she wanted to leave, that was up to her. He wasn't going to force her to do anything she didn't want to do. And apparently, she didn't want to be with him anymore. It had been inevitable, but it didn't mean he liked it.

CHAPTER 16

$\mathcal{V}$an had helped Phoenix unload her carload of shopping bags, but then she had plopped down on the new, shiny chrome stool at the breakfast bar to watch Phoenix unwrap her new kitchenware.

"What?" Van asked when she noticed Phoenix staring at her.

"I thought you were going to help me move in."

"Pfft," Van shook her head. "I helped you shop, and I helped carry things up the stairs despite my still-delicate condition."

That was stretching things. Van had been cleared by her doctor to resume her normal activities after her concussion, but she'd been using it as an excuse not to do anything she didn't want to do over the past few weeks. "Your condition is just fine."

Van shrugged. "Maybe, but I know better than to try and organize your things. Better to just watch you do it." Then she grabbed one of the apples they'd just bought out of the basket Phoenix had just poured them into, even though she had to reach over a fleet of shopping bags to do so.

"So, how long is your lease for?" Van asked.

Phoenix hadn't told anyone she was moving until this morning when she woke Van up and asked her to call in Clay and Bryant as reinforcements. It had happened so quickly. She'd gotten word that the first of the lofts downtown was finished and ready for rent—the fancy ones in the old factory that Minnie's dad hadn't needed the historical society's approval to renovate, and she'd sort of just jumped on it. Signed the lease before she had a chance to change her mind.

"A year. I figured we'd be spending enough time here that it made sense for me to get my own place."

Van bit into her apple as Phoenix unwrapped her plates and shoved them into the cabinet. She would wash everything later, after the clutter had been dispelled.

"Right. Makes sense," Van said around her apple. "And this totally has nothing to do with how you've been avoiding my dad for weeks."

Phoenix stilled, her arm raised, as she looked at Van over her shoulder. "Has he mentioned anything to you?"

Van snorted. "My dad thinks I've been through enough. He's not going to burden me with his troubles." Then Van shrugged. "Plus, I asked him, and he told me it was your story to tell."

"Fucking coward," Phoenix said into the cabinet.

Van was silent as Phoenix moved on from the plates to the coffee mugs. But after Phoenix had stacked the third mug just so, Van harrumphed. "Okay so maybe I wasn't being as direct as I could be, but come on. I have been dying to know the whole story for weeks, and you both act like it was some big secret that y'all were banging, but you've already admitted to it, so spill, sister."

"What do you say we try out the new coffeemaker?" Phoenix said first.

Van hopped up and started prying open the box with her fingernails. "Should I grab some popcorn too?"

Phoenix only glared as she cleared a space on the counter for the coffee pot. A few minutes later, they settled onto the bar stools, the only furniture she had so far. Phoenix clutched a brand new white mug full of steaming coffee between her fingers, trying to figure out what else she could say to put off this conversation.

Van said, "Well?"

Phoenix really didn't need the coffee. Her blood pressure was probably already endangering her life, but it was good to have something to do with her hands. Something to concentrate on as she took a deep breath, and said, "I was pregnant, and he didn't want us."

Why did nobody ever want her? Not her parents, not Robin. None of them had ever chosen her. For once, she wanted to be somebody's first choice. Phoenix's calm facade slipped as a tear escaped, the first she'd allowed herself to cry since her D&C more than a month ago. She hadn't had time for tears. One thing she had learned from Eve was that people who felt sorry for themselves never accomplished anything, they just festered in their self-pity until they wasted away. So Phoenix hadn't given herself time to grieve, because grieving felt like wallowing, and if Phoenix allowed herself time to wallow, she might cease to function altogether. Too many people were counting on her for her to allow herself that luxury. But with Van, Phoenix could finally let go.

"He didn't want me, and he didn't want our baby tarnishing his image while he ran for Congress." Phoenix's throat constricted, and she had to haul in air behind the sob clogging her throat. She opened her mouth to say more, but she couldn't speak.

Van's mug hit the counter with a *thunk*. And she pulled Phoenix into her dainty arms as Phoenix's one tear turned into a cascade of sobs.

Van held her, stroking her back, murmuring soothing whispers into her ear. Phoenix didn't know how long she cried. When she pulled back and dried her eyes, she saw that Van was wiping her eyes too.

"Why are you crying?" Phoenix asked.

Van gave a shuddering tearful laugh as she smeared her mascara over her cheekbone. "When you hurt, I hurt, Fe. I just wish you would have told me how much you were hurting."

"I didn't know how to tell you without making things complicated between you and your dad."

Van laughed for real that time. "Okay, so I know there's no way this situation was ever not going to be complicated, but you and he are the two people I love most in this world, and pretty much nothing you can do to each other is ever going to change how I feel about either of you."

Tears sprang anew to Phoenix's eyes. "I had a miscarriage."

"I figured," Van said.

"And he didn't even care, Van. He didn't care that we were losing our baby. I told him, and the only emotion he showed was relief."

"Ah, honey, I'm sorry." Van squeezed Phoenix's knee. Phoenix sniffed and picked up her mug, but the coffee had gone cold, and she set it down again.

"He cared more about his damn campaign and not having to make our relationship public than he ever cared about me."

Van frowned, as if she might say that she didn't think that was true, but what she actually said was, "You don't deserve that kind of bullshit. You are so amazing; you deserve to be celebrated. And if my stupid dad doesn't know that, then you are better off without him."

Phoenix found it hard to breathe again. "But I love him, Van. I still love him, and it hurts to be near him. I had to move out, or I was going to die."

Van shushed her and pulled her back into her arms. "I know."

"I wanted that baby," Phoenix whispered into Van's shoulder like it was a secret.

"I know that too," Van said.

And Phoenix felt so pathetic and so out of control as she asked, "But why didn't he want us too?"

Van shook her head against Phoenix's shoulder. "I don't know, Fe. Maybe he was afraid. I mean, I'm not defending him, but love hasn't been kind to him."

Phoenix couldn't even make space for that concept. Her life was not going to be ruled by someone else's cowardice. "Fuck his fear."

"Totally," Van said. She pulled back far enough to wipe Phoenix's freshest tears from her cheeks. "Please come to me next time. Even if it is about my dad. I don't care. I want to be there for you like you were there for me, okay?"

Phoenix nodded, wanting to remind Van that she hadn't

been there for Van like she should have been. That she'd been too preoccupied with the press and her pregnancy to be the kind of friend she should be over the last few months. But that was when Clay and Bryant burst through her apartment door, hauling Phoenix's mattress between them.

Both women stood and wiped their eyes, as Phoenix took charge, taking advantage of the help while she had it.

Van and Clay arrived home together the evening of the mattress moving incident. Clay carried two pizza boxes while Van held a large bottle of whiskey by the neck as they strode into the kitchen. He realized, with their dusty clothes, they must have been helping Phoenix move all day, but he didn't ask them how they'd spent their Saturday. Only pulled three rocks glasses from the cabinet and offered to pour them all a glass of the Irish whiskey his daughter favored.

"Thanks, Daddy," she said as she took her drink.

"We got a sausage and pepperoni pizza. I know it's your favorite."

Van pulled a slice off the other pizza, which was covered in green vegetables, and took a gigantic bite. That was one of the best things about his kids figuring out that they were in love with each other. Van was eating again, and she smiled. Not the smile she'd been giving him all summer, which was meant to be reassuring, yet only made him worry, but genuinely happy smiles.

Her grin grew brighter as Clay wrapped an arm around her shoulder and kissed her temple. Van beamed up at him and offered him a bite of her strange green pizza. He ate half the slice in one go without even blinking an eye. Then he flipped the lid on the pepperoni and sausage and grabbed his slice from there. The three of them sat at the breakfast bar eating and drinking whiskey for half an hour, and it was pleasant. They talked about how Robin was doing with the trial and his plans for his Congress run after the new year. They discussed how Van and Clay would be leaving soon to record her new album in L.A. and how the label had rented a house on the beach for them to stay in while they were there, since Van had sold her condo.

Then, like they had reached a prearranged point, Clay kissed Van on the top of her head and said, "I'm going to take Pebbles for a walk to work off all those pizza crusts you've been feeding her."

Van kissed Clay on the lips. "Let Butch follow you?"

"No way in hell," Clay said. "He's staying here with you."

Van rolled her eyes, but she smiled as she watched Clay clip the leash on his dog's harness and lead her out the back door. Robin loved seeing his daughter so happy. It was one of the more satisfying parts of parenthood; even if she had found the source of that happiness in an unorthodox place, Robin couldn't begrudge it of either of them. He'd watched them both struggle against their feelings for a decade, and he'd never seen either of his children more peaceful than they were now that they'd given in to their feelings for each other.

Van turned back to him, a wide smile still on her face as she knocked back the rest of the whiskey in her glass. "Piano?" she asked.

Robin did the same with his whiskey. "Sure." It had been weeks since they'd played together.

They settled in beside one another on the piano bench. She always sat on the soprano side of the keyboard, even though she rarely played. She could play, they had enrolled her in lessons by the time she was six, but the guitar had always been her preferred instrument. When they played together, Van usually sang, and Robin did all of the piano playing. He didn't mind, but as he set his fingers to the keys and asked, "What should we play?" Van hit him with the most direct stare he'd ever seen and asked, "So when were you going to tell me you've been sleeping with my best friend?"

And Robin's fingers slipped off the keys with a discordant clang. "Phoenix told you?"

"We've all known you two were sleeping together for ages, because, surprise, you two weren't as stealthy as you thought you were. But what I didn't realize was that you knocked her up and refused to take responsibility. How about you tell me about that?"

Van's voice was unforgiving, and Robin found himself placing his fingers to the keys and dancing out a few chord progressions out of self-preservation. "I didn't refuse to take responsibility. I told her I needed a few days to wrap my mind around the idea of having another baby, and by the time I did, she was miscarrying. I took care of her afterward, as much as she would let me, and I didn't want her to go through that. Your mother and I did three times after you were born. It was heartbreaking every time."

Van actually set her fingers to the keys and started playing one of the classical tunes he'd taught her when she'd been in middle school. "Yes, but you and mom were married. Phoenix was never more than your secret girlfriend. I mean, you never even told me about the two of you, and that's pretty shitty."

Van played a few more chords and launched into one of her own songs, playing with the piano keys until she found the correct notes, like she'd never played it on the piano before and was figuring it out by ear, from memory.

"I wasn't sure you would understand."

"You were afraid I'd be pissed at you." Her pointed stare said that she was indeed pissed at him.

Robin couldn't help the smile at his daughter's straight-forwardness. "Guilty."

Her hands fell away from the keys, and she said, "Look, I'm not going to pretend to understand it, because I don't. But I will tell you what I told Phoenix. You are my two most favorite people in the world, and I want you to be happy, whether you're together or not. And I will love you both, no matter what."

Robin pulled Van into his arms, hugging her tight. He was both relieved and proud at how big her heart was. "That's very generous of you."

"I know it is," Van said as she pushed against his chest. "It also doesn't mean I've forgiven you yet for breaking my best friend's heart."

"I—"

Van held her hands up. "I'm not looking for excuses or justifications."

"I don't have any," Robin said. Nothing he could say would be able to explain away how badly he'd treated Phoenix.

Van sighed and put her fingers back on the keys, tinkling out one of the warm-ups he'd taught her as a child. "But I also think you're hurting. And you have been for a while."

Robin placed his hands on the keys next to hers, and he played the opening chords of Van's first single. She laughed next to him, and it warmed his heart, to have her beside him, even if she was right, Robin had been hurting for a long, long time.

CHAPTER 17

"*D*arling!" Eve said as she grasped Phoenix by the shoulders and placed twin kisses on each of Phoenix's cheeks. "It's so good to have you back. I feel like it's been a millennia since I've had you all to myself."

"I've missed you too, Eve," Phoenix replicated Eve's preferred greeting before taking her place at their table. Eve had already ordered for them, croissants and fruit with mimosas, but almost never touched anything but her mimosa.

Phoenix had come back to L.A. with Van and Clay. They were busy recording her album; Phoenix was busy coordinating publicity and planning the next season of the show. She'd barely had time to think since she'd been back. With all the in-person meetings everyone wanted to have with her now that she was back in town, Phoenix didn't have the time to enjoy living on the beach again.

When they'd left Kansas, it had been gloomy and cold with misting, spitting rain. Phoenix shivered just thinking about it. She hated the cold. She had made it a point to step onto her patio every morning with her coffee and enjoy the sound of the waves crashing against the shore for exactly 2.5 seconds before she had to get dressed and dash off to the first of her million meetings.

She did not have time to remember the mornings last spring when Robin had joined her at the table on the patio. He'd worn that damn pair of gray sweatpants, and he looked better in them than men half his age. She did not have time to miss him cooking her eggs because all she had time for was a smoothie at the drive-through.

But today was Sunday, and Phoenix had no appointments, and Van and Clay were still in the stage of their relationship where they were having sex at every opportunity, so they hadn't been very good company since they'd been in California. Phoenix was trying not to begrudge them their time together. Clay was making Van happy, and she was writing again. She'd written twenty songs in the last two weeks alone. That was about nineteen more than she'd written in the last two years.

She was writing so much that Phoenix had a whole album worth of songs she was trying to sell—something Van had never done before. When Phoenix had asked if Van was sure she didn't want to save them for a future album, Van had only shrugged and told her she'd write a new album for herself when the time was right.

Phoenix was trying to learn to like Clay. She really was. He'd seemed less grumpy when they'd met for lunch a few days ago. Of course, the lunch had also been a photo op. They'd eaten on the patio at The Ivy. Van had been dolled up in a short skirt and torn top, closer to the kind of thing she wore on stage rather than her usual skinny jeans. Clay wore the designer equivalent of his uniform, worn denim and a gray T-shirt. But add the Ray-Bans and the high-dollar haircut Phoenix had scheduled for him, and he managed to look very Californian while maintaining his home-grown farm-boy persona.

He'd been relaxed, with one arm slung around the back of Van's chair and that stupid sideway grin of his. He'd refilled not just Van's water glass with the pitcher on the table, but Phoenix's as well, and she supposed that was something. Plus, he'd convinced Van to let Butch move a security team into the bottom floor of their house, which Phoenix approved of. Public opinion had largely swung back into Van's favor since the kidnapping, but there were still threats coming in. Phoenix dreaded how violent the threats would become once a trial date was set.

"Now, tell me darling, was it only this nasty business with Bishop keeping you in the middle-of-nowhere for so long, or did it have more to do with that delicious silver fox you were here with in the spring?"

Phoenix hid behind her champagne flute. "A little bit of both, perhaps. Robin was a good distraction, but really, that's where Van wanted to be. And with this new relationship with Clay—" Phoenix popped a slice of strawberry into her mouth since she didn't feel like she needed to finish that statement.

Eve's face lit up, just like Phoenix knew it would. "That child knows how to start the most scrumptious gossip. You'd think we were in Victorian London, the way everyone pretended to be scandalized about her sleeping with her stepbrother. But we all know everyone is absolutely delighted by it."

Eve drained her glass, and the server was there with a

replacement mimosa almost immediately. "And you, darling, don't think I'm not giving you any credit."

"I had absolutely nothing to do with Van and Clay getting together. I was against it at first, actually."

"Tell me it wasn't your idea to photograph him and Van together for the first time with his pecs out."

Phoenix felt herself blush, just a little bit. "Of course that was my idea."

"I would have done the same thing," Eve said. "And what do you know, the whole world loved them together, never mind the taboo. Now," Eve set down her glass in favor of the barest nibble of a melon slice. "Tell me about what you've been up to darling."

So Phoenix gave her the usual business update, and they discussed the song-selling venture and different ways to explore that avenue as long as Van kept creating new work. The fruit on the table was almost gone, and Phoenix had just finished half a croissant when Eve asked, "Now, tell me exactly how Robin Birch broke your heart."

Phoenix sputtered. "He didn't— I mean we— I don't—"

"Shhh," Eve patted Phoenix's forearm, her French manicure tapping against the china fruit platter. "I know I'm not the most approachable person in your life, but you're the closest thing to a daughter I'm ever going to have. With that, I've developed a bit of a mother's intuition when it comes to you, darling. I can tell that man made his way past those steel gates of yours and crushed your delicate little heart, so tell me what happened. I need to know everything."

Phoenix loved Eve. The woman truly did love her in her own way, even if she was likely more interested in the gossip than actually consoling Phoenix. She would also mostly keep it to herself. Eve was the sort of person of would only hint that she knew more about a given situation than anybody else, but she'd never divulge more than a vague detail. And, Phoenix wanted to talk about it. The initial shock had worn off, but the grief and betrayal Phoenix still carried weighed her down as much as if she were carrying a ten-ton boulder on her back. She was stooped, exhausted, and didn't even trust her own senses anymore.

Even though Robin had flat out said that he didn't want her to be a part of his life, had said that there weren't going to be any more kids in his life, the day after she'd told him she was pregnant, Phoenix still got the tingles whenever he was near. Her body had never lied to her like that before. Never once.

"Well, you heard the rumors that he's running for Congress, I'm sure?" Phoenix asked.

"Of course, darling. I'm assuming that's why he never contacted me about his screenplay. He gave all that up for politics."

"Apparently it's his life ambition," Phoenix said.

"Yes, I could see that in a man like him. Authoritative, successful, handsome. Which is what made him such a good match for my Phoenix."

Phoenix shrugged. "Yeah, well. He gave me up for Congress too."

"He didn't!"

Phoenix nodded. "His campaign manager thought dating a woman half his age looked bad and wanted us to get married and plan a family to help Robin's image, and Robin said no."

Eve had reached for Phoenix's hand across the table,

probably the most tender, sincere gesture she was capable of. "Did you want all of that?" Eve asked.

"I don't know. I wanted something, but we never had a chance to discuss it, and then I told him I was pregnant, and the next day he told his campaign manager that he was running as a widower whose only family were his adult children."

Eve's face crumpled into as close to a frown as she could get with her Botox, and said, "Oh, darling, I'm sorry. That's just cruel. And then I'm assuming you lost the pregnancy?"

Phoenix nodded. "I really wanted that baby."

Eve made a cooing noise. "Oh, darling, I know you did. You would make a fabulous mother. And I was always made to be an indulgent grandmother. In fact, I demand you make me a grandmother so I can spoil my granddaughter with teddy bears wearing diamond-studded collars."

Phoenix laughed, and she knew that was what Eve intended with her ridiculousness, but Phoenix said, "You're so sure I'll have a girl?"

"Absolutely," Eve said with a wide grin, "You'd be wasted on a son." Eve's grin turned to a smirk. "Besides, your Robin has already taken the only bird name that's appropriate for a man. And you'll have to name your child after a bird. I won't support any other outcome."

Phoenix rolled her eyes and pulled her fingers from Eve's. "That is so not going to happen."

Eve looked toward the restaurant's ceiling. "Oh, let a woman dream, will you?" Phoenix couldn't argue with that. She knew her mentor was far too realistic to be swept away by fantasies.

Phoenix spent the rest of the fall in L.A., meeting Eve

every week for brunch, just like she had before Robin, before Bishop had hurt Van and the tornado had wrecked Wellville and before Phoenix's heart had been completely ravaged.

It was comforting to settle back into a routine. And Phoenix had missed Eve. She was one of those people who wasn't very good at keeping in touch if you couldn't place yourself in front of her face on a regular basis. Phoenix understood that. They were both so busy.

Phoenix had even hired another assistant, who she'd basically tasked with helping her organize Van's album launch and tour. There were so many extra details to see to that Phoenix barely had time to think about them, and those were the sorts of details Bishop would have handled once upon a time. The label had basically given them Bishop the first time around, and now they were completely terrified to recommend anyone. It wasn't like Phoenix hadn't learned anything in the last five years. She could absolutely handle assuming Bishop's duties into her own team, she just wanted someone to ask her to do it instead of just assuming she would pick up whatever slack was left in the wake of this entire shit show.

Phoenix had been doing that from the beginning, and she was exhausted.

As much as she was dreading doing Christmas in Kansas because it meant seeing Robin, Phoenix looked forward to the downtime of the holidays. She managed to mostly avoid Robin, sitting as far away from him as she could at Christmas dinner and pretending he wasn't there was her best defense. That didn't mean she didn't feel his gaze on her throughout the meal, but having her own apartment in a different part of town gave her an excuse to cut out early, and she was so thankful for it, even if it was lonely going to bed by herself in the cold.

She had stayed one night at Minnie's. Which had been weird, because Rocco and his girlfriend had answered the door when Phoenix had shown up with soup in one hand and whiskey in the other. Minnie had sounded like she'd had a cold on the phone, and Phoenix liked to be prepared. Rocco had solemnly directed Phoenix to Minnie's room, where Phoenix had found Minnie on her bed in the middle of a pile of discarded tissues.

When Minnie saw Phoenix, her already red eyes filled with new tears, and barely choked out, "Bryant found out about Malcolm," between sobs.

Phoenix dropped her bags and joined her friend on the bed. After Van's kidnapping, Phoenix had managed to weasel the whole story out of Minnie. As a way of protecting herself and her son, Minnie hadn't told Bryant that Malcolm was his child. When she'd gotten pregnant, she'd thought Bryant was dating Van and lying to Minnie about it. But things had changed so much in the last six months.

Trying not to think about the mound of used Kleenex she was sitting on or Minnie's cold, Phoenix wrapped her arms around her friend as Minnie told Phoenix what had happened. Minnie and Bryant had been attempting to work past their deceptions and reconcile their relationship, but Phoenix had been waiting for this moment. She knew Bryant would be upset to learn that Minnie's son was actually his son too, but she hadn't expected him to want nothing to do with either Minnie or Malcolm. Phoenix had expected him to at least want to have a relationship with his son. She'd spent that entire night pissed as hell at him.

But then Van had called her the next morning. Bryant had spent the last two days locked up in his house, not answering her phone calls. The only reason she knew he was alive was because she'd asked one of her security guys watch the house. They'd tailed him as he'd walked to his neighborhood liquor store and come back home with as much whiskey as he could carry. Van was worried he was going to drink himself to death.

She and Clay took turns checking on him while Phoenix arranged Bryant's rehab stay. When they arrived in Florida, Phoenix practically cried in relief. They all needed a break. And while Bryant might hate them for a few weeks while he detoxed, Phoenix was glad for a reason to live on the Atlantic Ocean for a little while and just pretend. It wasn't like she didn't still have to work, or like Stark let them off the hook for their workouts, but it was on that beach that Phoenix actually had time to come to peace with what had happened with Robin. As much as she could anyway.

She'd given in to the tingles. She'd had months and months of really good sex. And sure, maybe she had fallen in love for the first time in her life, but that's all Robin was. Her first love. Everyone said first loves were the most difficult to get over. It was natural to grieve. Just like it was natural to consult her calendar and figure how close to her due date she would be had she not lost the baby.

So what if she still wasn't completely over it? She had lost the baby, and Robin had made his stance clear. He'd announced his candidacy only a few days after they'd left for Florida. There was no going back to the way things had been between them.

Especially after Eve had called Phoenix one day in late January. She hadn't even said hello, she'd just said, "Darling, when are you coming back to the correct coast? I have a favor to ask of you."

"In the next week or two," Phoenix said, pulling her sunglasses down her nose to make sure her freckles on her knees weren't getting too dark. "What's up?"

"Are you familiar with Leo Palmer?"

"The action star?"

"The very same."

"What about him?" Phoenix asked.

"I need you to date him. Hypnotize him. Do whatever it is you do to men. Make him better."

"I barely have any interaction with men," Phoenix's dry laugh had nothing to do with the ache in her chest. She hadn't been with anyone but Robin in more than a year, and she wasn't interested in anyone but him, even six months after she'd walked away from the asshole.

"It's not a hands-on favor, darling, just an arrangement. Just dates. If there are extra-curricular activities, that's between you and Leo."

Phoenix had done this sort of thing for Eve only once before. When a prominent actor in one of her projects was causing trouble and she needed to do damage control, Eve often paired her actors up with reputable off-screen industry people.

The last time Phoenix had done so, she'd been photographed all over L.A. with an aging TV doctor who had been going through a nasty divorce at the same time he'd been doing a movie for Eve. The divorce was public enough and far enough underway that Phoenix had been the rebound and not the cause of said divorce, but once the three months had been up, Phoenix had bolted. The dude had been a handsy asshole, and she didn't fault his ex-wife for kicking him to the curb.

Phoenix doubted that Leo Palmer would be any better. But he couldn't be any worse either.

"I'm still planning a tour and a wedding and—"

"It's only a few photo-ops a week, nothing more."

"And compensation?"

"Making Robin Birch green with jealousy isn't enough?"

Phoenix snorted into the phone. "No."

"Would you believe me if I told you that I put the property next to yours on the market explicitly so Van could buy it last fall?"

"I didn't know you owned that house," Phoenix said. "I thought a movie studio owned it."

"Yes, darling. My studio. And now your best friend owns it. I hope you didn't think that was a coincidence."

Phoenix opened her mouth to remind Eve that Van had barely had a chance to move in but stopped. It didn't matter, because Van would be spending time there in the future. And they would have the chance to be close as sisters again.

"Fine, but this is the last time, Eve."

"Whatever you say, darling," Eve said and hung up the phone. Phoenix rolled her eyes. Knowing Eve, she probably already had another project in mind for Phoenix come fall.

CHAPTER 18

*I*t turned out Leo Palmer was an idiot.

Phoenix had spent the last two months splitting her time between Kansas—where Van had asked her to be a part of her and Clay's house-building show and where Phoenix was helping to plan the wedding—and L.A., making plans for Van's tour over the summer. Whenever Phoenix was in L.A., she was going on Godforsaken dates with Leo Palmer.

They went to restaurants and movie premiers. He'd been her date during awards season, and suddenly Phoenix, who had always been present, but tangential in the tabloids, was front and center for dating the new action star. They were all fawning over what a cute couple the two of them were, and wouldn't it be great if Phoenix got married just after Van, and wouldn't their children be gorgeous?

Phoenix had been playing along with all of it because Leo Palmer had crashed his car into the front of pharmacy over Christmas. Which was kind of funny actually, because the man had enough drugs in his system to supply the pharmacy he'd crashed into. The official line was that he'd had too much to drink at a holiday party, but Phoenix had barely been around him a day before she noticed the pills. Phoenix really, really didn't want to know what they were, but Oxy was her guess.

She had trouble telling sometimes if the reason the only thing he could talk about with any vigor was working out was because he really was nothing more than a set of abs and a pretty face, or because he was so high that was the only part of his day that stuck. Either way, Phoenix was counting down the days to the wedding, which would mark the end of her contractual dating period.

Wouldn't all the gossip rags be surprised when Phoenix took Minnie to the wedding instead? She hoped at least one paper would propose that Phoenix had left Leo for a woman. Eve wouldn't be happy, but it sure would tickle Phoenix.

She did not have feelings for Minnie beyond the platonic, never had for another woman, but sometimes she wished she could. She and Minnie were in similar places and had been spending a lot of time together when Phoenix was in Kansas. As in, Phoenix spent almost every evening sitting at Minnie's dining room table.

What Phoenix did not expect when she arrived at Minnie's that night was to find Van at Minnie's table, sushi and bottle of wine already open between them.

"Rocco picked up Malcolm early," Minnie said when Phoenix dropped her bag on the sofa.

Van poured a third glass of wine and held it out for Phoenix. "And I forced Clay to go hang out with Bryant."

Phoenix had to stop her wince. She and Minnie hadn't spoken about Bryant since Minnie's breakdown after Christmas.

There were two names Phoenix and Minnie never said, out of courtesy to one another. Bryant and Robin were strictly off limits. Not that Phoenix didn't complain about how mad she still was at Robin after a few drinks. Because she did. She was still pissed and still getting the tingles whenever they crossed paths. Phoenix was mostly able to avoid him, but there were still some times when Phoenix had to communicate with him directly about the developing case against Bishop. It was looking like they were going to hold the trial in Kansas because the kidnapping charges were the main ones he was being arrested on. Bishop's counsel was, of course, trying to get it moved. Trying to have a separate trial for the assault charges. It was all still a mess, but thankfully, mostly none of it had to bother Van until the actual trial.

And Bryant. Phoenix hadn't told Minnie anything about him or his recovery. He'd been home from rehab for about a week, and they'd been taking shifts to hang out with him, to check in with him every day. It wasn't like he didn't know what they were doing, and when Phoenix had brought him a steak dinner from Henry's last night, he'd said thank you with a little too much emphasis not to let on that he was annoyed with their helicoptering, but also hungry. Bryant hadn't said anything about whether they should tell Minnie that he was sober or not.

Phoenix had asked him, and he'd said that was a situation he wasn't ready to confront yet. While Phoenix didn't want to push him, she also hated seeing how much her friend missed him. And she knew Bryant would eventually regret choosing not to know his son.

For now, though, he didn't seem to want to drink, and that was what was important. Phoenix couldn't keep herself from grinning with pride as Bryant explained his new routine, how he was going to bed before midnight and sleeping so well that he was actually jazzed to get up and work out in the morning before heading to the jobsite. He had seriously bulked up since Christmas. The way his biceps strained at his T-shirts could replace Leo Palmer's on screen in a heartbeat. Except Bryant had specifically asked not to go to L.A. any time soon. He'd go for the trial, if it ended up taking place there, but no appearances, no photo-ops.

Before he'd come back home, he'd told Van that he didn't want that life anymore. That he wanted to stay in Kansas and concentrate on his business. Phoenix could respect that and had done her best to facilitate it. When she'd said as much, Bryant had reached over her baked potato and squeezed her hand. "I appreciate that," he said. "I'm happy here, now, with the way things are."

And Phoenix was happy for him, she really was. But she wanted to see Minnie happy too. Phoenix didn't miss the resigned sadness in Minnie's eyes at the mention of Bryant's name. Or the way she had to force a smile when she said, "That'll be good for him and Bryant both."

Van grinned and said, "Besides, I have a surprise for you tonight."

That was news to Phoenix, who raised her eyebrows at Van in question.

"Oh, yeah. I am in major need of some girl time. Did you

know being engaged to man means you are basically around him all the time? Nobody fucking told me that."

Van and Minnie shared exasperated smiles. Van and Clay had been together for six months, and they had barely voluntarily left each other's sides in all that time.

"So, since my wedding is in, like," Van looked to the ceiling as she did the mental calculations, "seven weeks and none of us has a dress to wear yet, I arranged for a dress shop to come to us."

"I don't think there's room for that in here," Minnie said, glancing around her tiny apartment. It was barely big enough for her and Malcolm.

"Don't worry," Van said, sipping her wine with a mischievous smile on her lips. "They're setting up at my dad's place as we speak, and don't you worry." Van sent Phoenix a sympathetic look. "It'll just be us girls, so we can drink as much champagne and change as many times as we like."

Thirty minutes later, a car service arrived to pick them up. Butch, who had been waiting outside Minnie's apartment, walked them downstairs. Security had lightened somewhat over the past few months, but Butch or one of his top guys still accompanied Van everywhere she went, and Phoenix didn't see that coming to a stop anytime soon.

There was a full-sized semi-truck parked along the street in front of Robin's house, and Phoenix wondered if they were going to shop inside the container, but they went to the back entrance just like usual. Robin's living room, however, had transformed into a boutique. The furniture had been pushed back, a rack of dresses lined one wall, and someone had set up a dais and a three-way mirror in the middle of the room and a changing screen in the corner.

Van grinned as she watched Minnie take it all in with awe. Even Phoenix was impressed. This was the kind of thing Van could do on a whim but didn't do very often. And it was the perfect solution to the dress problem. Phoenix and Van had been able to square away the details of the wedding itself, but there hadn't been any time for dress shopping. Not that Phoenix or Van were all that big on shopping. These days, they were often approached by designers for any big event.

Van's wedding had been no exception, but everything anyone had approached them with had been white and extravagant and just completely wrong for Van.

The dresses on the rack now created a rainbow. As usual, Phoenix was drawn directly toward the blues. Minnie joined her there while Van gravitated toward the reds. "Wouldn't a red wedding dress be completely spectacular?" Van asked, pulling a dress out that had a deep V in the front and back and a full floor-length skirt. Van would look amazing in it, but Phoenix could already tell it wasn't right.

"Good evening, ladies." A tall blonde woman in a tailored suit and tall black heels emerged from the kitchen with a tray in her hand. Three full champagne flutes sparkled on top of the silver. "Are we gravitating toward the reds, Ms. Birch?"

Van skipped toward the champagne like a puppy. "I haven't decided anything yet, but I want to see everything."

"Very good," the woman said. "I'm Blake, and I have already pulled a selection for each of you, but you are, of course, more than welcome to choose from the collection."

Van clapped and followed Blake. "Ooo, I want to see what you have."

Phoenix laughed about how excited Van was, and she

and Minnie shared amused smiles. This wasn't how she'd expected to spend the night, but it was a lot more fun than the moping she'd planned to do once she'd returned home from Minnie's place.

"Wonderful," Blake said. "Bride first?"

"Please," Phoenix said at the same time Minnie said, "Absolutely."

The three of them made themselves comfortable as Blake presented Van with a tablet with photographs of the dresses she'd picked out for her. There were dresses in almost every color but white, and Van seriously considered a few of them, but only chose three to try on. One was a hot-pink dress with a tight beaded bodice and a skirt made of cascading silk tulle that reminded Phoenix of fuchsia clouds. Van looked adorable in it, but she decided it was too bright. The next one she tried on was similar in cut to the first but was a sapphire blue up top that faded into a shimmering silver at the hem. Van looked regal in it, but she smiled at Phoenix. "This looks like something you would choose; don't you think?"

Phoenix's fingers did itch to try it on for herself the more she looked at it. But her dress shouldn't be half so grand, not for this event at least.

The second Van emerged from behind the screen in the third dress dress, Phoenix knew that one was it.

She looked radiant, even with frizzy hair and zero makeup. She beamed as Blake motioned for her to stand on the dais. The black top was a long-sleeved lace number that cut off at Van's rib line and showed off just a hint of Van's toned stomach. The skirt was also black, high-waisted, short in the front and trailing the floor in the back in long, puffy waves. It was just the right amount of funky. Van twirled for a minute, then faced Phoenix and Minnie, and said, "Check this bitch out." Then she pulled on something and the long part of the skirt fell away, leaving Van in only the ruffly short skirt that was perfect for dancing.

"You have to get that one," Minnie said.

"I don't think I'm ever taking it off," Van said, facing the mirror again. "Do you see how big this top makes my boobs look? My boobs never look big."

Minnie snorted into her champagne flute. "Do you think they have a dress that will make my boobs look smaller?"

"Sorry, babe," Van shot over her shoulder as she cupped both breasts in the mirror as if unable to believe what she was seeing. "It's not possible."

Minnie looked down at her own ample chest. "Yeah. It's a curse."

Van blew a raspberry through the mirror, and Minnie laughed. Phoenix did too, and she realized as she watched Van twirl in the mirror again that she hadn't had this much fun in a long time.

Van did indeed keep her choice on the rest of the evening. Minnie ended up with a shimmery, silvery blue number. All she needed was the braid, and she could have passed for Elsa. Phoenix ended up with a dress that mirrored the concept of Van's, it had a sleeveless lace bodice and a full, cascading floor length skirt, but it was in a color Phoenix never would have chosen for herself. The shimmery champagne that she would have guessed would wash her out actually made her skin look smooth and her hair radiant.

They had all opted to keep their dresses on for a little while, just because it was fun, even though Minnie's needed to be taken up at the hem and Van's was too loose around her midriff. Phoenix's only needed the minor alteration of tucking the waist just a tad more to tailor it to her shape, otherwise, it was already a near-perfect fit. Blake had made the notes on the alterations and was packing up her mobile dress shop while three of them snacked on a fruit and cheese plate in the kitchen.

They were all a little tipsy from the champagne, and maybe they were singing a Kesha song at the top of their lungs, but Phoenix hadn't felt so good or so free in ages. She missed this ridiculousness. In the last year and a half she had forgotten what it was like to truly let go.

Until the security guard on duty opened the back door and a weary, exhausted-looking Robin Birch stepped into the kitchen.

The tingles hit Phoenix full force, even before his eyes landed on her. Minnie and Van were still singing about how they were motherfucking women, but Phoenix felt as if time had slowed. She lowered her champagne flute and watched as Robin slipped his messenger bag off as if the racket the three of them had been making hadn't even registered. When he'd hung the bag on the hook by the door, Robin's eyes went straight to Phoenix. He took in her dress, the champagne, the fruit tray. And then his gaze lingered over the bodice of her dress before slowly raising to her eyes.

Something Phoenix couldn't name slammed into her chest, and her tingles began to sing, even though Robin looked terrible. He'd lost weight, and there were dark rings under his eyes. His tie was crooked, and his shirt was wrinkled beneath his suit coat. His hair needed a trim, and the expression on his face was so guarded and so forlorn that

Phoenix almost went to him and pulled him into her arms without thinking.

But then he closed his eyes, turned his back, and disappeared down the hallway toward his office, and Phoenix told herself that he'd done this to himself. This sad, lonely life was the one he'd chosen, and it was the one he had to live. She, on the other hand, was choosing to be happy.

CHAPTER 19

*R*obin hadn't been able to get the image of Phoenix in that stupid gown out of his mind for days. Weeks.

Months had passed since Robin had been in her presence for more than a moment. Not since the intervention they'd had for Bryant. They'd seen each other in passing of course, but she was still having Amanda contact him most of the time if she needed anything directly.

So much had changed since that day in his office.

He'd worked himself to the bone over the fall and winter. But the water rights case was over, ruled in his client's favor. And once the case that had taken all his concentration had ended? Robin kept working. If he worked, he didn't have time to think about or feel his loneliness. Even with Van and Clay back in the house most of the time, the two of them were too besotted with each other to pay much attention to him.

He wondered if Phoenix was lonely too.

After the trial had ended, Robin had come home and slept for two days. Then John had started pestering him about planning his campaign launch in January, but Robin's heart hadn't been in it anymore. The lifelong ambition had started to feel empty, and though he allowed John to go ahead and launch, Robin had been having trouble mustering any enthusiasm for it.

He'd known something was wrong when the phone calls started coming in, news networks wanting to do interviews about his campaign, agricultural co-ops wanting to put him on retainer, offers for more work than Robin had ever dreamed of during those first few meager years of his and Caroline's marriage. The ones where he'd coasted by on nothing but bravado and a charming smile. This was what he'd worked his whole life for. But Robin couldn't make himself care.

He showed up when John asked him. He made the speeches. Sometimes he even wrote one. He talked to reporters on the phone, even called back a few of the potential clients. But mostly, Robin got up every day, put on a suit, and sat in his law office and worked on finishing the last book in his mystery series. The one he'd left unfinished since Mary Beth had passed.

When he was finished with that, he started querying. Every day he sent letters to dozens of agents.

And when he was done with that, he sat down and started on the screenplay Phoenix had wanted him to write.

By the time the kids were back from Florida to start filming the building of Clay's house while they planned Van and Clay's wedding, Robin had only done a nominal amount of legal work, and the bare minimum involved for the campaign. John was still pestering him daily about his duty. Robin had stopped answering his texts. He'd wrapped up some lingering cases. He'd forwarded his long-term clients to trusted colleagues in the area and found Adam another position. Without telling anybody, Robin started packing up his law office one carload at a time.

He hadn't told any of his family that he was retiring. He hadn't fully said the words aloud to himself even. Robin just didn't want to be a lawyer anymore. And he didn't need to be. He'd been one of Van's initial investors, and though he'd insisted he didn't need to or expect to be paid after Van's career took off, both Van and Phoenix had insisted that he take a percentage.

He thought, perhaps, after the wedding, after he'd taken a month or two to rest and to process everything that had happened in the last year and a half, he might regain some enthusiasm for his political aspirations again. He needed to find that enthusiasm, because Robin still wanted to do something that mattered with his life.

Despite the way that his writing was the only thing that mattered to *him* lately, Robin didn't think that counted. He had a sneaking suspicion that if he used his real name, Robin Birch could have a Top Five publishing deal by the end of the week, but he couldn't be both a congressman and a mystery writer, at least not publicly, so he'd been querying under the name Robert Ash.

The night he'd come home to find Van, Minnie, and Phoenix having a trying-on-dresses party in his living room, Robin had just come from one of the more obnoxious dinners he'd had in months.

He'd met John and Frank at Henry's, as they'd been doing weekly, to make all the meetings and planning and answering questions and having opinions on recent developments seem like less of a slog. But Robin couldn't even get excited about the bread. It had no flavor, and the part of his steak that he did eat only sat in his stomach like a stone as he listened to John, set out the details of the upcoming primary they had to win. They'd been talking about having the victory party in the private room at Henry's when Robin had checked his email. It had become a nearly hourly habit as he waited to hear back from agents.

Logistically, Robin knew why it was important to celebrate winning an unopposed primary. They wanted to proceed with confidence, with the appearance that they had the support of the people of Kansas behind them. But Robin was beginning to wonder if he wanted to proceed at all.

He'd locked his phone again in disappointment and tried to re-engage with the conversation, but all he could think about were the tweaks he would make to his query letter the next day before he sent out his manuscript to the next few agents on his list.

On the day in late April when Robin turned in his key to his office building and loaded the last of his things from the law office into his car, he had had three separate agents ask for the full copy of his manuscript, and he was feeling good about his chances of finding both an agent and a publisher in the foreseeable future.

The kids were so busy, they barely even noticed that he dressed in jeans every morning and went to work in his study instead of donning a suit and driving downtown.

There were days when he missed stopping by Revival for coffee or talking with people in a professional capacity, but it didn't take him long to figure out that he could pack his laptop and write for a few hours at Revival. This was more of an exercise in socialization than it was in work, because

Robin rarely got more than an hour's worth of writing done in an entire morning, but it was enough to buoy his spirits and keep him away from the blogs and gossip sites long enough not to obsess over what Phoenix was up to.

It was stupid, but Phoenix had spent most of the last couple of months in L.A. working on Van's summer tour while Van fulfilled her obligations in Kansas. And while Robin loved that his daughter had spent most of the last year living with him instead of halfway across the country, that Phoenix hadn't spoken to him directly in over six months was slowly tearing Robin apart.

Her absence had made such an impact that he'd completely changed the screenplay. It was no longer a screen version of his first novel, but another story entirely. Robin hadn't done anything with it. He still had Eve's card, but more than anything, Robin had written it to come to terms with the fact that for a few months, he'd known what it was like to be in love again, and then it had ended, just like it always did, and that was fine. He'd never expected his relationship with Phoenix to last. He didn't deserve a third love in this lifetime, but he didn't regret the time he'd had with her.

That there were pictures of her everywhere with some sculpted new movie star was none of Robin's concern, even if jealousy and possessiveness rose in his chest every time a new picture of them together surfaced. There were coffee dates, pictures of them together out in L.A. at night, at dinner or at clubs. He was an up-and-comer Robin had never seen in a film, and he'd never heard the name Leo Palmer before he started appearing in pictures next to Phoenix. But Robin sure as hell had watched everything the douchebag had ever been in after that.

The kid was the same age as Phoenix but clearly hadn't grown up yet. All his characters were immature and whiny, even when he was supposed to be the hero.

Robin despised him, but he knew that was mostly because Phoenix had moved on and Robin was still regretting how his doubts and insecurities had let everything that was good and passionate and real between them last year dissolve like he didn't care about her.

Because that was wrong. Robin had loved Phoenix Lambert with a fierceness that had only been rivaled by his love for Caroline, and the ache of not having her in his life was constant.

He'd been tempted every day to pick up his phone and tell her exactly how much he missed her. How much there was that he would do differently this time if only she would give him another chance to love her. How much he had wanted her, how sometimes he'd estimate how old their baby would be. Robin would spin elaborate mental narratives about what their lives would have been like had they stayed together, had Phoenix not lost the pregnancy.

Robin wanted that life, and he wanted everyone to know. Now that Bishop was awaiting trial for the kidnapping and the world was just as excited about Van and Clay's wedding as the happy couple was, Robin had more faith in his daughter's ability to adapt to change. Though he still wasn't sure about the general acceptability of a fifty-five-year-old man being in love with a woman who didn't turn thirty until November.

One night, only a few days before the wedding, Robin had been contemplating his conflicting emotions by letting them play out on the piano keys when Van joined him unexpectedly. She sat on the bass side of the keyboard and leaned her head against his shoulder. Robin welcomed the suffusion of warmth the action gave him and leaned over to place a kiss on the top of her head without his fingers ever leaving the keys.

"Clay's picking up pizza," Van said. "Don't tell Stark."

Robin chuckled. "I'll make sure to leave that out of the conversation the next time we have tea."

"Well, he'll be at the wedding," Van said, "So it is possible you two could speak."

"Fair enough," Robin said, then switched from the classical piece he'd been playing to one of Van's new songs.

She smiled up at him. "When did you have time to learn this?" she asked.

Robin only raised his eyebrows at his daughter and nudged her with his elbow as they neared the end of the intro. Van sang that song, and then Robin played the next, but when he'd started on the third, Van stopped him with a hand on his arm.

"Dad."

"What is it?"

Van bit her lip like she'd always done when she didn't want to have a conversation. "It's about the wedding."

"What about it?"

"It's more about you and Phoenix," she said.

"I'm not planning to bother Phoenix." Robin tinked out a few notes rather than meet his daughter's eyes.

"I was going to say that it might be the perfect opportunity to make amends," Van said.

When Robin turned sharply toward her, she grinned wickedly. "I mean, I don't want you to make a scene or anything, but as someone who loves you both, and who knows you've been thinking about each other—maybe one of you should actually do something about it."

Robin had been going to protest, but Clay came through the front door just then, and both Pebbles and Van jumped up to greet him.

That night, Robin scrolled through all of his old threads with Phoenix. The naughty pictures were still there, but Robin also read the mundane, everyday texts. The ones where they were comparing schedules or planning visits or when they were complaining about their days. The messages documented a connection he couldn't deny, and one he was prepared to humiliate himself to get back.

He didn't see Phoenix in person until the week of the wedding when she returned to Wellville, staying in her downtown apartment, of course, and spending most of her time with Van. Robin didn't begrudge the girls' time together, but he was jealous that there was no longer any reason for Phoenix to hang out with him in the evenings. As awful as last summer had been on many levels, having Phoenix by his side through it had made everything easier to bear.

And when he allowed himself the honesty, he was able to admit that he wanted her there.

Robin recognized that he'd be a much happier person if he focused on recognizing that his relationship with Phoenix was over. That he hadn't been there for her the way she'd needed him to be, because he had been afraid of his own emotions, afraid of the consequences of his actions— that acknowledging a relationship with this brilliant, unstoppable woman would have legitimized his fears for himself. That allowing himself to truly have her meant he could lose her the way he'd lost Caroline. In many ways, those fears had kept him from being the husband he should have been to Mary Beth. He'd married her; he'd tried to let go. He'd even been happy for a time with her. But Mary Beth hadn't been stupid. She'd known when it was time to leave. And Robin couldn't blame her.

He only wished she'd had a chance to change and blossom without him. He'd helped her find her footing, but she could have flown so far after she'd left him. Robin would have been so proud of her.

When Robin saw Phoenix standing on the dais as he walked Van down the aisle on her wedding day, his lungs froze. She was the most beautiful woman he'd ever seen, and he couldn't even breathe at the sight of her. Her hair was teased into fiery red waves, her skin glowed and shimmered. Her champagne-colored gown clung to her body in delicious drapes that teased and hinted at the form beneath. She was luminous, and her blue eyes barely rested on him before flitting to Van.

Phoenix might as well have been the sun for the light and genuine pleasure that radiated from her as she watched Van approach. She even glanced in Clay's direction and kept her smile when he met her gaze, as if the two of them had come to a truce. Robin was glad. The fewer things there were to trouble Phoenix, the better.

Robin attempted to keep his attention on the couple during the wedding, but his gaze couldn't help but stray to Phoenix. Through some twist of fate or, more likely, his daughter's meddling, Phoenix and Robin were seated next to one another at the reception.

Phoenix mostly ignored him, leaning in to speak to Van, who sat on her other side, but Robin felt her eyes on him just as often as he was tempted to look at her.

Bryant sat to Robin's right at the circular table, so Robin caught up with him. They hadn't seen each other much since his return from rehab, but Bryant looked healthier. Less drawn, less exhausted, more vibrant and alert. He was enthusiastic about the work he had lined up for the summer and couldn't stop talking about taking a larger role in the business as Clay stepped aside to make room for his burgeoning music career.

Despite his enthusiasm, Bryant would lose focus every few minutes as he scanned the ballroom.

"You expecting to find someone?" Robin asked.

Bryant shook his head but said, "I was hoping Minnie would be here. I haven't seen her since—"

Bryant cut himself off, and Robin knew what he didn't say. He hadn't seen her since just before his breakdown. The one that had spurred the intervention that had sent him to rehab.

"She's here somewhere," Robin said. "She's wearing a silvery-blue dress, if that helps."

"Did you see where she was?" Bryant asked, craning his neck to see around a large tropical plant next to one of the support pillars.

Robin was suddenly conscious of the whiskey in his glass as he decided to not take a sip just then. He set the drink down, and the glass clinked against the edge of his plate. "No. I haven't seen her today, but the girls went dress shopping together. They had someone come to the house."

Bryant nodded as Robin trailed off. His eyes flicked toward Robin's rocks glass. "You can drink in front of me, you know."

"Oh, I—"

Bryant raised his own glass of what looked like sparkling

water in salute. "I am in a good place," he said. "It's liberating not feeling like shit all the time, you know."

Robin nodded. "I'm proud of you. What you've been doing. It's not easy."

Bryant ducked his head, his cheeks tinged ever so slightly pink. "That means a lot. Thank you."

Shame and chagrin burned through Robin. He should have made more time for Bryant these last few months. He'd been so preoccupied with fulfilling obligations he didn't want to fulfill and with his own misery that he'd just assumed that with the rehab and Van and Clay hovering over Bryant like mother hens, Bryant hadn't needed anything else. Perhaps he'd been wrong.

"I'm sorry I haven't been more present the last few months," he said.

Bryant spun his glass of sparkling water and shook his head as he met Robin's eyes. "It's okay. You're doing important things."

Robin forced a grin. If what he was doing was so important, why did he feel like all he was doing was wasting his time?

"And you haven't spoken to Minnie since you've been back?" Robin asked.

Bryant swallowed and rubbed his fingers over his chin. "Not since everything came out about Malcolm. I want to—there's just so much to figure out. And while I know I'm more than just an addict, a big part of me is afraid that she won't let me into her life because of that."

Robin squeezed Bryant's shoulder. "You are so much more than your addiction, son." Bryant's eyes met his, gratefulness suffusing his entire bearing. Once again, shame stole over Robin for not being more present for Bryant during this time. Maybe he wasn't really Robin's child in the way that he could lay claim to Van and Clay, but Bryant was family nonetheless. And Robin was probably the only father Bryant had ever known. Robin should have taken that responsibility more seriously. He should have seen what was happening with Bryant before he'd nearly drunk himself to death. Robin promised himself that he would do better, starting right now.

"You have so much to offer," Robin said. "And the best you can do is to try to be there for your son, regardless of what happens between you and his mother."

Bryant nodded and clasped Robin's hand. "Thank you. I can't even begin to tell you how much it means to me to hear you say that."

"Just know that you can come to me," Robin said. "Anytime. For anything."

"I will. I promise." Bryant sat back in his chair and nodded toward Phoenix. "You gonna do anything there?"

Robin took a sip of his whiskey. "I was actually wondering if you could help me with that." And Robin laid out his plan.

Bryant's grin broadened. "About time," he said, but Robin pretended not to hear.

He'd assumed they'd all talked about the affair amongst themselves, but Robin wasn't necessarily keen to pay much heed to what they thought, good or ill, about his feelings for Phoenix. They existed. After more than a year of pretending they didn't—hell, it had been the better part of a year without her—Robin found he couldn't pretend anymore.

He only wished he had confidence in Phoenix feeling anything but animosity toward him.

Phoenix and Minnie danced for a long while before

Bryant practically pushed him out of the chair. The whole plan hinged on Robin breaking in on Phoenix and Minnie, whisking Minnie away into Bryant's arms, then returning for Phoenix. When Robin scared off Phoenix's dance partner, she somehow managed to look down her nose at him, even though he was a head taller.

"You're still upset with me," he said.

"Don't be silly," she said, still not meeting his eye. "There's nothing to be upset about."

"I'm so sorry, Fe," he said in his tenderest voice. "I never meant for any of this to happen."

Her eyes snapped to his then, but forgiveness was not in them. Blue flame burned there. "And what did you mean to happen?"

Robin didn't have an answer. Not one that she would like anyway, because he'd always meant for the relationship to be secret. To be temporary. The fact that he wasn't able to define temporary didn't help. That he hadn't wanted them to be over, that he was still mostly reluctant to go public, that he was certain it would cause a scandal, was nothing in the face of how much he missed her.

"That's what I thought," she said. "You're still embarrassed to be seen with me in public."

"I'm in public with you right now," he said.

Phoenix rolled her eyes. "This is your daughter's wedding. It's socially acceptable for the father of the bride to dance with the maid of honor. Now, if we went to Tessa's for brunch in the morning? Just you and me? What would your campaign manager have to say about that?"

"We've been to brunch before."

"In L.A. On a day when we managed to avoid the

paparazzi. But in Wellville? With the whole town swarming?"

Robin didn't like the sound of it. He didn't like the idea of the gossip that would ensue. There were parts of his life that he would like to keep private, and funnily enough, his private life was one of those things, but he would do it for her. "If that's what it takes to earn your forgiveness," he said.

Phoenix stiffened in his arms, then stopped dancing. "Why does that sound like I'm the one who has to do the earning when I don't give a damn what the world thinks. I love you, Robin. Love you. And the fact that I don't even register on the scale enough to tip your pride? That our child didn't? I'm not sure if that's something I'll ever be able to forgive you for."

His pride? Robin's temper rose. His pride wasn't what was standing in their way. It was her stubbornness. "If you love me so much, why are you with Leo Whatshisface?"

Phoenix's neutral expression turned into a sneer. "You actually think I have feelings for Leo Palmer?"

"You've been in public with him a lot lately."

Phoenix's lip twitched and her nose wrinkled. "That was a three-month publicity stunt that I agreed to because I was doing a favor for Eve. He is a child."

Relief was the first thing Robin felt, swallowed almost immediately by anger. "Why would you agree to associate yourself with him then?"

Phoenix pulled herself from his arms and shook her head. "Because I don't give a damn what the world thinks of me, Robin. And the sooner you figure out that it doesn't fucking matter, the happier you'll be."

She was wrong. It did matter. When you were trying to break into politics. All of it mattered.

When Robin didn't say anything, Phoenix said, "Congratulations on winning your primary," but Phoenix didn't stick around to hear his thanks. She disappeared into the crowd, and Robin had to force himself not to chase after her.

It took all his concentration to keep a smile on his face for the rest of the night.

CHAPTER 20

*P*hoenix had had one text from Robin since she'd abandoned him on the dancefloor at Van's wedding. A week later, he'd sent her just one sentence.

I'm thinking of dropping out of the race.

That was it. No explanation, no follow-up. Just that he was thinking about giving up on his dream. Phoenix wasn't sure what that meant. She definitely didn't know what to do with it.

Phoenix hadn't responded. She hadn't had time. Van's summer tour had kicked off three weeks after the wedding, and she'd been so busy while Van was on her honeymoon, organizing everything they were going to need, that Phoenix had only had time to think of Robin for the three seconds between collapsing into bed and falling asleep each night. Then, too few hours later, she'd be back up and on the phone while typing emails on one tablet and ordering supplies on the other. It had been a year of managing Van's career on her own, and she was seriously thinking it was time to hire a new manager. Someone they trusted. A woman, preferably.

Phoenix just didn't know who.

And she was too tired to think about it tonight. They'd just arrived in New Orleans after a quick Kansas City-St. Louis-Chicago line-up all in one weekend. Phoenix hated those weekends. There was barely enough time to sleep between stops, let alone see that everything was set up. But they'd have three days off in New Orleans before doing two shows there on Friday and Saturday.

Phoenix was so glad for her hotel suite. The first thing she'd done was draw a bath with the fancy soaking salts the hotel had provided and broke into the six-pack of tiny champagne bottles in the mini bar. The champagne was good, light and bubbly and not too sweet, and Phoenix drank the entire six pack without feeling guilty. Pleasantly tipsy, and with skin that felt like silk, Phoenix grabbed up the chocolate bar she usually hid in the minibar behind the booze she didn't like so she wouldn't eat it, and hopped in bed with her personal tablet.

She caught up with all the usual gossip sites, but everything seemed calm at the moment. Everyone was still trying to capture shots of Clay and Van together. There were a few tabloids already trying to invent "trouble in paradise" stories, but that was to be expected. Phoenix had never seen two people more ridiculously in love than Van and her new husband. And as loathe as she had been to admit it, Clay did adore Van.

Even if seeing them together made her miss the only love she'd ever known.

She missed Robin.

Every day. All day. She missed him so much there was a

constant ache behind her breastbone that she didn't know how to make go away.

Sometimes, when she was feeling vulnerable, and when she'd drunk the equivalent of two bottles of champagne, she Google-image searched him and mooned over how handsome and distinguished he looked. Especially when he was wearing the expensive suits Van had helped him pick out for his campaign, but which really, Phoenix had commissioned and said they were from Van. Robin would make a good congressman if he decided to stay in the race. She'd taken solace in the idea that at least he was doing what made him happy, but now, she wasn't so sure.

Not sure what to do with her unrest either, Phoenix opened the encrypted file on her phone that she only opened when she was feeling extraordinarily vulnerable, and got lost in all the explicit photos he'd sent her when they were heavy into their sexting phase. And when she was done with that and feeling extra pathetic, she opened up the novel he'd sent her and reread all her favorite parts. It really should be published.

And she still stood by her belief that it would make a good movie.

For the first time in more than a year, she remembered the document he'd shared with her, the one that he'd invited her to edit for him. The screenplay file he'd started but never done anything with.

She wondered.

Phoenix had to search pretty far back in her email history before she found the invite, but when she opened it, the document had more than a title page this time. It had 120 pages to it. That was a full movie.

Phoenix sat up straighter and took a great big bite of her chocolate bar. Holy shit, he'd actually written it.

She couldn't believe it. By the looks of the first few pages, he'd actually taken a lot of her suggestions into account. But then, it began to diverge. Instead of the lawyer-gone-rogue-detective simply seeking revenge for his dead wife, he found himself falling in love again and fighting it, but ultimately succumbing at the same time someone else caught his wife's murderer using the work he'd done.

It was an uneasy ending, one that left itself open for sequels, where the lawyer would turn private eye, and the new woman was set up to be not just the hero's plucky side-kick, but his tech-savvy partner, and it left Phoenix in tears.

Because the whole thing could have been a metaphor for her and Robin.

Only Robin refused to make space for her in his life the way his protagonist had done. And that was why she was drunk in an expensive hotel room in New Orleans while he was in his big, silent house back in Wellville. And that was the way it would stay.

When Phoenix woke up the next morning, her head felt as if someone had driven an ice pick into her skull from behind her left ear. Her tablet still lay on her chest, and she'd spent the entire night with her head propped up against the pillows at too sharp an angle.

She stretched and realized she'd forgotten to brush her teeth after the chocolate, but instead of getting out of bed to brush them, her body took over and unlocked the tablet. It was on its last ounce of battery strength, but it opened to her email. On the screen was an email she didn't remember sending to Eve the night before that read:

Do you remember that screenplay Robin Birch was working on last year before The Incident?

Well, he's finished writing it, and I think you should take a look at it.

Fe

Attached at the bottom was a copy of Robin's screenplay.

Phoenix groaned and covered her face with her hands. She hadn't just submitted his writing without his consent, had she?

That was an absolute breach of trust, even if they'd barely spoken in the last year. That would be like him selling her sexy texts.

Should she tell him?

Did it matter?

Eve received thousands of scripts a week, and she barely read any of them. The chances of her actually wanting Robin's were slim, Phoenix decided. So she probably would be fine. No need to mention it unless it actually came to something.

Only, after Phoenix forced herself through yoga and a shower and was sitting down to breakfast with Van and Clay in the hotel restaurant, her phone buzzed with an email.

The response from Eve read, *First thoughts. This could be something. Thanks for passing it along, doll. I owe you.*

Van and Clay didn't even notice her heart stop. That was the trouble with Phoenix being on her phone all the time, nobody noticed when she got a message that made her world begin to crumble.

She dashed off a quick, albeit rambling explanation to Robin, to which his response was *Well, thanks, I guess.*

And that was it. No anger, no outrage, no true delight, just reluctant acceptance that Phoenix had most likely just sold his script for him. She would be pissed as hell if someone had done that with her creative work without her permission.

And sober, she never would have dreamed of it. Had they been on better terms, she absolutely would have badgered him about it and peppered him with helpful critiques until he submitted somewhere just to get her to leave him alone, but she'd never do it for him.

Only she had.

And she couldn't let it rest, so that night, before she went to bed, she texted back *Again, I'm really sorry. Under normal circumstances, I would never. I was just drunk, and exhausted, and . . . I'm sorry.*

His text appeared in the time it took her to brush her teeth. *It is alright to admit that you miss me, Phoenix.*

She couldn't decide if it was a good thing that she couldn't detect any of the teasing pride in his statement that she would have found a year ago. There was pride all right, Robin's stupid overblown ego would never get over the fact that she liked him enough to want to sleep with him over and over again for months. Then when he got her pregnant and she actually wanted to keep the baby? Well, that had basically made him a fucking God, despite the fact that he didn't actually want to have a baby with her. No, he was proud that she was still attracted to him, he just wasn't smug about it anymore.

Phoenix scoffed and hid her phone under her pillow. Making space for his ego was absolutely the last thing she needed right now. She had a US tour to run, a European tour to finalize, and they were probably going to Japan in January. Phoenix didn't have time to devote to someone who didn't want her.

So she shoved Robin from her mind, and it worked for the rest of the US tour, but right about the time they landed back in L.A. at the end of July, Phoenix had a phone call—an actual phone call—from Eve, just as she was sitting down to brunch with Van and Clay. She wanted to know if Phoenix would mind if Eve hosted Robin for a week as she introduced him to some studio friends who were excited about his script to see if they could build up hype about a bidding war.

Wow. So Eve really liked the script, or she really liked Robin, Phoenix couldn't really tell. She was kind of a man-eater. Eve didn't have time to maintain an actual relationship but liked to have a handsome man on her arm. She used them like accessories, and Phoenix had never minded before. Eve never usually dated anyone she was working with, but she was clearly interested in Robin. The fact that she wasn't planning on buying the script herself but still hyping him up said a lot.

"That sounds like a great opportunity for him," Phoenix said.

"Yes, darling, it is. But you could be a part of it. Your name could open just as many doors as mine can these days, you know. Even in the film industry."

That was unexpected. "This is your specialty, Eve. And I have a world tour to finish planning."

"Well, I offered. And I won't step on your toes at all? I know you two had quite the affair. Just say the word and I'll call the whole thing off."

A heavy sinking feeling pulled Phoenix from standing to sitting. Eve really was interested in Robin. And the problem was, Phoenix could see him being good for her. He could be a grounding influence, and Eve would make an excellent politician's wife. "That was a long time ago. But does Robin have time to spend a whole week out here? The election's in, like, two months."

"Oh, didn't you hear, darling? Robin Birch is withdrawing from the congressional race. The Republicans are ecstatic."

That jump-started Phoenix's heart. She hadn't communicated with him since that day in New Orleans. Not a single word after his moronic ego had to have the final say. "No, I hadn't heard," Phoenix said. "How have I missed the news?"

"It hasn't gone national yet, darling. I just happen to have the inside scoop. I'll let you know how it goes. Now get some rest; I know how exhausting those tours can be. Kisses."

Eve hung up the phone before Phoenix even had a chance to respond.

Van looked at her with a bemused, questioning expression, and Phoenix realized her mouth was hanging open. She snapped it shut and said, "That was Eve."

"And?"

"Did you know your dad was dropping out of the congressional race?" Phoenix asked.

Van's eyebrows rose, and she shook her head. "He hasn't said anything to me. Granted, he's been a mopey bastard pretty much for the last year—" she nailed Phoenix with a meaningful stare, "But last I knew, he was still dead set on doing the political thing."

Clay cleared his throat and shifted in his seat. Van whipped her head toward him, her black hair flaring out as it followed. "You knew?"

Clay shrugged and spun his Bloody Mary. "We talk."

"Like that's an explanation," Van said, swatting Clay on his arm with her napkin. "Of course you talk, but why would he say something to you and not to me?" Van asked, sounding hurt. Phoenix wanted to know the same thing.

"It's not official yet," Clay said. "I'm sure he'll tell you before he makes the public announcement." Van still glared, and Clay leaned toward her, brushing a stray strand of hair out of her face. He flashed Van the crooked smile that made his dimple pop, and Phoenix had to avert her eyes. The two of them together made her remember what it had been like to have someone look at her like that, even if it had only been in private. "I think he just wanted to talk it out with an impartial party. All of his friends are working on the campaign, and he knows you'll support him whatever he wants to do. He just needed to talk."

Van still flopped back in her chair, arms crossed and pouting. "He is so going to be hearing from me about this." Then she turned to Phoenix, "How do you think Eve knew? Is that what she was calling about?"

Phoenix shook her head. "She was basically asking if I minded if she flew your dad out here to bone and find someone to buy his screenplay."

Van choked on her laugh, and then actually choked on

her smoothie. "Eve has the hots for my dad?" She wheezed after she'd sort of caught her breath.

"Apparently." Phoenix wanted to throw a tantrum like a toddler, but she had more dignity than that. She, however, did not have too much dignity to pout in the restaurant, because she crossed her arms and sunk back into the cushions.

"Doesn't she know?" Van asked.

"Of course she knows," The words came out harsher than Phoenix meant. "But it's basically been a year, and it's probably a good thing if he moves on."

Van rolled her eyes, and Clay only threw a skeptical glance her way. Fine. They were allowed to have their own opinions about the situation. It didn't change anything. She and Robin were done. They had been over for a really long time. She shouldn't care who Robin dated—or if he was having sex with somebody else—but the truth was, she really, really did. She hadn't been with anyone at all since they'd broken up, and she didn't want him to be either. Like, that tantrum might turn into a full-blown fire-breathing-bitch-demon storm at the very idea of Robin Birch in someone else's bed.

It was stupid for her to still be holding on to this. She knew she should be trying harder to get over Robin, to move on so that maybe she could find a man who would love her as much as she loved him. Phoenix deserved to be in a relationship with someone who not only worshipped her in private, the way Robin had done, but also thought she was worth putting before himself. Robin had never been able to do that. And that's why Phoenix would never forgive him.

If he would have asked, Phoenix would have moved to

be with him. She would have moved in with him in Wellville. She would have travelled with him to Washington while Congress was in session. Phoenix would have found a way to make everything work. But Robin had never asked. He'd never even asked her to stop sleeping in her basement apartment and stay with him in the main part of the house.

Was it too much to ask to have him magically wake up one day and realize that she was his equal? That if Van wasn't embarrassed by them being together, why in the world should anyone else be?

"And are you okay with that?" Van asked. Then hacked. "Sorry, there's still a blackberry seed in my throat."

Phoenix couldn't help the breath of a laugh that escaped her throat as Van made a show of not choking any longer. Then, when she'd made a sufficient spectacle of herself, she offered Phoenix a wide, blackberry tinted smile and said, "Well, are you?"

Phoenix only shook her head. She wasn't alright with it at all.

CHAPTER 21

*R*obin had thought he had good stomach for the show business industry considering how long Van had been in it now, and how masterful she and Phoenix were at playing the game. But spending the day with Eve, hitting one producer for lunch, another for drinks, then another for dinner, and yet another at some house party— Robin was wondering if he'd made a mistake.

He had a suspicion he was too old for this sort of life-style. Robin also did not have the kind of alcohol tolerance it required. He had been offered a drink at every meeting, and he was pretty sure he'd been sloshed since three o'clock that afternoon. At midnight, Eve was only just ushering him back into her car, not just steady, but alert and invigorated. Robin was afraid he was going to fall asleep the second the car pulled away from the curb.

"Well, that was a successful day," Eve said. She still looked magnificent in her white suit, her sleek blonde hair pulled back in tight twist. She had to be in her mid-forties, and she wasn't unattractive. Probably, she was beautiful.

Robin couldn't be sure anymore. Phoenix had been his standard of beauty for so long that anyone who wasn't her didn't even register on the scale.

Eve laid her hand on his arm, "What did you think, darling? The prospects look good, yes?"

It had taken him until halfway through their second meeting to realize she called everyone 'darling' like she thought she was Zsa Zsa Gabor without the accent. But she also hadn't stopped touching him all day long in a way that one, claimed him as her pet in front of everyone they met and two, said that she would definitely like to take off his pants.

It wasn't that Robin didn't appreciate that she was giving him what he was sure was the VIP Hollywood treatment, but he wasn't interested. Every other time she'd touched him that day, he'd skillfully maneuvered out of her reach so as to avoid embarrassing her, but now, he removed her hand from his arm by her wrist and replaced it in her own lap.

"I have no idea if what we did accomplished anything," he said. "But I'd be happy to talk to any of them about developing the idea further."

"Oh, each of them should be able to do your script justice turning it into a film. I'd go with Hollyrod myself, but he's not the easiest to work with. He has a temper and likes to ask for rewrites at the last minute, but his end product is always immaculate. What we need to concentrate on right now is making sure the project is firmly attached to the Birch name. That way we can be sure of making a big splash of it first thing."

"And if I'd rather use a nom de plume?" he asked.

"I think you'll find that that would be a mistake. The

reason I was even able to set up these meetings is that you're known. Everyone wants to know what would make an intelligent, successful, attractive man drop out of race for Congress, which he was *winning*, in order to pursue a career as a writer. And a writer of genre fiction for goodness sake. That's what will get the movie made and grab us attention at the box office."

Robin had suspected as much, but he'd been half hoping that wasn't the case. But, as much as he didn't necessarily want to explain his seemingly irrational change of course to the world at large, at least Eve de Silva wasn't expecting him to piggyback entirely off his daughter's fame. While he was more comfortable in capitalizing on his own infamy than he was in using Van's name, it still wasn't his first choice.

"I'm not sure that's something I'm interested in," he said, trying to sound authoritative and in charge, but the truth was, since Phoenix had left him, Robin hadn't felt in control of anything. He'd felt separated from himself, seeing each day pass like he was watching television. He suddenly felt like he was dying, like he'd been imploding since she'd gotten on the plane the day after her D&C. Phoenix had barely said a word to him since then, and it was coming up on a year since their loss. Because it had been their loss. Maybe at first Robin hadn't allowed himself to process what it had meant that Phoenix had been carrying his child, but he'd been thinking of almost nothing else since he'd turned in his keys to his law office. He and Phoenix could have been a family. They could have started a family of their own, and the thing that had been standing in their way was his pride and his fear.

Robin had done the math. His and Phoenix's baby would be almost five months old if things had gone differently.

She'd be learning how to sit up, becoming more alert to the world around her. She would probably still be keeping them up at night, but watching her grow along with Phoenix every day would have been totally worth it. That was the life Robin wanted. None of his ambition meant a damn thing if he didn't have Phoenix to share in his every day.

Clay had made him see that. The last time they'd been in Kansas, he and Clay had had coffee together while Van completed her workout. Robin had confessed that he wasn't sure he wanted to run for office anymore, and Clay had reminded Robin so much of Mary Beth when he'd asked, "Why are you in this race? Is it because you are the best person to serve the people of Kansas or because you want to add 'Congressman' to your job title?"

Robin had almost answered "Both," without even thinking about it, but stopped himself. Running for office had been part of his plan for so long, he had to think for a second to remember where it had originated. As he thought back, he realized it hadn't even been his idea. It had been his father's. Phillip Birch had been a mechanic who had wanted to pass his shop down to his son, but Robin had been more interested in books and music than he had been in internal combustion engines. When Robin had received a scholarship from the University of Kansas, he had known exactly what he'd wanted to study. English, then law, and to convince his father that this was the right path for him instead of staying in Wellville and taking over the shop, he and his dad had sat down and mapped out Robin's trajectory. His father had told him that if he didn't go into politics, didn't come back to Wellville and help the people who needed it most, he would be wasting his education.

That was why he'd brought Caroline back to Wellville

instead of taking the job with the law firm in Lawrence. That was why he'd run for city council all those years ago, why he'd joined the local historical society. He still cared about Wellville, thought that he would make a good congressman, but only if his heart was truly in it.

"It was my dad's idea," Robin said. "It's what he wanted."

"And what do you want?" Clay asked.

His heart had shouted that all Robin wanted was Phoenix, but what Robin said was, "Not to be in the spotlight."

Clay grinned as he sipped his coffee. "You're in the wrong family for that one."

Robin couldn't help how his lips twitched as he looked down into his own nearly empty mug of coffee. Clay might have a point about that.

"But if your passion isn't in navigating politics for the good of the people of Kansas, then maybe you aren't the right person for the job. And there's nothing wrong with that."

"I feel like I would be letting everyone down."

Clay scrubbed his hands over his jaw. "I mean, none of us really want the other guy to win, but there are other ways to do good."

"I'm not sure writing mystery novels is it," Robin said.

Clay cocked his head to the side. "Is that what you've been doing?"

Robin's cheeks burned as he nodded in the affirmative.

But then Clay shrugged like it was no big deal. "I mean, people can say what they like about Van's career, but look at all she's accomplished. All the money she's raised, the ways she's helping to change the conversation. She didn't have that planned when she moved to L.A. She just wanted to sing her songs on the street corner."

Robin shook his head. Van's busking days had never made him comfortable. "Thank God she's not doing that anymore."

Clay nodded in agreement. "She's moved on, and she's found her voice. Maybe you just need to give yourself time to do the same." Clay stood and rinsed his empty mug in the kitchen sink. "And maybe you try to work things out with Phoenix. If that's what you want."

It was what Robin had wanted. He just hadn't known how to go about it. All he could remember over and over was Phoenix walking away from him at the wedding. He didn't think she'd be interested, but Robin couldn't handle being so close to her and not asking. He knocked on the window separating them from the driver. "You got enough gas to get us to Malibu?" he asked.

"Yes, sir."

"Good," he said, then gave him Phoenix's address.

"Are we taking the scenic route, sir?'

"*No*. The quickest route possible." This was not a pleasure trip. Robin needed to get Phoenix now.

When he buckled himself back in his seat, Eve was watching him with a self-satisfied smile.

"What?" The question was almost a bark.

"That's Phoenix's address."

"And?" He'd basically reverted to a caveman.

"That's where we were headed already, but I wasn't sure how you'd feel about it. Now I guess I know."

"She knows we're coming?"

"Not at all," Eve said. "She wanted nothing to do with your trip, but since she's barely been anything but downcast eyes and sullen sarcasm since she miscarried the baby, I thought maybe she was lying because she thought you didn't want to be with her."

"You know about the miscarriage?"

Eve shot him an aggravated frown. "Darling, I know about everything. Just like I know how your screenplay is all about my darling firebird." She speared him with her glittering eyes, even in the dark. "Isn't it?"

"I—" Robin said, feeling the unsteadiness from the alcohol hit him all at once. He ran his hands through his hair.

Eve hummed. "Don't back down now," Eve said. "What are you going to do when we arrive?"

"Grovel my way inside if I have to."

"You won't have to," Eve said, and turned to look out the window as if it were daylight and she could watch the scenery pass them by.

They were silent the rest of the trip, and when the driver asked for the code to the gate, Eve and Robin said it unison. Good, Fe hadn't changed it.

The car didn't even pull into Phoenix's driveway, just idled in the street. Eve said, "Well, you're up, darling. I'll be in touch about the screenplay."

Robin stumbled up Phoenix's walk and rang the bell as he heard Eve's car pull away.

Phoenix was slow to answer the door. Robin rang again and knocked twice. When she did pull the door open, she was muttering under her breath about how she didn't get notified about a visitor, which meant she didn't realize how late it was. She had a glass of wine in her hand and wore one of those maddeningly loose t-shirts that fell off one shoulder over yoga pants.

Robin wanted to wrap his hands around her waist and walk her backwards into her house, then back her into the door, but instead he tried to stand straight, but overcompensated and swayed, giving away his level of intoxication. Phoenix wobbled a little bit herself as her eyes traveled from his chest, down his light gray suit bottoms to his fawn shoes and back up. Her eyes lingered on where his shirt was unbuttoned at the collar, then up to finally meet his eyes.

"Robin? What are you doing here?" she asked.

"I'm here to see you."

"But you're with Eve now." Phoenix's voice was, truthfully, a little slurred, but it was also soft and defeated. She sounded like she was a teenager instead of on the verge of her thirties, and Robin wanted to remind her of the woman she was.

He stepped into her house without being invited, and she stepped back to make room for him. He closed the door behind her, then using just his presence, backed her against it and thanked the universe that she wasn't the kind of person who hung decorations on the inside of their door.

"I am not with Eve," he said as rested his forearms on either side of her head.

She gazed up at him, a wine-induced glaze to her eyes. "But you were here to see her."

"I had meetings with her today." Phoenix's chin dropped, and he hated how defeated she was. This wasn't his Phoenix. His Phoenix didn't doubt herself. She owned the whole world. He wanted to see that bright fire burning in her eyes every day for the rest of his life.

Robin slipped one crooked finger under her chin and raised her eyes to meet his. "But I came here for you." Her eyes darted down again, and he followed them with his own. "I came here because you thought my screenplay was good enough to pass along to your mentor, and I wanted to do something for you."

Phoenix shook her head. "You're ashamed of me."

Robin's blood roared in protest as he stilled her motion with his hand. "I love you."

Defiance burned in the back of her blue eyes. "But you don't want me," she said. "You never wanted anything more than a mistress."

She raised her wine glass to her lips over his hand a took a sip. He allowed it, then pulled the glass from her hand and took a sip for himself. It was her favorite Pinot Noir. The taste he thought of as hers alone.

After tasting the wine, Robin needed to taste her. He set the wine on the side table by the door and cupped her chin with both his hands. "I was an idiot," he said, his lips so close to hers, he could feel her breath feather over his mouth.

"You were afraid," she said, the words hot and accusatory on his skin.

"Scared shitless," he said. "Because every woman I have ever loved has been taken from me."

Phoenix cocked her head to the side then. Her lips brushed the corner of his mouth as she spoke. "You're not to blame for any of that."

"But I don't want to—"

She pressed a kiss to the corner of his mouth as he spoke, and he cut off. "Shhh…" she said. "You can't worry about those things," she said.

Robin's heart beat so hard, he worried for his health. His breath was difficult to catch as he smoothed his mouth over her upper lip, so close to kissing her, but just keeping himself at bay. "I will never not worry about losing you."

"No one has ever wanted me," she said as her fingers bunched and wrinkled the lapels on his suit. He'd borrowed it from Bryant. It was one Phoenix had picked out for him to wear to an event when he'd still been with Van for the show. Robin had never allowed Phoenix to buy him clothes, but he'd wanted to wear something nice for her. Something that had nothing to do with that damn campaign. Something she would have approved of for what he was here to do, and he hoped she noticed.

He skimmed his lips over her chin and down her throat as she tilted her head back and arched against the door to allow him better access.

"My parents fought over who had to take me when they split, instead of who got to keep me. My stepfather would have let his son keep raping me. My stepmother was good to me when I moved in, but she thought if she gave me a little bit of CBD oil and some therapy that I should have been fine by the time I turned eighteen. When I told her about the miscarriage last year, she told me what essential oils I needed to use the next time I got knocked up."

Robin stilled, his lips below her right ear as her voice shook, and he stepped into her.

"Eve loves me, I think, but she holds everyone at arm's length, and then I met Van. She became my family. And then so did you and Mary Beth and Bryant." She paused, her hands fisting tighter. "And I guess maybe I can count Clay in that too. You were my family, and when Mary Beth was in that accident, it felt like I was losing my mom too."

Robin wrapped his arms around her, pulling her tight against him, and it had never felt so good to touch another human being as it did to have this woman in his arms.

"And I didn't want to be attracted to you. I didn't mean

for it to happen, but you were at my pool, and you put that damn towel around my shoulders, and I couldn't get you out of my head for six months, and it wasn't just the sex that was good." She sniffed, and Robin wanted to shush her, to tell her it was alright if she wanted to cry, but he didn't dare move lest it frighten her into cutting her confession short.

"We were good together, weren't we?" she asked.

Robin nodded into the crook of her shoulder. "We were."

"I looked forward to just spending time with you. I mean, the sex was fantastic, but I liked you out of bed too, and I thought you liked me."

"I did. I do."

She let out another shuddering sigh. "But you didn't want me," she said. "And you didn't want our baby, and you still don't."

The tears fell then. He held her as her cries wracked her small body. He could feel her ribcage expand and contract beneath his hands. Phoenix clutched his lapels, wiped her nose on his shirt and wept.

Eventually, he eased her to the floor so he could cradle her in his lap. He whispered comforting phrases in her ear, clichés like, "It's alright. Everything's going to be okay. I have you. Shh, it's okay."

When she was spent and lay limp and exhausted in his arms, he kissed the wetness from her cheeks. "I am sorry I let my fear hurt you," he said. "I was frightened then, but this year without you has been like dying a slow death."

Phoenix let out a laugh. It was soft, hesitant, but it was still a laugh.

"I have missed you so much. I have needed you so much. I love you," he continued.

She shoved at his chest, and Robin grabbed her wrist.

Her laughing eyes met his, and Robin pulled her wrist until her arm was wrapped around his shoulders.

She tilted her chin up and said, "If you kiss me now, I'm never letting you go."

Robin's heart swelled. "That's what I'm counting on," he said and finally allowed himself to kiss her. Her lips were soft and warm and salty from her tears. But she tasted like the heady mix of her wine and that missing piece of himself he'd misplaced the day Phoenix had overheard him make the biggest mistake of his life on that phone call.

Robin didn't ever want to give her up again.

CHAPTER 22

*P*hoenix woke up cocooned in the weight and warmth of a man's arms. She'd had to contort herself around to check for silver hair and the scar on Robin's shoulder from his wild, by-gone motorcycle days before she believed that last night hadn't been a dream.

She'd been drinking wine by herself, trying to calm the panic that had risen within her knowing that Robin was in town but that Eve was showing him around, being beautiful, successful, confident Eve. She was the woman Phoenix had always wanted to be, and Phoenix knew Robin would be attracted to that unstoppable energy.

Phoenix had drunk way too much wine. And thought she'd been hallucinating when Robin showed up on her doorstep at midnight. It had been the only explanation until he'd closed her door. Touched her, run his lips over her, and said the most beautiful things. About being sorry. About loving her.

Then she'd cried all over him like she'd wanted to do

when she'd lost the baby. She'd held all of that in for him for more than a year, and Phoenix just couldn't anymore.

It had been too big of a year. She'd lost Robin, then she'd lost the baby, then Van had gotten married, and Phoenix knew she hadn't really lost her best friend, but she'd seen a hell of a lot less of her since Van and Clay had finally given in to their feelings, and once they were married, they sometimes forgot other people existed. And while that was great for Van, Phoenix had felt lonelier than ever. Between the assistant and the new manager she'd hired, she had less work to keep her busy, and she'd been feeling completely lost.

She'd met with Eve a few times. Her mentor had offered a sympathetic ear, but she was still Eve. Still attempting to manipulate every situation toward her own advantage.

Phoenix just wanted one person in the whole motherfucking world to care about her and what she needed.

Last night, Robin had been there, apologetic, eager, and patient in that gentle yet forceful way of his. And when he'd finally kissed her, Phoenix hadn't had the strength to resist him anymore. He'd hurt her more than almost any other person alive could have, but he was also the only person Phoenix wanted to soothe her hurt.

She'd let him carry her to her bed, take off each piece of clothing one by one and lay her back on the bed as he'd tasted every piece of her body. His touch had been exquisite torture until he'd thrust inside her, and Phoenix had let herself get taken away with the moment. With the feel of him on her, in her, the pleasure of his lips, his hands, and his cock.

It was the most like coming home out of any orgasm she'd ever had.

But despite falling asleep in his arms and waking up multiple times throughout the night to make sure he hadn't sneaked away to his own bed the way he had done all those weeks they'd been living in his house after the tornado, Phoenix still hadn't expected Robin to be next to her when she woke that morning

She stretched against him, reveling in the delicious friction of his body hair over her skin. One strong arm tightened around her waist for just a moment before he leveraged himself on top of her. His lips latched on to one exposed breast immediately, and Phoenix undulated against his body.

Robin moaned, and Phoenix could already feel his erection pressing against her thigh. She opened her legs as she remembered one very important and potentially complicating issue they hadn't discussed the night before.

"I'm not on birth control," she said. Robin stilled and lifted his head from her breast, meeting her eyes in mild surprise. "I never went back on it after the miscarriage. I wasn't sleeping with anyone, and I was probably a little depressed, and it just seemed pointless."

A small, satisfied grin curled at Robin's lips. "I haven't been with anyone else in all this time either," he said. Which was a good thing, since they hadn't even talked about protection the night before, which had been one-hundred percent irresponsible of them.

"Yes, well, it's good that disease won't be a problem, but it's um, basically my fertile window so pregnancy might be something you want to consider before proceeding," she felt herself blush, which was silly, she and Robin had done this literally hundreds of times, "you know, without grabbing a condom."

Robin stroked her hair out of her face. "Would you still like to have a baby?" he asked.

Phoenix gave a quick nod. She'd never changed her mind.

"With me?" he asked.

Another nod.

Robin's lips landed on hers in a hard kiss as he slipped inside her. "You don't know how much I've wished things had gone differently last summer," he whispered against her cheek before moving into her. "I never got to tell you how I always wanted more children."

"You have?" Phoenix asked.

Robin answered her with a kiss. "I'm going to be home writing all day. Why not do it with a baby on my knee?"

"This is insane," she said, because this didn't count as a real conversation about the future of their relationship. Neither did last night when they'd both been emotional and intoxicated. But it didn't take long for her to get lost in the pleasure of the feel of him. The idea that they might be trying to make a baby on purpose was so heady that Phoenix found herself more excited than usual.

Robin was similarly enthusiastic, his thrusts hard and deep and long until Phoenix was moaning beneath him. His cock felt extra hard and thick as she spasmed around him, and his appreciative groan let her know that his climax wasn't far behind. Sure enough, his lips met hers as his thrusts became erratic. His favorite way to come had always been with his lips on hers, and it had always been Phoenix's favorite part, even better than her own orgasm, because they were sharing in the joy they were bringing each other.

They lay together for a few mintues, kissing and caressing until Phoenix's stomach growled, loudly. Robin laughed, still half on top of her. "Did you have wine for dinner last night?"

She stretched beneath him. "Basically. I haven't had time to hit the market."

"Then we should go out for breakfast."

Phoenix picked her phone up from the bedside table. It was already eleven. "We might be able to get reservations for lunch."

"What sounds good?" Robin asked.

Phoenix couldn't figure him out. He was being tender, caring, not at all freaking out that they'd just had unprotected sex twice in twenty-four hours during her fertile window, and he was the one suggesting that they go out in public.

"Pasta. Maybe pizza, but don't tell Stark."

Robin kissed her temple and pushed off the bed, "You know how often your trainer and I talk about you."

"Exactly," she said as he disappeared into the bathroom. "You have to learn to lie."

It took until she heard the toilet flush to realize that she was smiling as she stared at the ceiling. It had been a long time since she'd smiled just because.

When Robin emerged from the bathroom, he tossed his phone onto the bedside table on his side of the bed and dove under the covers with her. "Do you think you could get us a reservation at The Ivy on short notice?"

"Probably," Phoenix said, though her words were almost a laugh. "What did you do, google the place in L.A. with the largest paparazzi presence that also serves pasta?"

He kissed her shoulder. "What if I did?"

"They'd probably put us on the patio."

"Even better. Perfect visibility."

"We'd be all over the internet by dinnertime."

"Exactly."

Phoenix rolled to face him. "What is up with you?"

Robin smoothed a stray curl out of her eyes with a soft thumb against her cheek. There was so much tenderness in his eyes that Phoenix almost didn't feel her stomach growl again. "I want to show you I don't care if anyone has a problem with how much I love you," he said. "And that I want to tell the whole world we're together."

Phoenix bit her lip to keep it from trembling in relief. This was all she had ever wanted.

"Then let's go to The Ivy," she said.

Phoenix placed a quick, hard kiss on his lips, then slipped from bed, her phone in her hands as she made her way to the bathroom. "I'll call the restaurant, but you have to call Van and warn her."

As Phoenix shut the bathroom door behind her, she heard Robin issue a good-natured groan, but a second later, she heard him on the phone.

Then she let The Ivy know they were coming and sent a text to the guy she used whenever she wanted to make sure there were plenty of photos. Because if Robin was serious, she wanted this news fucking everywhere.

EPILOGUE

*T*he trial, which had ultimately taken place in California, had thankfully only taken a week. It had been one of the most exhausting weeks of Phoenix's life. She could only imagine how worn out Van had been by it all. They had all been there for the duration. Phoenix had testified. So had Minnie. Van had been on the stand for hours.

Phoenix had actually made Clay stop with her at a pharmacy and get his blood pressure taken on the way home from the courthouse. She'd been watching the vein in his neck tick at a concerning pace since Bishop had taken his seat on the defendant's side of the courtroom, but while Van was up on the stand, she'd been afraid the whole time that her best friend's husband was going to have a stroke. His blood pressure had been surprisingly normal, but the moment they'd gotten back to their house on the beach, Clay had gone straight for the whiskey and downed two shots.

He almost never drank, so it was obvious how much the

stress of the trial was getting to him. Bryant had been the one to take the bottle away from his friend and replace it on the shelf over the refrigerator. Then he'd pulled Clay into a fierce hug and told him that everything was going to be alright.

Van had gone straight upstairs to their bedroom and drawn herself a bubble bath so hot that when Phoenix entered the bathroom, she could see the steam rising from over the water. Minnie sat in the vanity chair, facing Van, her arms crossed over her abdomen, her face white.

"I never would have been able to do what you did today," she was saying as Phoenix took a seat on one of the steps to the tub.

"Me either," Phoenix said. "If anyone asked me to relive in public what I went through…"

Minnie nodded emphatically. "I was bullied out of finishing my degree." It was the first time she'd heard Minnie admit out loud that she hadn't actually graduated from Columbia, though Phoenix had suspected as much. She was sorry her friend had faced animosity and scorn for seeking justice for what had happened to her, but Phoenix was proud to hear her owning her experience.

"You were cheated," Van said, then swiveled her head toward Phoenix. "Both of you." She took a shuddering breath and sat up, reaching for the glass of champagne Phoenix hadn't noticed before. "It was awful and liberating and humiliating, and I never ever want to do it again, but it was also a little bit of closure, you know?"

"Even without knowing the verdict?" Phoenix asked.

Van nodded and raised her glass, "Yes, because I know I did everything I could to see that motherfucker behind bars."

Minnie also raised her glass and took a sip of champagne at the same time Van did. "Would you like some?" she asked Phoenix as she noticed her eyes on the bottle on the vanity. Even the idea made Phoenix's stomach turn.

Everything was making her stomach turn lately, and it was the best feeling in the entire world. Except she wasn't ready to share, not just yet.

"Not tonight. I have to go field all the fallout from today so we're ready to start fresh first thing in the morning."

Van reached a wet, soapy hand out of the tub, and Phoenix entwined her fingers with her friend's. "I don't know what I did to deserve you," Van said.

Phoenix gave her a tired smile. "Likewise." Phoenix squeezed Van's hand then pulled away. "Now, I have to go put your dad to bed. You know how cranky he gets when he misses his bedtime."

Both Van and Minnie laughed at that as Phoenix made her exit. They joked between them about Phoenix's partner being so much older than her, but Phoenix was grateful every day that Robin was there when she got home. Whether they were in Kansas or California, they didn't spend any nights apart anymore.

Robin was in Van's kitchen with Clay and Bryant, each of them with a bottle of Perrier in their hands. They'd had a couple pizzas delivered, and one was already almost gone.

"Make sure you save some of that for Van," Phoenix said, announcing her presence.

"We got a feta and spinach if you'd like a slice," Bryant said to her with a quiet smile, and she wondered if he knew somehow.

Bread and cheese had been Phoenix's enemy the last few weeks. Thankfully, Robin covered her grimace by wrapping an arm around her shoulder and placing a kiss on her lips. "I ordered you a garden salad," he said.

"With extra ranch dressing?"

"Of course."

Phoenix was not normally a ranch sort of girl, but just about the only thing she wanted to eat lately was a garden salad with tomatoes and cucumbers and strong red onions smothered with obscene amounts of ranch dressing. "Bless you," she said and stole the bottle of fizzy water from his fist and finished it off in one go.

Her phone buzzed in her skirt pocket, and Phoenix rolled her eyes. "It's going to be a late night yet, I think," she said.

"It's a good thing Minnie baked some of those vegan brownies you like," Robin said as he steered them toward the door. Phoenix was vaguely aware of him waving at Clay and Bryant, but all she could think about were the fudgy brownies Minnie made that were both vegan and gluten free and almost Stark proof.

"No she didn't."

"There's a whole pan just for you on the kitchen counter," he said as the crossed the few feet of beach that separated Van and Clay's back door from theirs.

"It's like she knows," Phoenix said. "Do you think she knows?"

"I think they all know," Robin said as he set the plastic box containing her salad on the counter and wrapped his arms around her from behind. He kissed her neck while she eyed the pan of brownies, completely ready to skip the salad that had sounded so delicious only minutes before. "Go ahead," Robin said with a nip at her neck.

Phoenix didn't need telling twice, she'd scooped the

brownie right out of the middle and shoved the entirety of it into her mouth in less than three bites. "What do you mean you think they all know?" Phoenix asked despite her full mouth.

Robin only grinned. "They've been waiting for this since we got back together."

"We've only been back together two months."

Robin fished a fork out of the silverware drawer, opened the lid on the salad, and handed it to Phoenix. "And how far along are you?" he asked.

Phoenix blushed. Because she was eight weeks, almost to the day. She'd called her doctor three days before her period was due. She'd already suspected she might have conceived, and even though she didn't have a positive pregnancy test yet, she wanted to make sure she was on progesterone supplements as soon as possible. Just in case.

So far, everything was looking good. Her doctor was happy with the numbers in her blood tests, and Phoenix was so much sicker than she was the last time around, she was confident she'd see this pregnancy through.

"I want to tell them," she said, just before shoving a giant forkful of ranch-soaked lettuce into her mouth. "But not until after the trial is over."

"Whatever you want," Robin said.

The day the verdict came down as guilty on all counts. Bishop's sentencing came down almost exactly one year to the day that he'd kidnapped Van. When the sentence was announced, Phoenix was glad she had good news to share. Because despite the guilty verdict, the judge had gone soft on the punishment. That Bishop had only gotten ten years, with the expectation that he would likely be out after five, had Van spitting mad.

"He deserves more," she said, as she cruised down the beach, irate.

"Of course he does," Phoenix said. Then, "Van, if you keep making me chase you, I'm going to puke."

Van turned at that, a reluctant smile tugging at her lips. "Oh yeah, and why is that?"

"Because I'm fucking pregnant with your sister, you asshole."

A huff of a laugh escaped Van's lips, even as her smile turned genuine. "You're so sure it's a girl?"

Phoenix felt her friend's eyes zero in on her still-flat abdomen. "I mean, I don't have it confirmed, but I think it's a girl. I've been calling her Pidge, but Robin has been pushing for Paloma, because he thinks it's more elegant."

"Paloma?" Van asked, cocking her head to the side.

"It's pigeon in Spanish. A bird name since both of us…" Phoenix gestured vaguely in the direction of their houses, and Van broke out into a grin.

"Oh my God, I can't believe you're actually fucking serious." She threw her arms around Phoenix's shoulders and squeezed tight.

"Serious enough to vomit all over you if you hug me any tighter."

Van laughed and pulled away. "Are you guys getting married?" she asked, a squeal practically invalidating her words.

Phoenix gave one short shake of her head. "I don't think so. I don't know. We haven't really talked about it, but we've chosen each other, and for right now, that feels like enough. I'm just happy that we have one another."

Van squealed again. "Oh my God, you two are sooooo adorable. You are the best sister slash stepmom slash best friend I could have ever asked for." Van threw her arms around Phoenix again. "I love you so much."

Phoenix held on to her friend, grateful for every blessing running into this woman on the street six years ago had given her. Friendship, love, belonging, a purpose, a partner, this child. "I love you too," Phoenix said. "But don't you dare ever call me your stepmom again."

THANK YOU FOR READING!

I hope you enjoyed reading *The Betrayal Incident*. Phoenix has been one of my favorite characters to write to date. She has a such a secret, raw vulnerability that she hides behind touchscreens and a too-long to-do list. But she also has no patience for anyone's bullshit, and I love that about her. It was a treat to finally dig into her softer side. Robin on the hand. . . Writing this infuriating man was like wrestling an alligator. I've never written a character before who wanted so much and was so unwilling to compromise. He fought me every step of the way until we finally—FINALLY—found a compromise he could live with. If you ever see me calling him, "Fucking Robin" on Instagram, just know it's because he's a stubborn asshole and not because he's not a fantastic match for Phoenix, mmkay?

Want to Connect with Me?

I am @marlaholtauthor on Instagram. I'd love to see your bookstagram posts or just chat about the book. I can't wait to meet you!

Finally, leaving reviews is one of the best ways you can support the Indie Authors you love. I'd be forever in your debt if you took the time to review *The Betrayal Incident*

Your message is very important to Phoenix, and she will get back to you as soon as she's answered the other five hundred notifications she received while nursing Paloma.

Author's Note

Thank you to everyone who has stuck with me throughout this series. Writing about three couples whose relationships all hinged around a central experience was a daunting endeavor. There was much flipping back and forth between manuscripts, comparing timelines, and general worrying about how much information was enough to make each book available to new readers but not enough to make the novel repetitive to readers who had started at the beginning. I tried to find a compromise between the two and ended up with a series that tackled some hard issues, but still delved into lifelong friendships, chosen families, and happily-ever-afters.

I invite you to journey along with me as I continue to turn tropes upside down, find new ways to torture my characters and generally revel in irreverence.